Praise, Vilification & Sexual Innuendo

or, How to Be a Critic

The Selected Writings

of John L. Wasserman

(1964 - 1979)

by Abby Wasserman

With a Special Tribute by Michael McClure

CHRONICLE BOOKS

SAN FRANCISCO

All articles are printed in their original form, courtesy of *The San Francisco Chronicle.*

The Now Society by William Hamilton. Distributed by Universal Press Syndicate. Reprinted with permission.

Michael McClure: "Inside This Hill" from *Fragments of Perseus* copyright © 1983 by Michael McClure. Reprinted with permission of New Directions Publishing Corp.

Cover photograph by Sydney Goldstein.
Cover and book design by Brenda Rae Eno.

Printed in the United States of America.

Library of Congress Cataloging-in-Publication Data
Wasserman, Abby.
  Praise vilification and sexual innuendo...or how to be a critic, the selected
    writings of John L. Wasserman, 1964–1979 / by Abby Wasserman.
       p.   cm.
    Includes index.
    ISBN 0-8118-0247-7
    1. Wasserman, John, 1938–1979.   2. Journalists—United States—
  Biography—Humor.   I. Title.
  PN4874.W29W37   1993
  070'.92—dc20   92-10867
  [B]   CIP

Distributed in Canada by Raincoast Books,
112 East Third Avenue, Vancouver, B.C. V5T 1C8

10 9 8 7 6 5 4 3 2 1

Chronicle Books
275 Fifth Street
San Francisco, CA 94103

Where, save perhaps for the Bible,
is the truth stated more simply?

JOHN L. WASSERMAN

"I admired the way John was able to review between the lines. He was the intelligent face you saw from the stage."

—Jay Leno

"It was great reading John again. His columns gave me a great deal of pleasure as did his company all those many nights in jazz joints."

—Clint Eastwood

"John Wasserman's work for the *San Francisco Chronicle* throbbed with life and the heartbeat of a city. It must have been fun to follow his wanderings and wonderings at the time; as represented in this book they still make good writing and good reading."

—Tom Wicker, Columnist, *The New York Times*

"Abby Wasserman has brought her remarkable brother back to life. A big treat awaits those who will be happening upon John L. Wasserman for the first time in these pages, for they will be discovering, as we did years ago, a writer of incomparable wit and charm."

—Ron Fimrite, Senior Writer, *Sports Illustrated*

"I had almost forgotten the privilege we all used to have of being able to open the *Chronicle* and read John Wasserman's regular dose of wit, wisdom, and sarcasm. Now that this wonderful collection has come along, I intend to take full advantage and read no more than one column a day, thus spinning out for as long as possible the highly pleasurable delusion that John is somehow back with us."

—Orrin Keepnews, Landmark Records

"[John] was a real presence, laughing, scratching, needling, roaring with laughter or listening with gratifying intensity. And what beautiful, crazy stuff he wrote! Inimitable, irreplaceable.

—Herb Caen, Columnist, *The San Francisco Chronicle*

CONTENTS

Introduction

I know a man whose trade is censure;
fools are his theme and satire is his song.
AMBROSE BIERCE

John Wasserman, my older brother, died February 25, 1979, on the eve of a
solar eclipse. Our mother reached me at 4 a.m. at my home in Maryland; the
sound of the telephone filled me with dread.

"Something terrible has happened," she said in a high, trembling voice.
I thought, it must be my father.

"Johnny has been killed," she cried. "What should I do? I don't know
what to do."

I was three thousand miles away and could only make sure that my
father and younger brother were on their way to her from their homes on the
North Coast. I made tea and sat up in bed until the light came, then went
downstairs to tell my sons.

My mother had said bitterly, "He was hit by two men in another car.

1

They were all killed." I could not summon outrage or tears. I went to the *Washington Star,* where I was a stringer, and sat frozen in front of a computer, unable to lift my fingers. Finally I typed slowly, deliberately, "John Leland Wasserman was killed last night near San Francisco." I wrote a eulogy, a confession of love and loss, and asked the Op-Ed Page Editor to consider running it. Beyond this, I was unable to take action. It took 48 hours of leaden indecision before I flew to California to join my family in their grief.

The morning of his death, John wrote his entertainment column for *The San Francisco Chronicle,* handed it in, had lunch with a friend and drove to a party at the home of record producer David Rubinson and his wife, Martha, in San Mateo. Other guests had gone roller-skating in Golden Gate Park earlier, including John's date, Dianne Walker, who always drove when they were together but had come in her own car. John was in a gloomy mood to begin with, and as afternoon wore into evening he drank heavily and argued loudly with his host. He stayed after everyone else, including Dianne, left, and the Rubinsons, upset with him and worried about his condition, made him promise they could drive him home. John handed over his keys to Martha and excused himself to go to the bathroom, then left the house, got into his car and drove away. He always carried an extra set of keys.

It was raining heavily, and visibility was poor. South of San Francisco he spun out on the wet pavement and got turned around, or maybe (it is not known) he left the highway and came back on the wrong ramp. For 30 or 40 seconds, he drove straight and steady in the right-hand lane, while opposing drivers frantically swerved to the left and right. Rounding a bend, he crashed head-on into a Karman Ghia, which burst into flames. John was killed instantly, as were the occupants of the other car—Bethanie Kay Sample, a 29-year-old TWA flight attendant from Indiana, who had lived in San Francisco 10 years, and her sweetheart and housemate, 20-year-old Richard Salazar, a clerk for the San Francisco Social Services Department and a native San Franciscan.

It was unclear at first who had been going the wrong way, but eyewitness accounts, and the fact that John's blood alcohol level was .26, nearly three times the level for legal intoxication, confirmed that he was at fault.

Traffic backed up for miles, and some of John's friends were caught in the mess. Fire trucks were still on the scene when Cyra and John McFadden passed. They had driven from Los Angeles that day and were exhausted, so when they reached home they ignored their flashing message machine and went straight to bed. A friend woke them with the news at 6 a.m., and Cyra immediately got on the phone to other friends. When she finally played the messages, there was John's teasing, deep baritone voice, saying, "Kyra the Elephant Girl! I'm having a party and you and John are going to be there!"

Before the day was out, others found John's voice on their answering machines, inviting them to a party or apologizing for not being in touch: "Hi, this is John, back from the dead. Sorry I haven't called."

Joan Baez answered her doorbell just before 7 a.m. to find her mother and a friend standing there to break the news of John's death before she could hear it on television.

Michael McClure was leaving home to watch the solar eclipse when his daughter, Jane, phoned. He, too, had passed the accident the night before on his way to a movie John had praised in his column.

Frances Moffat, the *Chronicle* society editor, had planned to watch the eclipse from her Telegraph Hill apartment window, but after hearing about the accident, she went into the street to join the crowd gathered there with their telescopes trained east. People's voices were hushed as they talked about John's death, she recalls, almost as if a family member had died.

For two hours the dark moon crossed the sun, turning the sky a dusky color. By 9 a.m. it was over, the last solar eclipse visible in San Francisco until 1991. The city took on its familiar sparkle and people streamed down the hill. Frances slowly climbed the stairs to her apartment.

Years later, her voice reflecting the sadness she had felt that morning, she said, "It was as though the light had gone out of San Francisco."

John Wasserman and his literary hero, Ambrose Bierce, began their San Francisco journalism careers at age 24, exactly 100 years apart. Flamboyant in dress and taller than the average man, each roamed a city that was anarchic, exciting and teeming with colorful characters, defining itself as a place where anything goes.

Both were acerbic humorists and prolific writers. Bierce produced three to four million words before he disappeared at the age of 81 into revolutionary Mexico, and John wrote two million words, give or take a thousand, in the 40 years of his life.

Bierce wrote longhand, and his pen was a stiletto. John typed, and he called his typewriter a weapon. He used this weapon for 15 years as a columnist and entertainment critic for *The San Francisco Chronicle.*

In fact, writing and laughter were his best things. His near-apoplectic laugh and brilliant wit generated laughter in others, and he was a restless stylist, always on the prowl for new ways to unleash a double entendre, turn a cliche inside out or polish a witty phrase. Yet he wrote loosely, with his shirtsleeves rolled up.

He *played* on the page.

Born August 13, 1938, just north of San Francisco, John was raised in Mill Valley, a small town of hills, meadows and redwood groves at the base of Mount Tamalpais. Our parents were Louis Wasserman, a first-generation American of Russian-Jewish parentage, and Caroline Leland Wasserman, from Minnesota Methodist stock.

Lou was a scholar, a philosopher who taught government and speech in high school while working his way through graduate school, wrote a book on comparative political philosophies and joined the faculty of San Francisco State, where he was a tenured professor. Caroline was a pianist, a schoolteacher, a political leftist and a professional puppeteer.

As a boy, John had two afflictions—asthma and siblings. I was younger by nearly three years, Richey a year younger than that. The asthma plagued his youth and kept him out of the Navy, to his great disappointment, and the siblings nudged him out of the circle of attention he craved. Richey came down with polio during the 1948 epidemic, and for the next three years Mother gave him physical therapy on the dining room table, until he recovered the use of his legs.

With Lou devoted to a scholar's life and Mother teaching or busy with Richey, John was left to his own devices. He read constantly (there was no television in the house), joined the Cub Scouts and collected pets, including a baby screech owl he found in the woods when he was 12, a dog named Jolly, a horse named Clover and parakeets, goldfish and hamsters. He wore cowboy boots and chaps our maternal grandfather, a pottery salesman and Plains Indian wannabe, made from buffalo hide. He learned to shoot a BB gun. He was musical, sensitive, verbal, sociable, eager to please—and iron-willed.

In his teenage years John became skilled at bridge, bowling, drinking and poker. He was a natural athlete with great strength in his arms, and little taste for team sports. An indifferent student, he loved to debate and test his wits. He was a person with many insecurities and a lot of anger, especially towards Lou, who seldom seemed satisfied with his sons' accomplishments.

John was an overpowering presence in my life: a protector, a nuisance, a force to be reckoned with.

On his 24th birthday he despaired of the future. He wanted to be a newspaperman, but despite several tries hadn't made it through college, and prospects were dim. He simply could not discipline himself to study; he hated doing what other people wanted him to do. He had worked on school papers and the copy desk of *The San Francisco Chronicle* and had been published in a small local paper, but this didn't impress Abe Mellinkoff, the City Editor at the *Chronicle*. "Go out, get some experience, then come back," he advised. So John went to New York, where he hunted for work and stayed with a maternal cousin whose cat made him sneeze. He was uneasy in New York; it swallowed him up. In mid-1962 he gratefully returned home, found work as a postman, caterer, furniture salesman and house painter, and tried the *Chronicle* again.

"I'll do anything," he promised Darrell Duncan, the Editorial Office Manager. "I'll sweep your floors." Duncan called when an assistant critic's job opened up suddenly in the entertainment department. John auditioned with a review of the Rock Hudson film "A Gathering of Eagles" and won. Bill German, the News Editor who cast the deciding vote, recalls that John's review "was the only one that didn't bore me."

His real life began.

The first year his writing was undistinguished, although he won a reputation for chutzpah by taking seven friends to his first nightclub assignment and leaving the club to pay the tab. By the second year he had gained confidence as a writer, and his humor began to surface at the same time as innovations appeared in San Francisco entertainment: topless dancers, improvisational theater, the new rock music, bodybuilding, mainstream porno flicks, punk rock. He started on the drama desk but soon wrote about everything that could loosely be defined as show business—from live sex shows to space shuttle flights to political rallies. For each subject he took seriously there were several joyfully *unworthy* of being taken seriously, and these provided his finest fodder.

John's best writing years were 1970 to 1979, when he had his own column, freedom to select his subjects and the drive to elbow conventional morality right in the chin. He invented a persona, Wassy, for some of his most outrageous commentary, and gave him two families. The first, wife Harriet and two children, didn't engage his attention for long, but the second—loving wife Tacit, three "nippers," little Mary Beth, little Tommy and little Billy, who had a wooden leg, and the family pet, an attack-trained Doberman named Fido—were straight men for Wassy, the long-suffering critic who, in pursuit of excellence in entertainment, was confronted by an unrelenting parade of sleaze and schlock.

John never married, although he was engaged once, briefly. In an era of unprecedented sexual freedom—post-Pill, pre-AIDS—he had one-nighters, affairs and a few long-term relationships without commitment. One of these, possibly the most serious, was with Charlene Spiller, a dashing, quick-witted entrepreneur John called "the funniest woman I know." Occasionally, she appeared in his columns as "Miss Spillet."

John was a dashing figure on the scene, six feet two inches, dressed in his signature black clothes and black cowboy boots, pale good looks accentuated by the dark attire. "He was magnetic," writer Don Asher recalls. "Beautiful face, and the glow in the eyes and the little boy's grin. The smile was so heartwarming and his sense of humor was so lively that he drew people to him. People loved him."

Few believed they knew him well, though: he had a way of dancing off when anyone got too close. He revealed himself most completely in his columns. They *are* John: passionate, whimsical, obliquely confessional.

When he joined the staff, the *Chronicle* was a writers' paper, boasting columnists Arthur Hoppe, Charles McCabe, Herb Caen, Ron Fimrite, Stanton Delaplane, Terence O'Flaherty and Ralph J. Gleason; critics Paine Knickerbocker, Alfred Frankenstein, Thomas Albright and Heuwell Tircuit; and feature writers Kevin Wallace, Carolyn Anspacher, David Perlman, Michael Grieg and Frances Moffat. Under the leadership of Editor Scott Newhall and in the company of this bright, unruly group, John's talent burst forth.

He loved the instant gratification of newspaper writing. He would call friends at all hours to demand a fact or read his latest creation, craving their outrage or amusement. When the first edition rolled off the press he'd grab a copy and stand in the mailroom chortling over his own wit. He disliked being edited and once jumped onto the copy table to dance a wild flamenco, tearing the copy to shreds while the Copy Editor gaped. He sought criticism from only one man on the *Chronicle*, Kevin Wallace, who had been a staff writer on *The New Yorker*. Wallace gave John the best advice a columnist can get: "Remember at all times you are the last word, the final authority, and your time is too valuable to waste in discussing mere trivialities. It is eternal verities you are getting off, brought to mind by this particular event or that, which in passing you do review without seeming to. My point is that the gods do not descend from Olympus, at least in spirit, so don't, because it could result in flyspecks on the charisma."

Occasionally, John spoke about leaving San Francisco to seek a larger audience. The 700-word column format suited him, but he was convinced he should do something more important. He wrote for *TV Guide, Saturday Review of the Arts, LIFE, Time* and *Variety,* and started several book projects, including a collection of his reviews of bad movies and a biography of singer Joan Baez. He spoke to Woody Allen and Robin Williams about breaking into screenplay or comedy writing. But he never seriously entertained the possibility of leaving the area or his column. He loved San Francisco for its beauty and vitality and because he was a home-town boy. There, he was at the center of things. As a columnist, he could satisfy his desire to be both participant and observer, and there was time left over to follow other interests—television, radio, teaching, production. He taught annual extension courses for San Francisco State on "Media and the Arts," featuring guest speakers drawn from his extensive show business and literary connections; one student called it "the best Monday night show in San Francisco." He organized the Bay Area Jazz Foundation and sat on steering committees, made public speeches, judged contests and used his contacts in the community to help young performers in whom he believed. When he died, San Francisco lost not only a popular writer but a catalyst.

I like to think that John knew, deep down, that he was perfectly placed, the right man in the right place during an extraordinary period in history. This "urgent kaleidoscope," as a colleague called him, was a match for an era that was wild and woolly, multicolored, bright, restless and overflowing with humor and imagination.

1

How to Be a Critic

If God had intended man to grovel,
He wouldn't have given us platform shoes.
JLW

John became a journalist on purpose and a critic by accident.

Lou, on the assumption that his eldest was college bound, urged him to take a typing class in his sophomore year of high school, and that qualified him for a journalism course as a junior. He walked into the course's first day, saw a typewriter on every desk, heard the teacher, "Dirty Jack" Gibson, crack a ribald joke and knew he'd found his home.

As a reporter on the school newspaper, John peppered articles with puns, name play and in-jokes addressed to members of his clique, the Green-bellied Potfish Gang. His nom de Potfish was Joaquin Bandersnatch.

The journalism room was on the ground floor. Every day John would come in, salute Gibson and dive through an open window. Then he'd reenter as though nothing had happened and get down to work, having purged for the moment his need to be outrageous. He was Features Editor that first year and Editor as a senior, and under his yearbook graduation picture he named his ambition: Journalist.

If the opening on the Chronicle had been in sports or news or business, or if he hadn't been home when Darrell Duncan called, it's possible John never would have been a critic, for he had no particular love for the craft. As a college freshman he'd written home that a teacher's detailed analysis of an artwork was "literally disgusting" to him. "Appreciation of the arts is a personal thing and should be acquired through experience," he wrote. "I would fight to my dying day anybody who tried to teach me culture."

"I'm very analytical in some ways," he told an interviewer in 1975, "but I loathe analysis in other ways. It goes through my whole life and I think it's because I don't like warts. Analysis tends to reveal warts. I tend to take things at face value." A deliberate choice to give the reader an informed first-hand report rather than an in-depth analysis defined his critical style, as did his flamboyance. "Critics are all performers, just like performers are," he told a class in 1976. "We don't write for the Chronicle because we desire to be anonymous and live in a cave on a mountaintop."

He took his work seriously, however. Being a critic gave him power, which he relished, and freedom. Nevertheless, he always regarded the profession with skepticism and its practitioners with amused intolerance.

HOW TO BE A CRITIC
December 6, 1976

Hardly a week goes by here at the ol' *Chron* without the appearance of some bright-eyed and bushy-tailed youngster at the servant's entrance, seeking guidance in rehearsal for the life of a critic.

"Oh, massa," they cry joyfully when finally granted an audience with one of the *Chronicle*'s legendary tastemakers. "You are so great, and we are so small. How do you do it? Reveal to us your secrets, esteemed *arbiter elegantiarum.* Cast upon our tepid waters the detergent of truth, that we may better swab clean the contusions and abrasions of a world gone mad with mendacity and sloth, and especially tell us that part again about the free ducats."

"There, there, small and irrelevant person," we say comfortingly. "Your guess is as good as mine, your quest a just one, your jest a question. Harken ye, and hence, lest thee find thyself up shithe creek without a pathel."

Well, you can see the problem. Not only is it almost impossible to provide these insights without sustaining serious tongue-injury, but there is more. Everywhere we turn, somebody wants to be a critic. Community groups seek our counsel, journalism professors call upon us for coruscation, learned publications beg our reflections, researchers probe our surcease, bureaucrats elicit our admonitions. In short, we barely have time to do our jobs, which may include, on a typical day, posting the morning's payoffs to a Swiss bank account, genuflecting to our superiors and otherwise preparing ourselves for the grinding task of dealing with mass adulation and the lunatic fringe, if there is a difference.

Yet what are we to do? We cannot coldly turn away these supplicants, and take a chance that they'll apply for our jobs, but neither dare we let them into the building, for the same reason.

Up to now, the solution has been simple enough: The *Chronicle* Dobermans are turned loose on them. But, while there is admittedly a certain charm to this approach, it is no long-term answer, either, especially if Mace gets legalized.

No, there must be a better way. How does one become a critic?

A good question. Determined to find an answer, I set to work: researched the current occupations of 11,000 ex-convicts. Perused a list of Cal diplomats who have graduated from the Fine Arts Department *imbecillitas cum laude.*

Dropped down to Stanford and learned everything there is to know about the X-Y-Y chromosome syndrome. Trotted over to the Napoleon Bonaparte unit of the Atascadero State Hospital for the Criminally Insane.

Visited Alcoholics Anonymous.

And so, with—I might add—the full encouragement and hearty derision of my colleagues, I have determined to resolve this question once and for all. I am now prepared to write a book entitled "How to Be a Critic."

It will be the definitive work: good-grooming tips, how to defend yourself and three chapters on filling out expense account forms.

Nothing will be omitted. No subject is too hot. Among the anticipated chapter titles:

Arrogance—How To Learn It.

Leaving The Theater Backwards (So As To Appear To Be Walking In).

When To Order California Wines. French Wines. Cash.

Self-Mockery (How To Fake It).

So You Want To Be Quoted.

Sarcasm, Vilification, Sexual Innuendoes And Other Basic Techniques.

How To Write In The Dark.

How To Write.

How To Doze Off.

Some Key Differences Between Stand-Up Comedy & Ballet.

Opera: Is It Any More Than "Arepo" Spelled Backwards?

THE CRITIQUED CRITIC

December 8, 1976

On Monday, we discussed the genesis of my current book and probable best-seller, "How to Be a Critic."

Today, without further adieu, let's get on with it.

Chapter One: The Critiqued Critic (How To Dish It Out, But Not Take It).

Early on, every serious critic learns one vital lesson: It is one thing to heap random ridicule and abuse on exponents of the performing arts. It is quite another thing to have random ridicule and abuse heaped on oneself.

The former process is legitimate, providential and much to be admired. The latter, a vicious, petty and unworthy pastime not fit for decent human beings.

Why is this so? Well, it's very complicated but, with a little help from Chita Rivera and Rex Reed, I think the answer will become clear.

The first thing to remember is that critics are paid to express their opinions; performers are not. This is the American system. Ergo, performers have no right to their opinions.

It's no wonder critics are astonished when criticized by their victims. Here a critic may have spent a lifetime preparing for his craft—looking up "fool" in Roget's Thesaurus, spending arduous months in high school, memorizing key passages in *TV Guide*—and along comes some dilettante who probably can't even type, yet has the gall to contradict our preconceived opinions.

Is it any wonder critics must contemplate this insubordination sternly, and with contempt?

OK, now exactly how do we handle this problem?

It depends. There are two basic parries for two basic thrusts. The first to consider is the I-Don't-Care-About-Myself attack. I first faced it years ago when singer Al Martino stated that he should punch me in the nose because I insulted his back-up group.

Do not be misled by the apparent selflessness of this tactic. Psychiatrists will tell you that this is known as the Nose-Transference Syndrome and is, in fact, indicative not of an indiscretion on my part, but of a deep-seated loathing by Martino for his own misshapen proboscis.

The proper retort? Say, quietly but firmly, "And so's your old man."

Another example: Chita Rivera, the Broadway musical star who is at the Fairmont, recently sent me the following letter: "Mr. Wasserman (note the cold formality), I have become unhappily aware of your comments. I think it might be proper for you to look up the word 'ghastly' in a dictionary. I think you would find the word more applicable to your manners than it is to the immensely gifted young men I have the privilege of working with."

Again, observe the I-Don't-Care-About-Myself tactic. The retort? Look up "ghastly" in the dictionary and it all becomes clear—a simple misunderstanding. Miss Rivera obviously thinks I was referring to this definition of ghastly: "Ghostlike; pale; haggard."

Not at all. Her immensely gifted young men are, in fact, tanned, rosy-cheeked and well-rested in appearance. No wonder she took offense. But, in fact, the definition I was referring to was "Horrible; frightful."

Lack of communication.

Now, finally, we come to Rex Reed. You have seen how to handle an irate performer. But how does the critic handle another critic? Reed is the master here, and I the chagrined upstart.

The background: Reed recently lectured at the College of Marin. I, attempting to help publicize the event, noted that he should be seen because he so vividly represents "the moron point of view." Subsequently, during a question-and-answer session in a local leather shop following his speech, he was asked about my comment. His reply was a model of the quick-witted, stiletto-pointed barb, and I am not ashamed to reprint it here.

"It doesn't take much intelligence," he said pointedly, "for a local critic to attack someone who is nationally known."

Bullseye.

IS THREE A SHROUD?

December 10, 1976

What do Alfred Hitchcock, Roman Polanski, Russ Meyer, Luis Bunuel and James Whale have in common?

What about Patty Duke, Katharine Hepburn, Barbra Streisand, Robert Redford, Jill Clayburgh, Robert De Niro, Warren Beatty, Margaret Hamilton, Finlay Currie, Elizabeth Hartman, Tuesday Weld, Lola Albright, Elizabeth Taylor and Allen Garfield?

Or "Jaws," "Super Vixens," "Phantom of the Paradise," "Obsession," "Taxi Driver," "The Goddess," "Alice Adams," "The Way We Were," "She," "The Wedding Party," "Deliverance," "Great Expectations," "Peyton Place," "Splendor in the Grass," "American Graffiti," "The Wizard of Oz," "The Hustler," "Lord Love a Duck," "The Old Dark House," "The Bride of Frankenstein," "Greetings," "Hi, Mom" and "Psycho"?

If you answered that they are, respectively, (A) film directors, (B) film actors and actresses, and (C) films—you are wrong.

What these 42 (forty-two) people and pictures have in common is that they all appear in Pauline Kael's recent *New Yorker* review of the film "Carrie," yet none of them is directly connected with the movie being reviewed.

And so we come to chapter three of my new book, "How to Be a Critic." Kael and I will split the royalties down the middle of this one.

As loyalists among you may recall, we are this week presenting the world premiere of the definite, E-Z Lurn-at-Home instructional text on criticism. On Monday, we discussed the need for such a book (Mary Ann is job-hunting again, after getting a hickey from Derek Cuisine). Wednesday we began with chapter one: The Critiqued Critic (subtitled Man Bites Dog, or, If You Don't Like It, Get Your Own Newspaper).

Today, our subject is: Cross-Referencing, *Obiter Dicta* and the Photogenic Memory—Is Three a Shroud?

Now, I know it may seem premature to tackle such a subtle concept when we haven't even touched the fundamental matter of How to Get in Free, but since this topic comprises one of the three main skills the major critic must master (the other two are, of course, Advanced Vilification and How to Get Quoted), it's never too early.

Now listen carefully. It's important. The essence of Cross-Referencing, *Obiter Dicta* and the Photogenic Memory is this: The more irrelevant data, obscure examples and vague illustrations you can inject in a review having nothing to do with the subject at hand—the more likely you are to be considered a major critic. Okay now, let us observe the master at work. Not only does Ms. Kael unearth five directors who did not direct "Carrie," not only does she reveal the names of 14 actors and actresses who are not in "Carrie," not only has she discovered the existence of 23 motion pictures that are not entitled "Carrie," but she also triumphantly introduces into the review Joyce Carol Oates, the *National Enquirer,* Andy Hardy, pre-Rafaelites, St. Sebastian, "Beach Party" movies and Cinderella (twice).

In one piece, then, Ms. Kael not only authenticates her consummate cinematic chops, but establishes her credentials in the areas of contemporary American fiction, the New Journalism, male adolescence, Dante Gabriel Rossetti, organized religion, Annette Funicello and the traditional difficulty of getting shoes that fit properly.

"But how," you cry, "does she do it?"

This, I submit to you, is virtuosity.

It's not easy, believe me. Most have the sense not to try. But, if you've set your sights on the stars, here are a couple of things to remember: First and foremost, get a job on a magazine or newspaper with lots of pages. Sure, I know that sounds obvious, but it's crucial. For, just in listing the above-mentioned extraneous movies and film personnel, Ms. Kael consumes some 94 words—often the entire length of reviews in more parsimonious publications.

Secondly, and you can't learn this in school, you have to have a photogenic memory.

It looks good to those who don't.

How Not to Get Quoted
April 20, 1977

For this fourth in a series of preview chapters from my new book, "How to Be a Critic," the editorial board of Random Souse has chosen today's topic: How Not To Get Quoted. How To Get Quoted is, of course, one of the more anxiously awaited sections, but we have decided not to print it until foreign paperback, TV, motion picture and serialization rights have been negotiated, which will be tomorrow. Since How To Get Quoted is among the three seminal lessons that must be learned by any aspiring critic (the other two are How To Get In Free and Basic Character Assassination), to reveal how to get quoted today, before the contract signings, would be not unlike putting the horse before the cart—you could step in something if you didn't watch your feet.

The first question that must be answered is, obviously, why would any critic wish *not* to be quoted? Getting quoted is what it's all about, *n'est-ce pas?* Judith Crist has only to say "I loved this movie," or Rex Reed to tell how he wept profound and honorable tears, and pretty soon you see "I loved this movie" and advertisements for Kleenex in every paper in the country.

Parenthetically, for those many of you who wrote in—yes, I will be including a chapter on When To Sob At A Movie—And How Loud.

To return to the subject—it is plain to see that all-out raves will invariably be quoted and all-out pans ("I puke on this movie"...Judith Crist) will invariably not be quoted. The problem surfaces when the critic basically likes a picture, but not enough to recommend it without qualification.

Since review quotes are generally short, if you wish to avoid being quoted, you do so in this manner: Do not say "I loved this movie," but rather, "I sort of loved this movie," "I loved this movie platonically" or "I am extremely fond of this movie, but my feelings have yet to coalesce into a deep commitment."

Thus, by either qualifying your endearments or making them impossible to take out of context, you prevent misleading quotes from appearing in print.

The trick is to write in such a way that you cannot be quoted without outright distortion. If this happens, you have grounds for a lawsuit, which will supplement your pathetic income.

An excellent case in point is "Black Sunday," the recent John Frankenheimer drama about a terrorist attack on the audience at a Super Bowl. It is a decent film, with some good chills and, if it never confronts the moral question it presents—is there anything wrong with killing 80,000 pro football fans?—neither is it an embarrassment. The problem was to say it was pretty good, without appearing enthusiastic.

A full-page ad that ran in this newspaper subsequent to the opening here indicates just how successful I was. The ad contains quotes from 64 (sixty-four) different critics, gleaned from newspapers all over the country, including at least three from the Bay Area. Yet there was none from the *Chronicle*. How was this done? How does one give credit without due?

It's simple. Damn with faint praise.

Example: "An effective entertainment." Flat, too many syllables and, of course, meaningless.

Example: "Generally taut and suspenseful." And the rest of the time?

Example: "No single irritation prevents one from becoming engrossed in the plot." Thanks for nothing.

And so it goes: "Opened yesterday at the Cinema 21"..."book of the same title"..."Romanian actor"..."the Goodyear blimp"....

You get the idea. Now go home and start mumbling. Until you have devised your own terms, here are some standard unquotable expressions with which you may wish to practice:

"Closing tomorrow"..."starring, in alphabetical order"..."may not be suitable for viewing by goats"..."replace after each use"... and, of course, the traditional "Not intended to be frozen."

IF YOU WANT TO GET QUOTED

April 22, 1977

Continuing today with yet another exciting advance peek at my new book, we come to the fifth—and, to date, most important—installment: If You Want To Get Quoted, Avoid The Word "Puke."

How to get quoted is important to critics. By getting quoted in other mediums and outlets, the aspiring taste-maker can reach an audience far greater than that which actually reads reviews. Very few people read reviews. Hundreds of people read ads. And let's face it: People do what critics tell them to do.

If, for example, a critic says, as did Penelope Gilliatt in last week's *New Yorker,* that "Robert Altman's '3 Women,' from a script by him, begins with closeup shots of young torsos in swim-suits walking gently thigh-deep in water, arm in arm with parallel parts of old people disfigured by age and feeling their way," then, by God, every thinking American will shout, in unison, "Huh?"

The awesome power of the critic.

That established, we move to the crux of the matter: How does one get quoted?

The key thing to remember is that it's not enough to like something; you must like it in the correct words. For example, words that will never be quoted include "swell," "nice," "pleasant," "agreeable," "enjoyable" and "puke."

Words that will be quoted include "greatest," "sensational," "magnificent," "hilarious," "gripping," "shocking" and "fornication."

A case in point is that of "Black Sunday," to which I alluded in Wednesday's column. In my review, I said things like "effective entertainment" and "generally taut and suspenseful."

I was not quoted.

More savvy colleagues, waxing eloquent with "A gigantic thriller!" "As riveting as a cobra in your lap!" and "Chills, spills and thrills galore!" found their words—and names—splashed across the movie pages of an entire nation.

But these are, admittedly, blatant; the driveling of amateurs. For a look at a true maitresse at work, we turn to a close personal friend and legend in the business of getting quoted—Judith "I Loved This Movie" Crist.

"Brace yourself," she says, "for 'Black Sunday'! It is without doubt the finest espionage thriller of recent years!"

Simple, yet eloquent.

Let us now dissect this deceptively puerile piece of prose.

First: Note that she includes the name of the film in the title and spells it right. Go ahead, laugh, but this alone has always given Rex Reed serious problems.

Second: Say the same thing twice for emphasis, preferably in the same sentence. E.g., "It is without doubt the finest etc. etc." If you were to simply say "It is the finest" or "Without doubt the finest," the readers might not understand. "But is it the most *unique* finest?" they would cry out in confusion.

Third: Talk directly to the reader. "Brace yourself!" she cautions sternly. Observe that closely. Most readers, you see, are uneasy when they walk into a theater. "Will I laugh?" they wonder. "Cry?" "Should I brace myself?" "Is it black-tie optional?"

No such ambiguities here. "Brace yourself!" she commands. "You'll love this movie!" "Don't watch the first 30 minutes!" "Not for the squeamish!" "Take a bath!" "Tie a yellow ribbon 'round the old oak tree!"

And so on.

Fourth: Speak with authority. "The finest espionage thriller of recent years." Never "May or may not, depending on your perspective, be the finest espionage thriller in recent years." Be certain.

Finally, fifth: Never, ever let on that you don't know what the picture's about, even if it's "Last Year at Marienbad." Here, Judy shines. "Espionage thriller!" she intones with authority. But "Black Sunday" isn't about espionage. Espionage is spying. The film is about political terrorism.

Yet is our girl bothered by this? *Non.* She says what has to be said, accurate or not.

And if you learn that lesson, you can skip one through five.

2

The Botulism on the Tuna of Life

> I picture Guy Lombardo snatching a fly out of mid-air.
> The fly is pregnant and has only one wing.
> And its back is turned.
> JLW

*The day after John's column "Suffer—the Little Osmond Brothers" appeared,
poison pen mail flowered on his desk, 50 adolescent girls wearing "I Love
Donny" T-shirts and carrying "I Hate John Wasserman" signs picketed the*
Chronicle, *and the Board of Copyboys, with honorary copygirl-in-residence
Pat Luchak (now Datebook Editor), awarded him an Honorary Degree of
Doctor of Musicology, Criticus Maximus.*

*It didn't take much for John to get a hate-on: slick packaging, shallow
talent, cloying material, child performers, the low-flying-airplane sounds of
mass hysteria.*

Tom Jones, Engelbert Humperdinck and Wayne Newton were cherished targets, although John had nothing against them personally. This was not the case with Jerry Lewis, the man he loved to hate. John had written about Lewis's outlandish demands for service when he stayed at the Fairmont Hotel in 1966. The star wanted a brand new, never-been-used limousine to meet him at the airport, a valet on 24-hour alert and a huge sign advertising his accomplishments in the lobby. Lewis responded to John's barbs with a vitriolic letter John read during his regular morning critic's spot on Frank Dill's KNBR-Radio show.

At a 1970 New York press conference, Lewis revealed his low opinion of critics and hatred of one, "a moron working for a San Francisco paper," who was "diabolically sick." Unquestionably John.

Around this time a friend in Seattle bought a duck for her children and named it "Wasserman" because, she wrote John, "the duck tried to act cold and hard but was really an old softy who liked nothing better than to have his neck scratched." When she relayed the sad news that raccoons had killed the duck, John shot back, "Jerry Lewis probably slipped the raccoons five dollars and told them to 'wring Wasserman's neck.'"

SUFFER—THE LITTLE OSMOND BROTHERS
February 9, 1972

Now that such show biz luminaries as Bob Dylan and John Lennon are over 30, those whining sycophants who once adopted "Never Trust Anyone Over 30" as some sort of in-group Pig Latin are in trouble.

A whining sycophant without a slogan is like an eye-makeup kit without mascara.

Fortunately, I have just discovered a fine replacement: "Never trust anyone under 15, especially if he is a singer." Let us all chant that for five minutes.

The inspiration for this catchy new slogan is, needless to say, the Osmond Brothers, who appeared here in concert on Sunday night. The Osmonds originally tried to make it in show business as singers and musicians. When it finally became clear that this was an impossibility, they formed their current act. This involves appearing en masse on stage (there are between five and 27 of them…no one has ever been able to make an accurate count as they are constantly in motion) in white, plunging-neckline jumpsuits, screeching at a volume which precludes intelligibility, pretending to play musical instruments and jostling about in what might be described as pre-1955 bad Motown unison show-and-tell.

The star of this spectacle is one Donny Osmond, a 14-year-old crypto-midget who need only simulate picking his nose to bring forth brain-shattering shrieks from countless thousands of horny 13-year-old girls. The show also features at least five other Osmond Brothers, but many are so old—some even as old as 23—that the capacity audience of Sunday night could not even remotely relate to them. One of them—Patti, Maxine or LaVerne; I always get them mixed up—even had dark splotches visible on his chest where his shirt V'ed. This was either hair or charcoal smudges. I asked several nearby girls to identify this substance. They thought it was a two-tone shirt.

The show opened with Bo Donaldson and the Heywoods, the worst rock and roll group in history. There were seven of them in yellow jumpsuits and sequins, playing what sounded like prerecorded Gary Puckett at the wrong speed and carrying on like a bunch of dancing bananas.

Then, *they* appeared. Bedlam, hysteria, a lung-breaking performance by that new, 10,000-voice singing group the Decibelles, Kodak stock up six points. I haven't seen so many flashbulbs since the Monkees at the Cow Palace in 1967. Hair tearing, knee pounding, eyes blurring, tiny bosoms heaving against training bras, hand-lettered signs thrusting out of the mass mess like toadstools.

They started with a song which sounded like "Bite Him Down" and one thing was immediately apparent. The Osmond Brothers were painfully, literally painfully, loud. Combined with their own ham-fisted playing (drums, guitars, bass, electric piano) was an eight-piece back-up band and a crazy person at the volume controls. By comparison, the Who's Civic Auditorium concert sounded like two moths locked in mortal combat.

Surely, I said to myself, this cornucopia of riches cannot continue to expand. Wrong again. Out came yet another Osmond—Muhammad, I believe—who is eight years old and as cute as a Presto log.

Muhammad, a regular pee-wee Wayne Newton, stands approximately two feet seven. He immediately launched into "I Got a Woman" and "I'm Evil," all the whilst bumping and grinding from one end of the stage to the other and producing pelvic thrusts Lamaze never even thought of.

Finally, Donny sang "Your Song," "Go Away Little Girl" and—prepare yourself—"Sometimes I Feel Like a Motherless Child." That, of course, was the real humor of the program. "Sometimes I Feel Like a Motherless Child" is a kid's song like "Animal Farm" is a kid's book. Donny, on the other hand, thinks that "Hold On, I'm Comin'!" is the theme song of St. Bernard dogs in the Swiss Alps.

You Asked For It

August 21, 1970

Jerry Lewis, the noted sideshow display, recently held a press conference in New York during which he expressed his contempt for most United States film critics.

He did, however, single out three he respected: one who "cares," another who "examined my work," the last who "pointed out several of my mistakes to me."

In the past, I have been loath to take Lewis and his films seriously. The French do, and I suspect this is because they consider Lewis's cinematic buffoonery an accurate reflection of the average American.

I prefer to see them for what they are. Apparently, that's not good enough for Jerry. He wants to be analyzed coolly and thoughtfully. OK, sweetie....

"Which Way to the Front?" is the latest. It was produced by Lewis, it was directed by Lewis. The producer and director arrived at a meeting of the minds and hired Lewis as star.

The film is set in 1943. Lewis is the richest man in the world, but he is also bored. Then he gets a draft notice. Excitement. Except he is ruled 4-F, he is rejected. Rejection makes him behave strangely. His eyes roll like doughnuts in an earthquake. He utters strange squeaks and grunts. His palsied arms jerk every which way.

Then he has an idea. He stops grunting. He will form his own army of mercenary 4-F'ers and assorted servants, train them, drive his yacht to Italy and win the war for the Allies by kidnaping and impersonating a German Field Marshal and promptly ordering the entire German army to retreat to Tivoli Gardens.

The result is grotesque, tasteless, cute, obvious and extremely tedious. The latter conclusion has nothing to do with Lewis as a human being. As a director, he just appears incapable of creating a film which holds the eye and imagination.

But the rest of it balances on the Lewis humor, and the Lewis humor rests on the Lewis person. Let's look at a few specifics:

1) For openers, Lewis sucks on a pacifier. This is supposed to be funny. It is intended to be incongruous—high-powered corporation executive sucks on pacifier. It should be deflating; instead it is just stupid. For at this point in the film, Lewis is establishing himself as a character of genuine—not sham—dignity. The incongruity isn't funny. It's just incongruous.

Lewis seems no longer willing to play the fool—he now wants to be an idiot with a presence. He wants to be Jerry Lewis AND Rod Steiger. Unfortunately, it can't be done.

2) Lewis goes for the obvious. There are endless "Heil Hitler!" gags. There is mocking of German accents and Japanese buck teeth. A black man is named Lincoln; German generals are named von Schlitz, von Busch and von Heineken. There is more.

3) Bad taste and humor don't mix. The script—which Lewis presumably approved—includes this exchange: The character of Adolf Hitler, represented by a crypto-pansy, tells Lewis that "More people died last year from smoking than from bombing." To which Lewis replies, "What will you do about that?" To which Hitler replies, "Increase the bombing." That is only a sample.

4) Is derision, mockery, cruelty funny? We are asked to laugh at what are considered deficiencies in others—accents, infirmities, deformities. Lewis invariably includes, as director or actor, the equivalent of epileptic fits in his films. These are not affectionate portrayals. They are twisted.

Well, this tedious business has gone far enough. But I could hardly ignore altogether Jerry's cry for assessment.

THE BOTULISM ON THE TUNA OF LIFE

July 25, 1973

No one has ever said that the lot of a newspaper critic is an easy one.

Al Martino once called to say he should punch me "in the nose," a thinly veiled reference to a physical deformity over which I have no control. Jerry Lewis wrote me an unsigned crank letter. It arrived postage due. Like a fool, I paid it.

Mort Sahl has accused me of taking bribes, Mel Torme has noted on every radio and television station in the Bay Area that I was a "boob."

Of course one may look at this merely as botulism on the tuna of life. There are also rewards in this job. Most critics are well-paid (many over $100 a week), held in awe by the general public and loved and respected by the performers who so often profit from the trenchant and perceptive comments made in these pages. To be sure, there are occasional moments of hostility when these remarks take the form of personal attacks on the performer's family and sexual afflictions.

But that is understandable and such moments pass. Often, the entertainer winds up thanking the critic and taking the advice offered. One has only to note the many show business retirements and suicides to confirm this fact.

Imagine, then, my shock and dismay at a phone call received last week from the Circle Star Theater in San Carlos: "I regret having to say this, Mr. Wisselman," the voice said, "but we have been told by the office of Mr. Gordon Mills to refuse you admittance to the theater during the forthcoming engagement of Mr. Tom Jones. We cannot, of course, stop you from purchasing a ticket but we will not be responsible for any untoward event should you try to gain admittance. There will be no free passes. You will not be permitted to sit in your favorite seat near the men's room. You will not be supplied with your usual stockpile of air-sickness bags."

People, I was dumb-struck, not even capable of summoning my usual jaunty retort, which is "And the same to you." Banned from the theater by Mr. Gordon Mills, manager of Tom Jones and Engelbert Humperdinck. Barred, ousted, ostracized, a leper of the Great White Way. My mind reeled. What had I ever done to Tom Jones and Engelbert Humperdinck?

Oh, sure, I have previously made some thoughtful evaluations of their respective talents, hairdos and ticket prices. But that's kid stuff. Old show biz pros know the score: "Just spell the name right."

Tom Jones and Engelbert Humperdump.

My mind raced feverishly. What to do? My first thought, naturally, was a law suit. Restraint of trade, denial of due process, abrogation of equal protection; a constitutional case if ever I heard one. I contacted the American Civil Liberties Union. They said take two aspirin and go to bed.

I approached the Managing Editor. "Go to the concert, you clown," he said curtly, giving me his Master Charge card to jimmy one of the side doors. Weeping with thanks and reassurance, I plotted my next move.

"We will not be responsible for any untoward event ..." the Circle Star had said. Sounded ominous. Tom Jones is, as we all know, veritably surrounded by a host of fierce bodyguards and policemen. What if they should catch me?

"JOURNALIST BEATEN TO PULP," the headlines flared in my mind. "Mysterious assailants, wearing Tom Jones Fan Club buttons, dump critic in vat at Rice-a-Roni factory," the story began. "He gains 20 pounds."

A disguise, that's it! Over to the Opera House for Brunnhilde's costume from "Goetterdaemmerung." They'd never hit a 250-pound woman with antlers.

A quick phone call and I've got Ward Dunham, mammoth bartender person at Enrico's, for my escort. He brings a squirt gun filled with Wish-Bone Italian Dressing. We're off.

We enter the theater in the darkness and slink to our seats. "Hey, take off them horns," snaps the guy behind me. "Shhhh," I retort. The show starts with the Jeff Sturges Universe band, then the Blossoms singing group, comedian Norm Crosby and, finally, "The Body and Soul of Tom Jones." I watch the show for an hour: Tom kissing the girls, Tom sweating profusely, Tom twirling his buns and inspecting his crotch for possible rips in the seams, Tom singing his heart out on his theme song, "I Who Have Nothing."

And suddenly, it all becomes clear. How could I have been so blind? What an idiot I'd been to go when I was asked to stay away!!

Gordon Mills was trying to do me a favor.

SPRINGSTEEN AND HALLOWEEN

November 3, 1975

I have seen the future of Halloween. Its name is Bruce Springsteen.

Yes, indeedy, Friday night turned out to be yet another in the classic annual series of Hallowmas eves and, as is my will and wont, I spent the evening hopping from fete to festivity, frolic to spree, gala to revel, throughout the entire Bay Area and Polk Street, all in order to bring you this exclusive Monday morning report on everything that has occurred since last we spoke.

Since Halloween's chief mummery promised to transpire at the Oakland Paramount Theater, the evening was logically enough begun in that venerable venue. It was apparent that this was not just another rock concert when Bill Graham himself, costumed as an aging rock producer, appeared on stage and announced the imminent appearance of Mr. Springsteen and his E Street Band.

As you know, we have all been waiting with unabated breath for the appearance here of Mr. Springsteen, the noted Bob Dylan imperson-ator and scrivener of such acclaimed rock poetry as:

"The door's open but the ride it ain't free
And I know you're lonely
For words that I ain't spoken."

Well, we certainly is, and the evidence was a sold-out house of screaming degenerates and my trusted associate, Joel Selvin, whose de-tailed report on the proceedings may be found elsewhere in these pages.

At any rate, Springsteen assumed the stage in his own Halloween costume, a pre-menopausal ensemble comprising dark glasses, black leather jacket, soiled white T-shirt and pre-worn Levi's. In addition to his legendary Dylan impressions, he also did interpretations of what a man looks like when (A) riding a motorcycle, (B) suffering from food poisoning, (C) experiencing a nervous disorder and (D) protecting from assault his private parts.

One can only assume that the performance reflects a conscious attempt on Springsteen's part to make utter fools of those who have sung his praises.

Nothing Sacred—Dogwise

April 12, 1971

She slunk into the *Chronicle* offices like the veteran television star she is—hair long and sleek, enormous brown eyes, petite 74-pound body drawing stares with every step.

Then she barked. The spell was broken. And drooled on my typewriter. The final blow—Rudd Weatherwax, her sexagenarian sugar daddy, confessed that she is actually a boy. A transvestite, if you will, a female impersonator. Lassie bowed his head forlornly and dribbled on my telephone. Nothing, it would appear, is sacred.

Lassie was here to push his new dog food, Recipe. "Lassie is the Colonel Sanders of dog food," said Rudd Weatherwax. Recipe ("Eat the food that Lassie Eats!") is a secret formula of meat, carrots, peas, onions, beans, celery and two vitamin and mineral-packed "chew" biscuits, marketed by Champion Valley Farms. It is available in three varieties: "Liver and Bacon Dinner," "Hearty Meat Stew" and "Robust Chicken Stew."

Weatherwax ran down a few facts on the history of Lassie. He (Weatherwax, not the dog) was an animal trainer in Los Angeles in 1942 when Metro-Goldwyn-Mayer auditioned collies to play in the first Lassie film. Originally, a girl dog was sought, as the Lassie of "Lassie Come Home" was a lady. But the selected bitch (the dog, not Weatherwax) proceeded to lose her hairy chest during molting season and Weatherwax's collie, Pal, was hurled into the breech. Pal's son Lassie started the 17-year television dynasty in 1954 and the current animal, Lassie IV, has been taking care of business for three of his five years.

"I don't believe in working a dog too long," Weatherwax explained. "I train them for two years, and work them for five years. Then, when I retire them, they've got a full life ahead. They have a good life. The first Lassie died at 18, his son died at 19." The current stable includes the working Lassie, his dad—now retired—and his son Laddie. All are Laddie until they become Lassie. It gets confusing sometimes around Rudd's place.

When you hear Lassie bark on TV, it's Lassie. But when he growls ferociously, it's a German shepherd, also owned by Weatherwax, dubbed in. Collies, you see, have a terrific snarl but not much of a growl. And when Lassie whines, it is actually Lassie the First—preserved on tape lo these 30 years. Nobody could touch the original, whine-wise.

Each Lassie has fathered his successor. The main requirement for a prospective Lassie is the white blaze on the nose. If an entire litter arrives sans blaze, well, it's back to, uh, work for our boy. The other sons and daughters are not sold, but a paw-print birth certificate identifies them as authentic.

Weatherwax does not test the babies for IQs. "Once I've started on a dog, I've never failed to make a Lassie out of her," he said, momentarily forgetting himself.

In Germany (Lassie is syndicated in 27 foreign languages), a German bark is dubbed in. Presumably the dog also clicks his toenails together.

Training is accomplished "by reward...but I'm firm with them." He grabbed Lassie by the muttonchops to demonstrate, shaking the dog gently. "You shake 'em and talk mean; then babytalk 'em...." Goo, goo, he said.

Three decades of woofing all the way to the bank has left Weatherwax decently attired with money. "Well, I wouldn't say I'm a wealthy man, but I don't have to work. Let's put it this way. I'll say my ex-wife is a well-to-do woman." Lassie smirked approvingly.

How Soon They Disremember
December 21, 1977

By golly, to think I had almost forgotten. Thank you, Rod Stewart, for making it happen for me again.

I speak, of course, of that unique event of contemporary American culture—the superstar rock and roll show.

Sometimes, the memories fade. You go to your "Close Encounters of the Third Kind," all bundled up in a warm theater, or your Oscar Peterson solo program at the Great American Music Hall, and you forget the raw...how to describe it?...the raw *uncooked* quality that only superstar rock and roll, executed before 14,000 howling fanatics in an enormous hall, can produce.

Rod Stewart, one of the major stars of pop music, sold out the Cow Palace Monday night and again last night—his first appearances here in some two years.

I was there Monday. And they came flooding back, those misty sensations, in a torrent of rushing currents, a rippling tidal wave of deja vu, a tsunami of nostalgia, brooking no rivulets of streaming fluoridation.

You forget what rock and roll can be.

You forget that heady aroma of a hundred gallons of cheap red wine, spilled on the pavement, rushing up to embrace you like an old friend as you kick your way through a ton of trash and broken glass left in the parking lot by the swine who happily milled there only hours before.

You forget those fabulous frisks at the outer door, those friendly hands of "special" cops who go through your belongings and pat you down like a very special criminal.

You forget the electricity of those first steps into the lobby, and the comatose faces milling about, so stoned they can't focus their eyes.

You forget the assault of sound that greets you as you enter the main room, so loud that conversation is shouted or not at all, so distorted that the term "music" is rendered euphemism.

You forget the challenge of picking your way to your seat through bodies slumped on the floor, trying ever so hard not to step on anyone, trying ever so hard not to slip in the rain puddles of soda pop spilled everywhere.

You forget that you don't have a seat, for this is "festival seating," which means that all the hassle involved with knowing where you'll be located is obviated.

You forget how the fireworks go flying through the audience, landing in a crowd of people who have nowhere to go, and maybe, if you're lucky, seeing some woman's hair set afire. What a flash.

You forget how truly bad the music is under these circumstances, how unintelligible the lyrics, how drearily sung by truly ordinary talent.

You forget the ritualized, stylized, synthetic spontaneity of the performances, artifice as energy, rehearsed intensity of leaps and bounds so tired and flabby that the entire show has a double chin.

You forget the patter, and the proper answers to questions like: "Hey, are you grooving?"

You forget the skill and timing with which Rod Stewart shakes his red satin-clad buns, or drops his red, gauzy blouse off one shoulder.

You forget how often he does it.

You forget the shrieks and howls that each pathetic spasm engenders.

You forget the songs, and their titles.

You forget the genuine contentment that accompanies the realization that, after 40 minutes, you have seen all there is, if anything.

You forget the inner peace that consumes you as you put on your jacket, fold your notebook, cap your pen and head for the exit.

You forget the skill required to avoid coming in contact with anyone as you leave, and the deep satisfaction which comes from knowing that, once again, you have avoided contracting a communicable disease.

You forget the freshness of the air as you step outside, walk briskly past the Daly City paddy wagon and climb into your car for the intoxicating escape back to civilization.

You forget, if possible, that it ever happened.

THOSE KUTE KING KIDDIES
October 10, 1973

It's not every day one is privileged to be present at the worst performance of all time.

Such moments are to be treasured, for they happen no more than four or five times a year. This particular catastrophe was all the more to be valued for its serendipitous nature.

My original plans for Saturday night were to catch Deodato at the Berkeley Community Theater. But, alas, Deodato kept his unique record intact. Twice he has been scheduled to play in Berkeley and twice he has cancelled.

So there I was, footloose and fancy free, a virginal Saturday night staring me in the eye. What to do? I pored through the newspapers, scoured the neighborhood telephone poles and called the Convention and Visitor's Bureau, which suggested I try some jazz at the Blackhawk.

Finally, I narrowed it down. There was "Four Hours of Kung-Fu

Action" at the St. Francis. Al Rik at Lefty O'Doul's piano-bar. The King Family was in Marin. Or I could go to bed early and catch the Rev. Daniel Panger's Sunday morning sermon at the Fellowship of All Peoples Church—"Flying Makes Me Nervous."

You've already guessed. I chose "Flying Makes Me Nervous." Unfortunately, the old expense account is a bit anemic this month and 2041 Larkin is two-bits Muni bus fare.

It's ironic, isn't it, that decisions which can change your whole life are so often made on the most pedestrian grounds. Two-bits for the Rev. Panger against $40 cab fare to the Marin Civic Center. No contest.

The Marin Veterans' Memorial Theater is a lovely auditorium with comfy blue seats, good acoustics and a spotlight operator who pursues his craft in the same spirit that others devote to Pin the Tail on the Donkey. All in all, the perfect installation for the King Family. Although I had never before seen them perform I had, of course, heard a great deal about their show. Still, I determined to go with an open mind. Just because they're Bebe Rebozo's favorite rock group doesn't mean they're not good.

The printed program alone was impressive. Forty-one numbers by the King Family, Sisters, Cousins, Kids and Husbands. Running the whole gamut from "Five Foot Two" to "Me and My Shadow."

Then they appeared, 19 strong, ranging from sexagenarian Alvino Rey to the King Kiddies, three of the cutest little nippers you ever saw, their tiny bodies swaddled in psychedelic Pampers.

The entire company launched into a number called "Side by Side by Side," which was, I've got to admit, pretty good. To make it visually striking, they matched the lyrics to the choreography, so that every time they'd say "side by side by side" they'd move around so that they'd wind up standing next to each other.

You'd expect a letdown after that but they kept up the pace. There was plenty of nostalgia about the King Sisters' mom and dad, with some swell pictures of them. And lots of jokes about what a big family it is. "When we were married," quipped one of the husbands, "the minister said, 'I now pronounce you man and mob.'"

But there was seriousness, too. The King Cousins sang "When Are You Gonna Learn" (about how kids and parents sometimes don't understand each other) and Alvino Rey presented his guitar interpretations of what he called "the three most beautiful tunes ever written." Those are

"Dixie," "Yankee Doodle Dandy" and "Be Kind To Your Fine-Feathered Friends."

What can I tell you? How to express the magic? Would it be enough to mention that there wasn't a wet eye in the house? Could I convince you by saying that they received a sitting ovation?

Well, it's true; all of it.

The rest of the first half matched this standard, capped by the King Sisters telling the history of their family, in story and song, from 1347 to the present. They told of their parents' lives, they told of their children's lives and their grandchildren's lives. They told of their husbands' lives. The told of their aunts' and uncles' lives. They told of the lives of every human being they had ever met. And they told of their goldfishes' lives.

Then one of the King Kiddies, cute as a speckled pup, took the microphone and announced intermission. One of his mothers scolded him for being impertinent. "Well," he exclaimed, his tiny eyes sparkling like sequins, "people have to have some times to go to the bathroom!!!"

How true, small person. There is a time for everything. A time to reap. A time to sow. And a time to go to the bathroom. And stay there.

Wayne's Just Like People
December 13, 1971

Wayne Newton, the noted castrato and trained killer, returned to the Bay Area on Thursday night for seven performances of fun, excitement and humility.

Newton, about whom I am currently writing a television series entitled "This Is Your Schtick," is not, of course, a true castrato. Castrati were an early version of today's counter-tenor; that is to say, a man able to sing in the soprano range. It is exactly this talent which has led Newton to become a brown-belt in karate and marry a beautiful airline stewardess. You call a karate brown-belt snotty Italian names at your own peril. Fortunately, Newton recently revealed that he doesn't attack hecklers, but rather walks away with dignity, knowing that he has probably saved their lives. I would sincerely hope that he continues to meet adversity in this manner.

The opening night show was vintage Newton. He opened the show with a couple of zingers, "Rock-a-bye" among them, then gave way to comedian Dave Barry, a last-minute substitute for comedian Jackie Kahane. Barry, who has quit wearing his toupee since playing Bimbo's several years ago, was extremely effective with the audience, bringing it to a state of laughter and mirth.

After intermission, Newton reappeared with two young ladies and assumed the stage. The ladies, who assumed the orchestra pit, were Glow Jones and Maggie Thrett. They were dressed in floor-length white dresses, thin of thickness and slit of thigh. When they sang, they tended to produce some elemental hula motions simultaneously. This was very interesting as each possesses your better-quality fanny. Maggie Thrett, I believe, is an actress who is temporarily retired from motorcycle gang films. She is gorgeous.

Meanwhile Newton sang "Put a Little Love In Your Heart" and "For Once In My Life" and stated that "You are stuck with me for the next few minutes." This last brought a heart-warming round of applause for his self-effacing attitude. He told the audience how fabulous it was, then described his Arabian horse ranch and a dressage maneuver called a "piaffe." Now, "piaffe" is pronounced "pyaf," but Wayne doesn't know that. He thinks it's pronounced "pee-off." He had us in stitches.

Then he slid into "Red Roses For a Blue Lady," and "Danke Schoen," modestly confessing that "these have been the most important songs in our career and the songs that made us famous." I looked around the stage like Sherlock Holmes but he was the only one there.

Getting serious again—"In our opinion," he continued, "this is one of the prettiest songs of the year." With that he launched into "Love Story," bringing it alive to everybody at the part where it says "I reach for her hand" and he reached out his hand just like he was reaching out his hand. "It's amazing how many people confuse folk music and Country and Western music," he explained a few minutes later. Then it was joke time.

"Were you there when the ship hit the sand," he said, that mischievous little grin flouncing from lip to lip again. It reminded me of my favorite religious song, "Were You There When They Crucified My Pomeranian?" Then he sang "Help Me Make It Through the Night" and told the audience that "Yoar reely sumpin."

Now things got serious. "This is the most requested song we've ever had during our show business career," he said, wrapping an arm around himself. It was, needless to say, "Danny Boy." It included his quoting from a new non-existent letter that has apparently taken the place of the old non-existent letter from which he used to quote. "Dear Mom," this one begins. And it is better than the old one, because Wayne was apparently there when Mom read it. "Now the mother's old hands begin to tremble," he explained.

At the end, the audience rose as one but do you think Wayne went around combing his hair or buffing his fingernails? He certainly did not. He just stood there in his beloved Christ-on-the-Cross position, head bowed, arms extended to each side, palms out, eyes brimming, overcome with the totally unexpected and spontaneous heartfelt tribute of the audience.

Like last time.

REVELATION NUMBER 16
January 28, 1976

And I heard a great voice out of the Palace of Cows, saying to the 18 Berserk Behemoths: Go your ways, and wrestle, and pour out the bile of the wrath of God upon the Ring. All at the same time.

And the first, called Andre the Giant, went, and poured out his bile upon the Masked Invader, and there fell a noisome and grievous sore upon the Masked Invader, who had the mark of the beast, and he was hurled from the Ring, and the Men of the Helmets did take him and lead him from the Ring, and he was vanquished, and then there were 17 Berserk Behemoths.

And the second, called Moondog Mayne, poured out his bile upon him called Dutch Savage, and it became as the blood of a dead man, and every living soul in the Palace of Cows did cry out and thrust arms to the sky and they were glad.

And the third, the Great Fuji, poured out his bile upon him called

Mr. Saito, and the Fountain of Pers-pire became blood, and the Masses said, "Great Joy" and "It looks like ketchup!"

And I heard the Angel of the Soiled Collar say, "Thou art Righteous, Andre the Giant, which are, and wast, and shalt be, because thou hast thrown the Masked Invader from the Temple, and now, even as we speak, art thrashing Pedro Morales about the head and shoulders, doing unto him Contusions and Abrasions."

And it was good, for they have shed the blood of the Participants, and given the audience satisfaction, for they are worthy.

And the fourth, called Ray Stevens, poured out his bile upon Bobby Jaggers, and power was given unto him to rend his face and hurl him from the Ring, and the Masses were glad, and sayeth, "Break his back!"

And the Masses were scorched with heat, and blasphemed the Men of Helmets, and the name of Roy Shire, called The Promoter, who hath power over these Plagues, and they repented.

And the fifth, called Pat Patterson, poured out his bile upon the seat of the beast, who was, in this case, Rocky "Soulman" Johnson, who was full of darkness, and he gnawed his tongue with pain, and was hurled from the Ring and called Eliminated.

And the sixth, Dory Funk, Jr., poured his bile upon Andre the Giant, and joined with Ray Stevens to hurl the Mammoth One from the Ring, that the way of the King of the Hill might be prepared.

And I saw three unclean spirits like frogs come out of the mouth of the Masses and out of the mouth of the False Prophet, which was called Show Biz.

For they are the spirits of devils, working miracles, which go forth unto the Box Office, seeking tickets to the Venue, to gather them to the battle of that great day of him called Shire, who hath dubbed it Battle Royal.

And behold, for I come as a thief, bearing Comps. But blessed is he that watcheth, and payeth, and keepeth his garments, lest he walk naked and they see his shame and think that he taketh not what transpires with solemnity.

And the seventh, Great Fuji, poured out his bile into the air, and sand into the countenance of Ray Stevens, who cried out and flung himself about the Ring in Throes, and then there was one, and there came a great voice out of the temple of heaven, from the throne, saying: It is done, Great Fuji hath profited seven silver talents and a lovely trophy.

And there were voices, and they did say Boo, and they did say Hiss, and thunders, and lightnings, and there was a great earthquake as the Masses began to pummel one another in the Aisles, such as was not since men were upon the earth, and especially since the Marquis of Queensbury.

And the Palace of Cows was divided into three parts: Pro-Fuji, anti-Fuji and Undecided, and there was venting of spleen and beating of breast, and great Babylon came in remembrance before God.

And every island fled away, and the mountains were not found, and the Tribe of Drools did reign.

And there fell upon men a great hail out of heaven, every stone the weight of a Wrestling Fan, and they blasphemed God because of the plague of the hail, for the plague thereof was exceedingly great.

AND NOW, BILLY GRAHAM
July 26, 1971

Several years ago, John Lennon said of the Beatles, "We are more popular than Jesus." This provoked a predictable response from the lunatic fringe, but of course, what he said was true. He did not say, "We are better than Jesus," just more popular. Record sales continue to bear this out.

It is interesting to note that the last show business act presented in a Bay Area baseball park—before Billy Graham—was by the very same Beatles. They gave their last formal public concert at Candlestick Park in the summer of 1966.

Graham opened a 10-day gig Friday night at the Oakland Coliseum. And, incidentally, outdrew the Beatles on opening night. The Liverpool moppets did about 28,000; Graham pulled 31,400. Of course, his price was right. Free.

The Billy Graham Revue, subtitled "Northern California Crusade," comprises music, song and patter. The opening night show got off to a leisurely start (Never give the audience your best shot early; build) with a 5,000-voice choir, a hymn and a prayer by Grady Wilson, "Associate Evangelist." That's Rev. Wilson's title, not the name of his prayer. Then George Beverly Shea and the choir rendered "How Great Thou Art," the Elvis Presley tune.

So far, not really socko. But then, you had to wait a whole act for the nude scene in "Hair."

Next appeared the Danniebelles, a female vocal quartet that falls somewhere between the Supremes and the Mormon Tabernacle Choir. They sang "God Is Not Dead," a moving little piece that forcefully answers the question posed by a recent *Time* magazine cover.

Then, a respite for the "Offertory Prayer." W. Robert Stover, president of Western Girl, stated that "there is no remuneration to Dr. Graham." This went over very big. Even Joan Baez charges two bucks a throw....

Three musical numbers followed—the Danniebelles with "Amazing Grace" (the recent Judy Collins hit, but done to the melody of "Danny Boy"), a sing-along on "His Name Is 'Wonderful'" and George Beverly Shea, who knocked off "He Touched Me" in a snappy fashion.

At this point, a couple of criticisms. The sound system is tinny and Cliff Barrow, the choir conductor, needs to tone down his gesticulations a bit. He looked like Zubin Mehta trying to fly.

Well, by now, the opening acts had done their job, the audience was warmed up and the star appeared. Speaking in a strong, commanding voice (three distinct echoes to each word in the cavernous Coliseum), Graham immediately established his schtick for the evening: "Jesus Christ Superstar," after the rock opera of the same name—another sharp show biz tactic. If you wish to enlarge your audience, include material which will appeal to those not already on your side. Example: Frank Sinatra's recording of "Green." Sinatra buffs will love it because it's Frank; those interested in ecology (or money, for that matter) will be drawn to the subject matter.

From that point on, we were Billy's. "You may never have another moment when you stand before God as you do tonight," he said. (Let the Listener Know He's Special.) "Bring a Bible...we're not here to put on a show." (Audience participation.)

"You don't have rock operas about Mohammed or Buddha." (Relevance.) "I do not understand The Trinity...how can my little finite mind understand that?" (Just folks.) "Where you are 100 years from now may be decided tonight." (Tantalize. Create Suspense.)

Then, just as fever pitch was reached and people were flipping through their Bibles like a lady trying to find a plumber in the Yellow Pages after the toilet backs up, came the "Invitation." This is known as the Let Them Down Gently technique. In supper club singing, for example, you will notice that the Big Ballad—the "Climb Every Mountain" or "You'll Never Walk Alone" or "The Impossible Dream"— invariably comes one or two songs before the end. Never at the end. (Let Them Down Gently.)

The "Invitation," in this case, consisted of an invitation to come on down to the playing field and "Declare For Christ." Several thousand people did this. My mind immediately flashed to Nancy Ames shaking hands with ringsiders at the Fairmont. And, finally, came an encore "Benediction," a number of dubious hit potential but perhaps appropriate as walking music, since that's what most people were doing at the time.

What can the neophyte entertainer learn from this? Well, aside from a few obvious tricks of the trade, the greatest lesson is that the bigger you are, the more jealousy will follow you. Some people call Billy Graham a "Counterfeit Christian." Even as he was doing his number inside the Coliseum, gossips and speakers of vitriol were distributing leaflets outside. "Facts you ought to know concerning counterfeit Christianity," one said sternly. Citing II Cor. 5:15, it grumbled that "When a person becomes a Christian, his bad habits leave him and he acquires new desires. Vainglory and exaltation, such as is common in the entertainment world, is abominable to him—prompting him to LEAVE same immediately."

Nonsense.

3

Topless

Statistically, the Composite Topless Dancer is 647 years old,
has a 1,028 ½ inch bust, a 700 waist and 1,016 hips.
She is not overweight, however, being 152 feet,
eight inches tall and weighing a fragile 3,506 pounds.

JLW

Weaned on classical strip-tease, John never took topless dancing, San Francisco's answer to the death of burlesque, seriously. But it had its charms— pretty young women, live music, a two-drink minimum, $1.50 a drink, and the same press agent, 320-lb. Davey Rosenberg, one of North Beach's most colorful characters.

John commemorated each anniversary of Carol Doda's first topless performance at the Condor with a feature story. Once he conducted a survey of club dancers and as part of his composite portrait, presented a grand total of their vital statistics.

The Topless allowed him to loosen up his writing and to indulge his considerable fascination with San Francisco's underbelly and women's overbellies.

In 1966, as the Alcoholic Beverage Control Board labored to revoke the liquor licenses of clubs featuring topless waitresses (claiming that nudity and liquor were a dangerous mix), John joined in the fray, making appearances as an expert witness to testify that topless dancers did not appeal to prurient interest, did not offend community standards, did not incite to violence and would not hurt a fly.

In San Francisco's flesh parade topless followed burlesque, bottomless dancing followed topless, and bodybuilding—bare pecs after bare mams— brought up the rear. John met Arnold Schwarzenegger in 1975 on the set of "Pumping Iron." At first, Arnold says, he thought John was a priest because he was dressed all in black ("Was the Catholic Church sending someone to cover bodybuilding?" he wondered), but after they became friends he started buying black shirts, too. John introduced the charismatic bodybuilder to people who might be able to help him in the entertainment business and even threw parties in his honor. At one of them, Arnold walked out with New Yorker cartoonist William Hamilton's date.

Like John, many of the key players of the Topless Era are gone. Davey Rosenberg and his public relations partner, Peter Marino, died in the '80s. Blaze Starr's autobiography was made into a movie starring Paul Newman as Huey Long. Carol Doda opened a lingerie shop in San Francisco, got a 900 number and started a rock and roll band—Carol Doda and Her Lucky Stiffs. The Condor is now a bistro owned by topless entrepreneur Walter Pastore. Arnold Schwarzenegger has made millions playing a movie robot avenger. He married Maria Shriver, a niece of John F. Kennedy, befriended George Bush, and has political ambitions in the state of California.

Look Ma, No Bra

July 12, 1964

On January 31, 1964, Judy Mac marched onto the hot-lit stage of the Galaxie and started Swimming.

Few present then realized that waves from this historic plunge would, within six months, threaten to engulf all of North Beach.

The vivacious dancer is still packing the club and considered by connoisseurs to be the freestyle champ, but in one respect, the act is old hat.

That is, she still has her clothes on.

This may sound only reasonable to those who have not made the Broadway scene lately, but to the regular melange of swingers, tourists and itinerant poets who answer the weekend cattle call, it closely resembles a hardening of the creative arteries.

For a violent competition for the North Beach-cum-Swim dollar has led to the most outlandish proliferation of new gimmicks since the advent of Prohibition.

The Swim and audience-participation dancing at the Galaxie have been answered by stage-like dance floors, writhing waitresses, fluorescent lighting, champagne showers and finally, the coup de bare, designer Rudi Gernreich's topless suit.

Leading the charge to glory is the Condor. Populated by midgets, pugilists and, circumference-wise, the largest press agent in the world, the club sparked the rock 'n' roll revival on Broadway in 1962.

But more recently, genial Pete Mattioli was in a dither. George and Teddie were gone, everybody else had rock 'n' roll by now, and the newly-installed $3,000 white piano that goes up and down like a yo-yo was not exactly setting the show biz world on fire.

Genial Pete was down, but not out.

Then, "Eureka, we'll drop it," he said, approximating Archimedes, and a new era was born.

Dropped was dancer Carol Doda's top, upped were the attendance figures, and everybody is joyous once again, including Carol.

"I don't mind wearing the suit," says the platinum-haired 23-year-old. "It's right for me. I'm really not a great dancer, but a lot of great dancers don't get the audience reaction that I do."

Truer words were never spoken.

Meanwhile, at the rival Off Broadway, owner Voss Borreta was not to be caught napping. Some weeks ago he built a champagne shower stall into a wall and installed Swimmer Dee Dee, a voluptuously constructed young lady who is somewhat less enthusiastic about the topless than Miss Doda.

As kindly patron Borreta put it, "Well, you know, she has, uh, well...more."

Before the June 18 revelation at the Condor, Dee Dee had contented herself with a bikini, but upon hearing the news she rose to the occasion like General Meade facing Pickett's charge and whipped off her top.

Of the frilly she has sewn to the suit's narrow straps, she thoughtfully explains that "It's sexier with ruffles. People have to watch more carefully. It COULD be vulgar, you know. Of course, I do not refer to my counterparts."

One counterpart to whom she does not refer—Tosha, the 74-pound Japanese doll at Big Al's—is less gung-ho yet.

"I've been brought up as a good Catholic," moans the tiny dancer, "and this is all very embarrassing for me."

Big Al, who grumbled, groused and finally bribed Tosha to join the fun parade, has taken steps, however, to preserve her feelings. The room is darkened and fluorescent lights illuminate her near-costume, often leaving something to the imagination.

"It was a hell of a job, at that," muses Big Al. But the topless is not a cornucopia of dollars everywhere.

The Peppermint Tree is doing SRO business by letting the audience provide the floor show, an innovation which is finding increasing acceptance up and down the road. Their dance floor ("largest in North Beach!!") is both elevated and specially lighted, the better to see and be seen.

"It swings, and we like to dance and meet people," suggested visitors Lola and Sherry. "We used to go to El Cid but this is bigger and more people can see you. And you can watch and pick up new steps." Among other things.

And down at Tipsy's, rugged individualist Pee Wee Ferrari is the Beach's answer to Billy Graham.

"We absolutely are not going to sink to the topless, or have a strip in here," he says firmly. "A lot of ladies resent it. Anyway, who needs it?

Once we get the fluorescent lighting in, and the band keeps imitating the Beatles, and Shannon's bikini is specially treated and...."

But the saddest topless tale of all comes from Karl Morales, owner of the Bunny Room. "Oh, we tried it a couple of weeks ago, and it was great, the place was packed. But the people were so bug-eyed nobody drank. They just sat there, clutching their glasses.

"I spent 26 bucks on that crummy suit."

There Are Two Things in Life—Work and Sex

September 20, 1970

As Louis Armstrong and Pearl Bailey approach the end of their highly-publicized and historic appearance here at the International, an equally historic engagement is being played out at the Aladdin.

Lili St. Cyr, a giant in the history of the strip-tease, is making her final offering to the fantasies of mankind. After some 30 years on stage, much of it spent in a tub, Lili is ready to hang up her $1,000 gowns and $1.98 bath towels for the peace and quiet of her home, her cats and her lover.

Lili has talked of retiring for years, but it now seems likely that she will carry through the threat. Although her body is still that of a woman 25 years younger, what was previously a job, a vocation, now has become a trial and a tribulation. The stage lights are a bit lower these days, a bit dimmer, and something has gone out of her bumps. But she's still the class of the field, the most elegant stripper of them all. Her retirement is the end of an era.

I've known Lili for more than six years but never cease to be amazed at the contrast between the private woman and the public performer. There is still a girlish lilt in her voice, an implied naivete that has not been extinguished by 5,000 nights in a saloon. Although it is hard to accept, I do not exaggerate when I say that she would look more at home at a PTA meeting than in Las Vegas.

I descended to the backstage dressing rooms, dodging Minsky's showgirls and dancers, and knocked. "Don't come in," she called through the door like a girl getting ready for the prom, "I'm not dressed."

Eventually she was and I sat down amidst the tools of the trade—make-up regalia, bare bulbs blinding a large mirror, ash trays (although she doesn't smoke), underwear hanging from hooks, a wig, the performing wardrobe, a wrinkled bed for between-shows reading. She doesn't mix during off-hours.

Her manner was subdued, as always, except for giggling at innocent intrigues and gossip.

The obvious question: Won't you miss performing after all these years, show biz in the blood, the smell of the greasepaint, the roar of the crowd?

She looked as if she had just gotten a whiff of tear gas. "I hate it...I haven't been enthusiastic for 10 years. And I just can't face any more openings. Never again! It's terror...before the last one I was shaking like a leaf, I started to stutter, it was so bad that I had to get help to put on my false eyelashes.

"Anyway," she concluded, veering away from the re-lived experience, "God knows it's about time."

Lili does not now and never has liked music or children. They both make her nervous. She has said that there are only two things in life...work and sex. She has been married six or seven times ("Usually because it made the man feel more secure"), the last from 1959 to 1964 to a Hollywood special effects man. Generally, she has favored large, rugged types—often younger.

Her present soulmate is a sometime soldier of fortune some 20 years her junior. Lili's age has been printed often but she has finally reached a point of sensitivity. "Maybe they've forgotten," she says with an amiable, yet hollow laugh. "Just say that she's growing old gracefully." The leisure hours of her retirement will be filled with aforementioned-items and her boutique, The Undie World of Lili St. Cyr.

Back upstairs, a baggy pants vaudeville comedian named Irving Benson was on. "I couldn't get lucky in a girl's prison with a handful of pardons," Benson cracks. Silence. "I thought I got rid of you creeps after the first show," he grumbles. Laughter.

A production number—"The Sacrifice of the Aztec Maiden," or some similar documentary—followed, and was in turn followed by the show's other solo stripper, Diane Lewis. Miss Lewis is a beautiful black-haired girl who specializes in traditional strip—a ramp-stripper, I believe they're called. Miss Lewis waltzed on stage, removed offending garments from time to time, engaged the floor in mortal combat, flung her excellent body from hither to yon, peeled to an itsy-witsy teenie-weenie strategic patch and vanished.

"And now, the Aladdin Hotel takes great pride in presenting Miss Lili St. Cyr...."

She glides on in an elegant midi-and-boots outfit, lounges momentarily on a convenient couch, stalks the stage like a tiger queen, strips, takes her fabled bath, towels down, knocks off a couple of grinds and reclines again on the couch. Not much in the description, but then neither is Ella Fitzgerald when described as a vocalist.

MAMA'S NEVER SEEN ME NUDE

June 11, 1975

The nicest, most unpretentious performers I have met in 12 years of lurking about the periphery of show business have been the old-pro strippers and veterans of the skin trade.

Lili St. Cyr, Tempest Storm, Sally Rand—each, without exception, combines personal dignity and an almost child-like innocence quite absent in the younger generation of ecdysiasts and their less ceremonious counterparts, the topless dancers.

The reasons for this, other than a gracefulness that sometimes accompanies the aging process, would appear to lie with two factors. The first is that when these women began working—from 25 to 50 years ago—both ends of the word "strip-tease" meant something. Today, only the former is operative. And the key component, the tease, required some class, some thought, some originality. Artful disrobing involves style; taking off your clothes does not.

The second factor, perhaps, is that strippers were, in the public mind, ipso facto, sinful ladies. And, just as I have never read of a high fashion model who wears anything but dungarees and a floppy shirt around the house, there was doubtless a compensatory need for these

Fallen Women to assume off-stage an almost exaggerated level of decorous propriety.

Whatever the case, and for whatever reasons, these stripper babes are terrific and late last week I finally got to meet the one remaining old pro whose path has not cleaved San Francisco in the last decade. Blaze Starr is her name and the Palace Theater, 53 Turk Street, is her game— at least through tomorrow night.

As is traditional, Blaze's name, age and measurements are as often whimsy as fact—but her credentials are imposing, her past colorful. She is, with Tempest Storm (Lili St. Cyr has, as far as I can determine, retired), the sole remaining burlesque superstar, she is being paid $4,000 a week for her labors here, she was once the bejeweled mistress of Louisiana Governor Earl Long, she was stabbed nearly to death resisting robbers who came for those jewels one night, she is financially independent—if not independently wealthy—and has recently published a book chronicling these festivities, catchily entitled *Blaze Starr: My Life as Told to Huey Perry.*

Her real name is Fannie Belle Fleming, her age is 43 (in 1967, she was revealing her age as 30, but imploring an interviewer to "say 29… it's good for business"), she freely admits to a recent chemotherapy face-lift but sternly denies any artificial input for her quite ample breasts; her measurements are 38 ("double-D"), 25 and 37 (they have been reported, variously, as 40-24-38, 40-23-38 and 48-24-36) and is a less-than-sylphlike five feet six and a half, 135 pounds.

She was born in Wilsondale, W. Va., happily refers to herself as a "hillbilly," was reared a strict Baptist, has been stripping for 26 years and relies—unlike her contemporaries—not on lithe sensuality of movement but bawdy comedy and discreet audience participation for her success.

"Ah don't dance," she drawled after the 4 p.m. show, jammed without complaint into a tiny backstage dressing room. "Ah do comedy and bounce. Ah can't dance a step."

She was nude, save for some panties, and bustled about looking for her clothes. "Lemme just get mah britches on," she said amiably, "and we can talk." She fastened on her Bali bra ("They sent me 50 of 'em a couple of years ago"), manipulated her breasts into the cups ("get in there, kids") and reflected on Blaze Starr.

"Ah'm Fannie Belle Fleming," she said. "Ah separate mah personal life from Blaze Starr. Ah'm not interested in fancy clothes and jewelry, but nothin's too good for Blaze. Ah see that Blaze has everything for the stage. She's been good to me...."

She paused for a moment, then spoke brightly. "Even mah mama gets a big bang out of me now. 'Course mama's never seen me completely nude; only down to pasties and a G-string." She shook her head, thinking about the new requirements of stripping. "If mah mama ever saw me out there like that," she concluded, "ah think she'd chase me all the way down Turk Street...."

A Superlative Bodybuilder
March 29, 1976

The worlds of show business and sport generally overlap on only one level—that of entertainment. But on Saturday night in San Jose, the two became one.

The occasion was the "Mr. Western America" and "Mr. California" bodybuilding contests, staged at the beautiful new Center for the Performing Arts.

The competition for the two titles was the sport.

But the superstars of the evening were not vying for these titles, which are, in the pantheon of bodybuilding, small time. These giants were men who erased boundaries between show biz and sport. Their names—Ed Corney, Robbie Robinson, Joe Nista Jr., Frank Zane, Ken Waller and Arnold Schwarzenegger—will be unfamiliar to most people, as is their game. But I assure you that no superstar performer was ever greeted with more appreciation, awe or astonishment than were the gentlemen named above.

And one of them, Arnold Schwarzenegger, has done what Frank Sinatra did for boy singers, what the Beatles did for rock groups, what Arnold Palmer did for golf and what Babe Ruth did for baseball—he has transcended the world of his counterparts and changed the face of his profession.

What Arnold Schwarzenegger did on Saturday night was show business.

Schwarzenegger, an Austrian in his late 20s, now living in the United States, is one of the handful of bodybuilders ever to become well known outside the confines of this strange little world where men develop their upper-arm muscles to an expansion which equals the waist measurements of a particularly svelte woman; in Schwarzenegger's case, biceps measuring 22 inches in circumference. He has been given the imprimatur of legitimate athletics in the pages of *Sports Illustrated*, is the focus of a fascinating book called *Pumping Iron,* the star of an upcoming film of the same title, and of yet another film entitled "Stay Hungry." The six-two, 240-pound muscleman dominates his field to a degree no man has before him.

What he and the rest did on Saturday night was both bizarre and breathtaking. In individual performances that lasted no more than 90 seconds, each man contrived to exhibit, to a capacity house of 2,000 or so (at no less than $10 a person), every major muscle group in their body, in a sculptured relief that has about as much in common with the average man's body as does Michelangelo's "David" with Porky Pig.

The logic of competitive bodybuilding escapes me, but the results—and the incredible amount of work implied—are extraordinary. That bodybuilders are an exhibitionistic, narcissistic lot is undeniable, but the same statement may be made for Barbra Streisand and Sammy Davis, Jr. That they are athletes is also fair; certainly if golfers and place kickers are so considered.

The difference is that, while athletes rarely do exhibitions, and performers rarely compete, bodybuilders are both and do both.

And so, when Arnold Schwarzenegger came on Saturday night— after Mr. California was crowned, after Mr. Western America was crowned, after his counterparts had done their 90 seconds, and 20 minutes of "Pumping Iron" was screened—the electricity swept through the audience just as surely, if with somewhat more restraint, as it did 50 miles away, at almost the same moment, when the Who thundered into their first number at Winterland.

Out he strode, his blond head a pin-point, almost comical, perched above massive, smoldering, shuddering shoulders and chest, his walk one of purpose, his manner one swagger short of arrogance. Up to the stage he climbed, past the ersatz Greek columns, oblivious, surely, to the Muzak strains of "Exodus."

A moment's pause, and then the poses, one after another, front and back, this side, the other side, each for only seconds, yet requiring such strain that he was puffing slightly when it was over. Total concentration. The best.

I wouldn't know a body if I saw one. But I do know something about superstars and show biz and charisma. You ought to catch Arnold Schwarzenegger's act some time. Note the name. You won't be required to spell it.

BLIND FAITH REWARDED
July 14, 1976

Perhaps I should have suspected something when Marinoberg-Rosearino, the giant flackery operated by David Rosenberg and Peter Marino, rang up on Friday afternoon and informed me that the Cadillac limousine which was to convey me that night across the bay to "Bodybuilding '76" at the Oakland Paramount Theater had been involved in a collision at the airport and was, for the foreseeable future, *hors de combat.*

But, as love is blind, so too is my admiration for Marinoberg-Rosearino and the two distinguished gentlemen who direct its world-wide operations.

After all, Rosenberg, whose gentle corpulence and generous nature have earned him the sobriquet "The Kris Kringle of Pubic Hair," and Marino, whose penchant for understated elegance in his attire has made him the envy of every pimp in the Bay Area, had never before led me astray.

Despite his lifelong reluctance to meet the English language on a one-to-one basis, Rosenberg has had a way, over the years, of meeting challenges head on, whether it be chaining a topless dancer to the Golden Gate Bridge in order to protest the rising suicide rate, or referring with withering sarcasm to members of the Alcoholic Beverage Control Board as "them cruds."

For his part, Marino has taken equally gutsy positions on contemporary public issues. A founder and past president of Odd Lib, Marino has also spearheaded the drive to have cotton, wool and flax placed on an

Endangered Yarn list, ban their use by the textile industry and encourage a return to more traditional fabrics like leopard skins, whale pelts and, of course, his personal favorite, rat fur.

"God's clothes," he calls them.

So it was with buoyant spirits that I anticipated "Bodybuilding '76" at the Oakland Paramount last weekend. There would be Franco Columbu, "The World's Strongest Man Born in Sardinia," Ed Corney, "Mr. Universe," Rick Wayne, "Mr. Foster City," half a dozen other musclemen and a terpischorean bevy of bounteous beauties, known as the Margo Tembey Dancers.

Earlier, I had asked Marino the classic question: Why?

"We feel," he had said, carefully weighing his words, "that these people have something to say about the contemporary inability of human beings to relate to themselves and their cybernetic environment, while still being able to enjoy Orowheat Seasoned Croutons."

"That's troo," Rosenberg said quietly.

"You see," Marino continued, "we'll start with a classical *pas de quinze* by eight bodybuilders and seven dancers, giving way to a toga-clad behemoth, alone on stage, silhouetted against a screen on which is projected a picture of the universe.

"Into this tableau will whirl a mysterious figure, a woman, clad all in lavender, wispy chiffon sashes seeking freedom from their bounds as she flies about the stage until—get this—she sees this toga-clad behemoth. 'Hark!' she says. 'Who art?'

"The figure is silent. She goes up to him. She is perplexed. Again, she cries: 'Who art? And whence?'

"The figure remains silent, disdaining her queries. Yet she is intrigued, inquisitional. 'Art thou deaf and dumb, mammoth person?' she persists. 'Doth thou think thy is Helen Keller?'

"No longer able to contain her pique, she rushes around him in ever-narrowing circles, rending and tearing at his garment, seeking to dispel his equilibrium. Soon, he is down to his briefs. Still, he will not speak. Her love has turned to contempt. 'Cat got thou tongue?' she taunts."

"Wait a minute," I blurt to Marino. "Is that it?"

"Oh no," he replies hastily. "There's much more. The girls dance, the men pose, there'll be some nice recorded music, some tasteful ads for gymnasiums, balloons will fall on cue from the ceiling and Franco

Columbu will blow up a hot water bottle until it bursts." Rosenberg nodded, his eyes misty. "It'll be grate," he said.

Well, as I said earlier, Marinoberg-Rosearino had never led me astray.

And they didn't this time.

That's just the way it happened.

4

Green Door to the Ultra Room

This is what investigative sexual reporting is all about,
sweetie. Slogging through uncharted swamps of irrelevent data.
Laying bare hitherto unsought information. Answering questions
no one has asked. Discovering, as it were, cures for which
there is no social disease.

JLW

*The transition from semi-nude and nude dancing in bars to pornographic
feature films and live sex shows took place in the late '60s. With the 1970
release of "Behind the Green Door," one of the first hard-core feature films to
have some sort of plot and to appeal to couples as well as stags, pornography
entered a new front-room phase. Filmmaker Alex de Renzy, theater owner Les
Natali and Jim and Artie Mitchell, who were both, were the main players in
this new scene.*

The Mitchells were Barbary Coast characters from Antioch, a Sacramento delta town, who made hundreds of stag loops before hitting it big with "Green Door," starring Marilyn Chambers. The film drew 60,000 patrons to the brothers' O'Farrell Theater in its first 24 weeks.

John liked the Mitchells because they were intelligent mavericks who knew how to treat their friends. Their office on the second floor of the O'Farrell was like a clubhouse, with its pool table and refrigerator stocked with beer and other potables. There were drugs for the asking and plenty of scantily clad women about. Among other denizens were Maitland (Sandy) Zane and Dan O'Neill from the Chronicle, Warren Hinckle from the Examiner and Hunter S. Thompson.

John was powerfully attracted to sleaze—strip joints, porno filmmakers, hookers, hit men—the antithesis of his middle-class upbringing. Pornography was doubly attractive because it was also a free-speech issue. The new sexual freedom brought out a new breed of would-be censors. Under California's Obscenity Law, Penal Code Provision 311a (declared unconstitutional in 1974), police could arrest not only theater owners and performers, but all personnel. It was out-and-out harrassment, John believed, meant to punish. The Mitchells, who were arrested many times, chose to fight. John was invited to join a superior legal defense team headed by attorney Joseph Rhine, his partner Michael Kennedy, Kennedy's wife Eleanore, who coached witnesses in court demeanor and dress, and psychiatrist and forensics expert Martin Blinder.

Blinder testified on "prurient interest" while John handled "community standards." They called themselves the Batman and Robin of Pornography and almost never lost a case.

John once told a group of students at San Jose State that pornography was "possibly anti-human," and he decried its lack of eroticism. He confided to Annette Haven, a sex-film actress with whom he was intimate, that he had been "desensitized" early on by watching a barrage of hard-core films. The Rhine-Kennedy defense team used the technique on juries to reduce the shock value of a film on trial.

Blinder claims he and John had no qualms about defending pornography: "From my perspective and John's, there was only one point of view, and that was that these films were harmless. It was a nice amalgam of justice, show biz, law, psychiatry and doing the right thing." If he hadn't hated studying so much, John might have been an attorney, for he found court combat exhilarating. The money wasn't bad either—he was paid $500 a day, double what he made in a week at the Chronicle in 1970.

The Mitchells and their sex show performers provided spice at John's parties, but "Party Artie," the younger brother, could be explosive. At a 1978 bash, Bill Hamilton accused him of producing child pornography, and Mitchell pushed him violently, breaking his drawing thumb. Attorney (now Speaker of the California State Assembly) Willie Brown, a guest, offered to mediate a settlement. Bill and Artie were ordered to pay John $1,000 each because they'd ruined his party. Jim Mitchell paid his brother's part in cash and John wrapped the money in butcher paper and put it in the freezer, where Ward Dunham located it after his death.

Great American Music Hall owners Tom and Jeanne Bradshaw, the Chronicle and the Mitchell Brothers paid for John's wake at the Music Hall. "We're really going to miss that guy," Artie told Tom, "but we showed him a good time while he was with us. Did I ever tell you about the orgy we threw for him and Sammy Davis, Jr.? Wassy had been to a few parties he claimed to be orgies, but this was the first real orgy he was ever at."

On Feb. 27, 1991, two days after the 12th anniversary of John's death, Jim Mitchell shot his brother Artie to death. Michael Kennedy flew in from New York to defend him on a first degree murder charge. He won, in a way. The jury was not persuaded by the defense contention that Jim was trying to get his brother into treatment for alcohol and drug addiction when the intervention went awry, but they didn't buy first degree, either. Jim was convicted of voluntary manslaughter and sentenced to six years in prison. He is free, pending the outcome of an appeal.

Annette Haven married, went back to school and completed an A.A. degree in speech and behavioral science. She only works in sex films now that depict "safe sex in a safe manner." Her former co-star, "Johnny Wadd" Holmes, died of AIDS. Sharon McNight, who directed them in the Mitchell Brothers' sex farce "Autobiography of a Flea," became an award-winning cabaret performer. Marilyn Chambers married Linda Lovelace's ex-husband, Chuck Traynor, and has a child. Lovelace has written two books alleging physical brutality by Traynor, including forced sex with animals; Gloria Steinem wrote the foreword to her last book.

The O'Farrell Theater, with one Mitchell Brother at the helm, continues to offer movie screenings, staged sex acts, a shower show and the Gallery of

Gynecomania, where each customer can focus on areas of interest with his very own flashlight.

LINDA'S GOURMET TASTES

May 2, 1973

You know the television commercial in which the man with an upset stomach moans "I can't believe I ate the whole thing," then pops a couple of Alka Seltzers?

Well, Linda Lovelace likes that commercial so much she inscribes a version of it on everything she autographs. "To John," she wrote briskly, "I CAN believe I ate the whole thing! I love it!"

Without going into Linda's gourmet tastes, suffice it to say that the ebullient and wide-eyed star of "Deep Throat" wafted into town last week, settled in for an hour or so at Perry's on Union Street, dazzled the great and near-great of journalism and revealed her thoughts on literature, thespianism and how a young girl bereft of conventional talent might get ahead in show business.

The questioning began in the dignified and thoughtful manner for which journalists are so justly renowned. "Do you wear a bra?" inquired a middle-aged social scientist, ignoring the overwhelming visual evidence at hand. "Ha, ha, you are a cluck," several of us more hip observers said to him. "Oh, no," Linda said prettily. "Well, gosh," the columnist said, chagrined—"I don't go to those movies."

"How did you get started in pornographic movies?" a syndicated savant queried after much thought. "Uh, umm, I don't really know, aah, umm, I guess...well, it was...uh...."

"Okay," I interjected, "then how did you get the job in 'Deep Throat?'" "Just a minute," the syndicated savant said irately. "Let her finish her answer."

Linda is 22 years old, has curly brown hair and bright eyes. She was wearing a perky yellow hat, a brown leather jacket, a yellow sweater and no make-up. As is true with many of the new breed of sex stars, at such times as she keeps her mouth shut and her clothes on, she could easily pass for a meter-maid or an aging girl-scout.

The world's first authentic pornographic film star was here to promote her new book, "Inside Linda Lovelace." Predictably, she had some assistance—"with the vocabulary"—but it is otherwise her very own autobiography. She allowed as how she was born in the Bronx ("The Bronx? Why, I was born in the Bronx, too!" exclaimed an astonished film critic), has never been married, does not consider herself an actress ("I'm a Linda Lovelace," she said sweetly) but confesses that she can "sing—ha ha—and dance, ha ha ha."

I asked her about a photograph recently printed in a scandal sheet which purported to show Linda and a German shepherd involved in activities not sanctioned by the Golden Gate Kennel Club. "It wasn't me," she cooed, "they just put my name on a picture of someone else."

Ah, the travails of stardom. Soon as you get big, they try to knock you down. Well, I never really thought it was Linda, anyway. After all, she's a Star, the focus of attention. The couple in the photograph had assumed the canine-superior position.

The Harder They Fall

October 19, 1977

In the several years now since renowned porno profligate Harry Reems has retired from filmmaking in favor of defending himself against the lunatic crusades of the United States Attorney's office in Memphis, his de facto heir clearly has been John "Johnny Wadd" Holmes, a lad of extended renown in the business of whipping it out, getting it up and placing it where the sun rarely shines.

Thus it was not surprising when the Mitchell Brothers, those noble crusaders in the cause of free enterprise, announced—hard on the heels of Rudolf Nureyev's unprecedented organ solo in "Valentino"— that they were bringing young Wadd to town in order to prove, "hands-down," who is the biggest of them all.

"Nureyev, Schmureyev," they snorted, in that eloquent little way they have.

I arrived at the O'Farrell Theater's Ultra Room at 9:30 on Saturday night, the second of a four-day, 36-performance engagement.

That's correct. Thirty-six performances.

"You will see," said the ad, "Holmes and two of our most sensual Ultra Women performing acts you never thought possible!"

Mercy! I never thought three dozen performances in four days was possible, never mind what the acts were.

Before the show started, I interviewed several of the fools in the audience ($15 for a private booth at night, $12 for the corral).

Why are you here? I asked Joaquin Bandersnatch (not his real name). "Hey," he said casually, speaking quite clearly despite the fact that he was wearing a nylon stocking on his head. "You know, like, what is here? If this were somewhere else, then here would be there and there would be here, you know what I mean?"

And you? I asked Etaoin Shrdlu (not her real name). "Gee," she began, "well, you see, my boyfriend here" (she nodded toward Bandersnatch, who had cut some holes in a large brown paper bag and was placing it over his nylon stocking) "always says that 'It's not how long you make it, it's how you make it long,' and, to be candid, I'm not sure what that means."

The show started. Two scantily clad young ladies appeared in the Ultra Room and walked around for a while, adjusting their clothing and checking for lumps. After a few minutes of this, the room went dark and then was lit up by a flash. It seems they had found a magic lamp, fondled it in time-honored fashion and become the recipients of three wishes.

"We wish a person with a gargantuan member would appear here and take us on a magic carpet ride to the pinnacle of sexual ecstasy," they cried.

The room went dark again. The lights came up. Johnny Wadd had magically arrived, wearing a costume that identified him as the Caliph of Puerto Rico.

"Ooh, ahh," the young ladies said, tearing at his gaudy togs. "For wish No. 2, we want him to be our slave."

Wadd shrugged and asked them if they would like a Danish. "No, no, oh Keeper of the Great Appendage," they howled. "We want to see your noble thingie."

Wadd looked relieved, there being no place he could get a Danish at that time of night, anyway, and peeled off his bespangled bloomers.

"Ooh, ahh, gasp, gurgle," the girls gulped, unashamedly ogling the great dangling participle confronting them.

"But it seemeth to be dozing," they moaned in dismay. "Let's see if we can slap some life into it."

With that, they began vigorously pummeling the inert article, feigning mouth-to-mouth resuscitation and otherwise endeavoring to emulate the ancient miracle of the Princess and the Frog.

Alas, it was all for naught. Despite the most earnest of entreaties, the star of the show remained in a state of arrested development for the duration.

It was the first time I've ever heard an actor in a non-speaking role booed.

As Wadd valiantly fought off anguished tears of humiliation, the girls, contempt distorting their otherwise dreary features, summoned up their third wish. The lights went off again. When they came up, Wadd had went.

"Acts that you never thought possible!" the ad had promised.

That much, certainly, Johnny Wadd delivered.

A Tonier Kind of Sleaze

October 8, 1976

"The Autobiography of a Flea," which is now at the O'Farrell, is indisputably fleaist, and a traditional sex farce at its heart.

Directed and adapted (from an anonymous Victorian novel) by Sharon McNight, "Flea" has the most elegant pornographic appearance of any film made to date (as my colleague, Stanley Eichelbaum, noted, it looks like "a hard-core 'Barry Lyndon'").

It is grandly photographed, features a handsome cast, a sprightly score, more than a little humor and solid technical credits (more than solid in the persons of art director Gerd Mairandres and cinematographer Jon Fonatana).

But where it differs from conventional hard-core films is its tone.

The sex scenes are a part of the story, they are integral and motivated, and they are handled with a certain restraint. The reason for this may be traced to director McNight, who is not a pornographic filmmaker by profession, has extensive experience in legitimate theater and music, and as a result, brings few hoary cliches to her first such endeavor. She is interested in making a film, first; pornography, second. It shows.

Even the cast is upstanding, with Jean Jennings, a 19-year-old ingenue, playing the 14-year-old heroine with appropriate blankness, Paul Thomas (of "Beach Blanket Babylon Goes Bananas") as the sex-crazed monk with aplomb, the very lovely Annette Haven providing a smoldering sensuality to contrast Jennings' nymphet, and such other worthies as John C. Holmes, Dale Meador and John Leslie growing excited at the slightest drop of their drawers.

This is not to say that "Flea" does not contain its share of dirt and filth, but the presentation is stylish and, ironically, this has led to some concern on the part of the producers, the eminent Mitchell Brothers, that some of the sleazos who regularly frequent their theaters may disdain "Flea" for a more raunchy alternative.

That would be unfortunate, for if pornography is ever to become erotic, it will only be when relatively classy productions like this prove their box-office mettle.

GRAB THOSE MEMBERS WHILE YOU CAN
January 24, 1977

If one is to judge from "Kansas City Trucking Company," which is currently breaking house records at the Nob Hill Cinema, all truck drivers are:

1) Hung like Clydesdales,

2) Horny as goats, and

3) Gay as Tchaikovsky.

I'm not sure if all this is true, of course, as my only previous exposure to the sub-culture was "Truck Stop Women"—first of the now notorious "truxploitation" films—but I can tell you that 11 fellows in the audience were fondling CB antennas for the entire duration of the picture.

Well, in any event, I have now seen my very first full-length male homosexual hard-core pornographic movie. It was a swell experience.

Gay pornos ("gornos") are relatively new, as you doubtless know. Back in the good old days, like the middle '60s, when female "beaver" films were all the rage, the industry catered primarily to the heterosexual trade. Oh, sure, there was the occasional male "beaver-with-stick" flick, but these were the exception and generally screened only in old culverts.

Then, five or so years ago, along came the famed Wakefield Poole with "Boys in the Sand" and "Bijou," as well as the militant gay-porno ("gorno power") demonstrations. The rest, needless to say, is history. Accusations of "pornist" and "truckist" were bandied about, jockey shorts were burned on the steps of City Hall and Assemblyman Willie Brown introduced a bill in the state legislature to legalize male pregnancy.

Now we have the "Kansas City Trucking Company" and the Nob Hill Cinema, which is a members-only club. Well, as I like to say, you only go around once in life, and you've got to grab for all the members you can.

The Nob Hill Cinema and Arcade is a tidy little theater, serves free java in the lobby, and charges $5 to see "Kansas City Trucking Company" ($3 for weekday matinees when, I was informed, "we get a lot of businessmen").

In addition to the $3 or $5, you must pony up $1, if you have never been there before, for a year's membership card. Only members are allowed, like at the Pacific Union Club. I am now a member.

"The Nob Hill Cinema-Arcade is a members-only social and artistic facility dedicated to cinema and conviviality," my membership card says. This means you can do convivial things in the facility you can't do in the Curran or at a Board of Supervisors meeting. Which is where the Arcade comes in.

The Arcade is at the rear of the theater; a 30-foot hallway with lots of little rooms off it. The rooms have doors on them, but no lights inside. If you misplace your car keys or handcuffs in one of these rooms, you are in trouble.

Each room has one wall with oddly shaped apertures in it.

To again quote my membership card, "We believe in an atmosphere of freedom for individuals. If you are harassed or restricted by any unwelcome police agents or entrappers, please notify the management and we will provide legal representation for you at our expense."

Talk about a guarantee! I looked about. Only welcome police agents were in view. I returned from my tour just in time for "Kansas City Trucking Company," which is about a group of truckers engaged in an unrelenting 75-minute frenzy of masturbation, fellatio, sodomy, and unusual acts perpetrated against automobile windshields.

Subsequently, I spoke with the writer-director, Mr. Joe Gage. "I'm not sure I got the part about ejaculating on the car windshield," I confessed. He shrugged. "Nothing mysterious," he said. "Perhaps you've forgotten that he was standing on the hood."

Of course.

Peeping Tom in the Ultra Room
January 17, 1977

With the recent debut of Ultra Room, their latest brainstorm at the O'Farrell Theater, the notorious Mitchell Brothers, called "The Potentates of Porn" by *Time* magazine, have established yet another beachhead in their life-long quest for the ultimate fulfillment of public sexual fantasies.

The brothers—Jim ("James") and Artie ("Bob")—are, of course, wizened veterans of this pursuit at the tender ages of, respectively, 33 and 31.

After absenting themselves from the premises of San Francisco State's eight-millimeter home movie department in the late '60s, they opened the O'Farrell and commenced shooting and showing the first of hundreds of nudie "loops"—10-minute extravaganzas displaying nubile maidens engaged in naked-ironing and teaching old dogs new tricks.

Subsequently, in the late summer of 1969, they (and Alex de Renzy) broke the open-to-the-public hard-core pornographic film barrier and went on to produce "Behind the Green Door" (excepting "Deep Throat," probably the most famous pornographic film ever made), "Sodom and Gomorrah" (the first big-budget hard-core flick), "The Autobiography of a Flea" (the most elegant such effort) and, of course, made Marilyn Chambers a household (detergent) name.

But now, with Ultra Room, they have outdone themselves. In an arena—pornography—that has been combed, sifted, raked and circumscribed for centuries, the brothers have come up with what may well be an authentically new and unique gimmick.

Physically, Ultra Room, which opened January 4 and is still being refined, is properly kinky, but nothing you couldn't find in "Mondo Bondo." It is, indeed, a room, elevated a couple of feet off the floor, maybe 20 feet long and 10 feet wide, turned out in black vinyl and mirrored walls, awash with your standard household array of stainless-steel trapezes, chrome chains, velveteen whips, ropes, handcuffs and the odd pulley, and completely encircled by private viewing booths within which the observer, his wallet now lightened to the tune of 10 smackers, may for the ensuing 30 minutes visually peruse a quartet of unclothed young ladies disporting and frolicking through a variety of colorful practices, including self-abuse, crimes against nature, counterfeit torture and ensemble pseudo-lesbian theatricals.

It is—depending on your moral posture and past experience in the world of commercial public sex—erotic, appalling or simply bizarre. Or all three.

But that's not the secret of Ultra Room. Live sex shows are not new, nor are cute little brass-studded size nine black leather harnesses by Rudi Gernreich. Why, your humble correspondent himself has, in the line of duty, seen exhibitions in Amsterdam and Copenhagen that made the activities of Ultra Room seem almost coy.

No, the secret of Ultra Room is that it exploits the most forbidden, hence exciting, of all forms of voyeurism—that of the Peeping Tom. Not only is the show watched (in most cases) in total privacy—behind closed doors—thus assuring safety from capture from without, but, further, it is watched through one-way mirrors, so one is also spared surveillance from within.

The illusion, then, is complete. For practical purposes, one is now invisible, and invisibility is, to the voyeur, the ultimate fantasy. The fact that the girls within, if they play their assigned roles properly, appear totally oblivious to onlookers as they act out their own fantasies, completes the clockwork orange.

It's genius, I tell you, pure genius.

And the end is near.

Green Door to the Ultra Room

May 30, 1977

I don't know exactly what she did, but Marilyn Chambers must have been a very naughty girl last week because the Mitchell Brothers spent the whole weekend punishing her.

Miss Chambers is, of course, the noted movie star and soap-flake flack who became a household word among the trench-coat crowd several years ago when she starred in "Behind the Green Door" and "The Resurrection of Eve."

The producers of "Green Door" and "Eve," it need hardly be pointed out, were aforementioned James and Arthur Mitchell—those pubic-spirited civic leaders who currently operate the Museum of Modern Fornication at 895 O'Farrell.

The dedicated duo, having made a star of Miss Chambers, then watched benignly as she left their aegis, hooked up with legendary sexologist Chuck Traynor (once Linda Lovelace's favorite lozenge) and went on to conquer new worlds.

"Hey," James would shrug when queried about her defection, "like, you know, since the Willie Brown bill, defection is legal in California, right? Hey, no hard feelings."

And there, for years, it rested as Marilyn spurned hard-core life for the stage, recording, conventional films and the joy of authorship. In three words, she went legit.

Then—and now it may be told—the fateful day when she and Sammy Davis, Jr. were watching some dirty movies together in his private screaming room. Marilyn was interviewing Sammy for *Genesis*. They were reminiscing about the good old days. "Hey," Sammy said, doing his now-classic imitation of James Mitchell, "you know, like, whatever happened to the Bros.?"

A lightbulb flashed above Marilyn's head. She tried to commit an unnatural act with it, gave up and laid a finger aside her nose. "Hey," Davis cried, "I love it! We'll call it 'Deep Nostril!' Shooting starts tomorrow!"

But Marilyn had shallower things on her mind. How about an interview with James and Arthur for *Genesis* magazine? They were, after all, now nationally acclaimed as the Potentates of Porn (*Time*) and the Ultra Room Usurers (Herb Caen).

It'd make a great piece.

"And so," James giggled when approached with the idea, "would you. How 'bout doing a guest stint in the Ultra Room while you're here? Hey, frankly, it's been in the artistic toilet since January. Sure, we're making a couple of bucks but the reviews have been terrible."

Marilyn and Chuck put their heads together. "C'mon, gumdrop," she implored. "I haven't done anything really filthy in years." "I know, honey," he said soothingly. "But we're not giving anything away. None of this 'for old times sake' stuff. The terms'll be stiff."

"Oh, thank goodness," Marilyn sighed.

And so it came to pass.

The Ultra Room was darkened as Marilyn scooted in and assumed a supplicant's posture on the floor. (Supplication is, of course, covered by the same bill as defection.)

As the music and lights came up, she slowly arose and commenced dancing. She danced and danced, kicking her legs out as if emulating a soccer player. (Curiously enough, emulating a soccer player remains illegal to this day. No one knows why this is.)

After a while, two toga-clad figures entered the room. "Whom are you?" Marilyn cried in alarm. "What do you wish? Can't you see I'm dancing and dancing? Are you the fuzz, disguised in plain-togas?"

"You should be so lucky," they snarled, doffing their togas to reveal an arsenal of straps, whips, chains, feet-cuffs and zucchini. "We're here to torture you and inflict unbearable pain and make you say 'ouch!'"

"Oh, goodie!" Marilyn trilled. "How did you know I was a vegetarian?"

Well, the rest must be left unspoken. Suffice it to say that, by the end of the 20-minute show, the Ultra Room looked like a tossed green salad, with Marilyn and a side of Louis dressing.

Show business is my life.

SEX AND THE FAMILY UNIT
May 9, 1977

As you are no doubt aware, there is a major flap raging today regarding the excess of dirty sex so prevalent in contemporary life and the dictionary.

Concomitantly, there is a great crying out for more wholesome, family-oriented entertainment—for movies, plays and live sex shows where a typical American family such as mine (myself, my wife Harriet, our nine-year-old Billy, our 12-year-old Sally)—can attend as a family unit.

In recognition of this need, I determined on Saturday to scour the city from pillar to post in search of such diversion. Unfortunately, my wife Harriet and the milkman were going over the week's dairy needs. "Never mind," I soothed the kids. "We'll do it on our own. Now put away those vibrators, hang up your leathers and let's go!"

Our first stop was "Odyssey—the Ultimate Trip" at the Presidio. Terrific, I said to myself. Kids love science-fiction.

"Odyssey," which was directed by Gerard Damiano, who also directed the laryngological instructional film "Deep Throat," is about a couple, Sleazette and Scarfo (not their real names) who have lost interest in each other in, shall we say, the Biblical sense.

"You don't know anything about the Bible," Sleazette snarls scornfully at Scarfo. "You think missionaries know everything." "Oh yeah!" retorts Scarfo, from his characteristic prone position, "and so's your old nan!"

This exchange, overheard from the floor below by Sleazette's wealthy grandmother, who has her ear pressed to the dumb-waiter, so enrages the elderly crone that she orders the servant from the room and, as the film fades out, engages in a frenzy of self-abuse with her newly purchased Cuisinart.

Next it was over to the O'Farrell, which was showing "Teen Cruisin'." "Teen Cruisin'" is about a young lady, the Nut House Nympho, who escapes the local loony-bin and drives up and down Main Street in a beat-up van, luring unwitting passers-by inside, where she forces them to indulge in a variety of unnatural acts with cashews.

"Gee, dad," the kids whined after a couple of minutes, "that's so passé. Can't we please see the Ultra Room? Huh, dad, huh?"

Hey, how do you say "no" to a couple of cute moppets?

We walked across the lobby and snuggled into a private booth with 11 members of the Vice Squad—they'd been there on a stake-out since February—seven representatives of the Board of Supervisors and 800 Japanese tourists.

"Gee, dad," piped up little Sally, "this is neat. It's just like watching mom and Auntie Sue in the sauna at home." "Not quite, honey," I corrected gently, "your mom and Auntie Sue are making movies."

Then it was time for something more serious: "Long Jeanne Silver" at the Screening Room. Good, I thought. Kids love pirate movies. We went inside. Long Jeanne Silver was performing with her left leg, which is, shall we say, underdeveloped. Angrily, I grabbed the little shavers and headed for the box office. "Hey," I said angrily, demanding my money back. "We thought this was a pirate film." "No, no," the cashier said mollifyingly. "It's a *private* film."

Exhausted by now, I took them to see The Arena, which is the Sutter Cinema's copy of the O'Farrell's Ultra Room. But it was no dice. "Jeez, dad," piped up little Sally. "Sure, they're indulging in foreplay, artificial stimulation and auto-eroticism, but you promised us the torrid entwining of sweat-slickened bodies engaged in a ritual of love as old as time itself." She had a point. Crestfallen, I gathered up the little nippers and headed for home. Harriet, my wife, was supine on the kitchen floor, surrounded by milk bottles, butter cubes and other dairy products. "How'd it go?" she asked brightly, toweling off the last of the cottage cheese. "Aw, it was okay, mom," little Billy said, "but if you've seen one exploitation of the psycho-sexual anxieties which appear endemic to our culture, you've seen them all."

"Gee, dad," piped up little Sally, "maybe next time we could catch a Disney flick." So it had come to this. Harriet and I exchanged meaningful glances. "You think they're ready for that?" I whispered. "Why not," she replied with a shrug. "It can't be that much more unrealistic."

HONEYSUCKLE DIVINE BLOWS HER HORN
January 15 & 17, 1979

"The Mitchell Brothers' O'Farrell Eros Center is pleased to announce," the tintinnabulous press release rang out, "the exclusive premiere engagement of Miss Honeysuckle Divine, January 12–18.

"Note to Assignment Editors: This story may be too controversial (hot) for some reporters. Do not send any rookies who might be squeamish or offended."

I folded the announcement into a paper airplane and sailed it into the Managing Editor's coffee.

"Nu?" I said casually.

"Of course it's new," he snarled. "Can't you read the date?"

"I mean, like so what else is nu," I said casually, ignoring his unilingual limitations. "So you got another tough assignment and you're looking for someone who can handle it. You're desperate, you got your rookies, you got your squeamers, you got your offenders. You're up against it. You need a guy who's been there. You need a guy who's seen it all and actually done it twice. You do the only thing you can do. You call in Ned Miller, a West Coast newspaperman."

"For God's sake, Wasserman," the Managing Editor says irritably, throwing his hands in the air and inadvertently knocking his Tinker Toys off the desk in the process, "take off that stupid costume, get your clothes out of the phone booth and get me a story."

"Right, Lois," I say casually, ankling out of his office without so much as a backward glance.

I don my foul weather gear, ring up my beautiful wife Tacit and break the news gently. "I may not be home for dinner, dear," I say. "It's a big one this time. Honeysuckle Divine. Could be that Pulitzer we've been waiting for. The Eros Center. Sex, nudity and perversion. I'll probably want to take a tub afterwards."

Suddenly, little Tommy came on the phone. How rude. "Daddy, daddy," he cried, "can I go, huh, please, huh, daddy?"

"Sorry, you little nipper," I said gently. "Daddy's got to handle this one his own way. Anyway, nobody under six allowed."

"Oh, darn," little Tommy said. "Well, then, how about if I ravish little Mary Beth?"

"Only," I remonstrate gently, "if you and your sister reconcile afterwards and view it as a growth experience."

I wend my way through the 895 O'Farrell copulation complex: The Sinema, now nearly a decade old, the fabled Ultra Room, where I once broke my nose on the two-way mirror, the Kopenhagen Lounge, where maidens play hide-and-seek with Japanese tourists, and the newest house of congress, the Gallery of Gynecomania.

The press is everywhere. I spot Irv Silver of the Pleasanton "Pervert," Tom McCall of the Foster City "Face-Sitter" and 19 editors from the *Sun Reporter.* Two guys who claim to be from channel 7 arrive. One of them is doing a lead-in:

"At this hour tonight, police from nine Bay Area counties are involved in a house to house search for the time—right now, even as we speak: at this hour. They began earlier today, at that hour, and now, at this hour, which is later than what it was earlier, we have learned exclusively that it is now, which is prior to a subsequent hour, or, in other words, subsequent to a prior hour."

"Nice going, Van," I whisper.

Miss Honeysuckle Divine shuffled on stage, towing a shopping cart. "You don't need to clap," she said cheerfully. "I've had too much of that in my life already."

She is dressed in a formless frock, wears no visible make-up, has lanky brown hair, shuffles along in bulky, styleless platform shoes and tows a shopping cart laden with a mop, a tin horn, several containers of Jergen's lotion, cans of talcum powder and plastic bags filled with Ping-Pong balls. If she were a contestant on "What's My Line," she'd have a longer run than "Fiddler on the Roof."

Honeysuckle Divine's line is the public pubic propulsion of provisions from what people used to perceive as private parts.

She is also a musician and philosopher.

Since much of what Honeysuckle says—never mind what she does—is unprintable in this newspaper, I have decided to adopt an appropriate euphemism for purposes of substitution where necessary. This euphemism is "nickson." E.g., "That, sir, is a piece of nickson." Or, "If you believe that, you'll believe that chickens have nicksons."

The pre-performance press conference commenced with the familiar show biz litany: born in Illinois, raped in the ear as a child, recruited by the local police chief to work in his whorehouse ("I said no...I was nicksoning morning, noon and night, but on my own time. I'm an independent thinker"), left to seek her fortune in Washington, D.C. ("but I wasn't as lucky as Liz Ray, my tape recorder kept breaking down"), worked as a stripper and hooker ("with government officials, but I don't kiss and tell") and eventually developed her unique maneuvers as the result of an accident that even "nickson" can't salvage for discussion here.

As she spoke, she busied herself signing the Ping-Pong balls ("Merry Christmas 1979—Honeysuckle loves your nicksons"), meticulously wrapping each in individual baggies and flinging them to the giddy throng like a glowing bride dispensing bouquets to eager attendants.

Honeysuckle on conventional sex: "I don't indulge in sex much anymore. I used to, morning, noon and night. I guess I just nicksoned my brains out. I haven't had sexual intercourse for more than two years. I'm in my rest period." She smiled cheerfully, "Oh, maybe a few harmless nickson jobs now and then...."

• On the Guinness Book of World Records: "Oh yes, I'd like to be in it. They have the shotput, don't they? How about the nickson-put?!"

• On marriage: "I had a boyfriend once. We was going to get married. But we broke up because he was starting to get weird."

• On the significance of a proper diet: "Oh, it's very important, 'cause it won't do if it's drunk. I stay in training just like an athlete."

Then it was show time. "I do a clean act," she began happily, removing the mop from her shopping cart and propelling it about the stage by employing a motive force not generally associated with housework.

"Now," she said brightly, "let's do some sing-alongs." Out came the tin horn, in went the tin horn and out came one of the most moving versions of "Jingle Bells" it's been my pleasure to hear.

"She has a nice personality," observed one of the TV guys.

Next, Honeysuckle blew out some candles ("They love me at birthday parties"), delivered an extended panegyric on the merits of Jergen's lotion ("I'd like to do a commercial for them, but they won't let me") and followed that by unleashing a veritable Niagara of the estimable unguent.

Finally, Honeysuckle Divine lay supine on the floor, dabbed talcum on her publics and effortlessly sent billowing puffs of white powder into the air.

"We have," the TV man cried exultantly, "a Pope!"

5

Movies That Suck

A couple of weeks ago I received an irate letter from a
couple who had gone to see "The Car" on my recommendation that
it was the worst movie in history. "Sure, it was terrible,"
the letter said, "but it was just dull and stupid—no style, no pretensions,
no *fun*." Well, as I said in my reply, "Please suck a parakeet,"
but that, of course, resolved nothing.
JLW

*John was best known for his reviews of "movies that suck." People couldn't
help going to films he panned because the reviews were so much fun they were
convinced the movies must be, too. They usually were not, and he received
occasional indignant letters from readers claiming he'd misled them. His bad-
movie reviews aren't really reviews; they are humorous essays, satirical songs.*
Throughout the city readers Xeroxed them for friends and passed them

around their offices on gloomy Monday mornings. John received countless thank-you letters, a few expressing sympathy that he had to sit through such turkeys even though it was for a good cause.

John wanted movies to be good. When they had something to say and said it well, he was laudatory and thoughtful. But if a movie was bad, no matter how sensitive the subject, he sharpened his carving instruments.

He irritated a lot of directors, especially Russ Meyer, who once stormed into the newsroom demanding that he retract his review or, better yet, be fired. John had taken a group of friends and two bottles of champagne to Meyer's "Faster, Pussycat—Kill Kill" and they hooted and hollered through the screening. John's rationalization to the Managing Editor, Gordon Pates, was that "you don't have to pay close attention to a Russ Meyer film, just sort of keep an eye on it." As for the champagne, it was split among eight people so he couldn't possibly have been drunk. Pates believed him but forbade any more friends at screenings. "That was the end of our fun," says Joel Pimsleur, one of the revelers.

Director Mark Lester, on the other hand, wrote to thank John for his hilarious pan of "Truck-Stop Women," claiming he understood the spirit of the movie. That film starred Claudia Jennings, "Queen of the B's." Clint Eastwood remembers John loved a Claudia Jennings movie: "The movie was trash but she was always a little above quality. She was his mystery woman."

John told Alan Farley on KALW-Radio, "The hardest film to review is a mediocre one, 43 or 38 on a zero to 100 scale. Then one is just sort of helpless. Only when the film is insulting can it be repaid in kind, with a sledgehammer or stiletto, whichever mood strikes me."

JUST GET INTO GEAR AND GO
May 20, 1974

"Truck-Stop Women"—the very name sings with intrigue, allure, beguilement! Who are these women? Why are they called women? Was the original title "Truck-Stop Babes?" "Broads?" "Chicks?" "Cookies?"

Do we see the fine hand of the Women's Liberation movement here? Are these union "Truck-Stop Women?" Scabs, mayhap? What about the Teamsters?

And why are they stopping trucks? Are they really that strong? Are the trucks moving? If they're not moving, how can they be stopped? What about existentialism? If a tree falls in the forest, and there is no one there to hear it, does it really fall? Or is it simply that the rest of the world has turned sideways?

These and other questions lured me off to the Golden Gate I, New Mission and El Rancho Drive-In the other day to see some answers. "No Rig Was Too Big for Them to Handle," the ad said. "Double-clutchin', gear-jammin' mamas who like a lot of hi-jackin' by day...a lot of heavy truckin' by night!"

My kind of flick.

Mark Lester is a young man who wants to direct motion pictures. That's not the plot, that's real life. So he came up last year with a film called "Steel Arena," which told the tale of professional stunt-drivers. "No Rig Was Too Big for Them to Handle," the ad read. "Double-clutchin', gear-jammin' papas who like a lot of hi-jinkin' by day...a lot of heavy puckerin' by night."

My kind of flick.

But Mark found himself saddled with reality in "Steel Arena," mainly because it was based on a real person, who starred in the film. Still, it made money and that's the name of the game. "It made money," Mark told Mr. Big, "and that's the name of the game. Gimme some more."

Mr. Big said "dig" and that is how "Truck-Stop Women" came to be.

"Now," Mark said, fondling his Arriflex, "let us make a movie about teats and violence." "Hold on, you fool," said Mr. Big, "teats are on cows. The SPCA will be on your case so fast it'll cloud your lens."

"Drat," said Mark. "Well, then, how about using girls instead?"

And so it came to pass that Mark hired Claudia Jennings, noted actress (she starred here in "Lenny"), former Playmate of the Year and recently crowned "Queen of the B-Movies," to star in "Truck-Stop Women" and remove her blouse.

With those two problems solved, he moved on to less important matters. He hired Claudia's roommate, songwriter Bobby Hart (formerly of Tommy Boyce and Bobby Hart fame) to pen some trucking jingles and warble same.

He hired some other actors, who refused to allow their real names to be used in the credits (they are billed as Lieux Dressler and Dennis Fimple, if you can believe that) and lined up skin-pic superstar Uschi Digard for a "mammeo" (the new Screen Actors Guild designation for a short, shirtless role; previously called, clumsily, a "mammary cameo").

Finally, he rented a number of enormous trucks, assembled all manner of pistols, rifles and machine guns, ordered 300 cases of Heinz tomato ketchup and fleshed out the cast with 35 outpatients from the Menninger Clinic. Still, he found himself with more than $30 left in the budget. Paul Deason was promptly commissioned to help him write the script. Deason is one of those legendary Hollywood screenwriters who can type without moving his lips.

The result, the first truxploitation film, is delightful. It's a terrible movie, of course, but it's a terrific terrible movie. That is because Mark Lester is entirely without pretensions. No artsy-craftsy stuff for Mark. He knows what sells. Action, killing, sex and trucks. The staples of human existence.

And anyway, no film with a song lamenting the life of a cattle-hauler, entitled "Bull-Shipper's Blues," can be all bad.

Go, Mark, go.

You'd Scream, Too
November 21, 1974

"The Texas Chain-Saw Massacre" is only as strong as its weakest kink.

That, it turns out, is screaming. Marilyn Burns, the heroine, screams without surcease for the last 45 minutes of the picture, thereby setting a modern record. Of course, this is understandable. For, during that memorable period, she is attacked by a Texas chain-saw massacre person, bound and gagged, beaten with a stick, put in a canvas bag, frightened by corpses, chased through the orchard by a monster, injured by jumping through a second-story window, forced to supply blood to a thumb-sucking dead person, obliged to sit in an armchair, the arms of which are really arms, beaten about the head and shoulders with a hammer, sliced with a razor blade and addressed in a rude fashion.

You'd scream, too. As did the audience, which was composed of a lot of weird people come to see what all the flap was about.

The flap, of course, occurred a week or so ago when "The Texas Chain-Saw Massacre" had a sneak preview at the Empire. The preview audience, apparently expecting a Walt Disney movie, was outraged, and demanded their money back. "Ugh, what a disgusting movie," they said, having no clue whatsoever from the title.

To be sure, it's not a fun movie. As a matter of fact, it's pretty gruesome and grotesque and sadistic and ugly. But I survived and, to show my contempt, ate two hot dogs and some popcorn, to boot.

If you've seen one chain-saw massacre, you've see them all.

XXXX-RATED

December 12, 1969

Nude. Nuder, nudest. Nudely, nudeness, nudity. Naked, bare, unclad. Unclothed, bereft of raiment, sans duds.

The above words have been bandied about with increasing license during the past few years. The corruptive potential is immeasurable. Fortunately, however, not everybody is toadying to the so-called "sexual revolution." San Francisco's distinguished afternoon daily has taken a stand. The ad appearing therein for a new film at the Surf/Interplayers Theater is printed as "XXXX Restaurant." Good for you, distinguished afternoon daily! This writer wishes to join hands and hearts with you.

"XXXX Restaurant" is a 1967 effort from the alleged king of pop art, Andy ------. It stars Viva, Taylor Mead, Luis Waldon and Brigette Polk and is the third of a trilogy preceded by "I, a XXX" and "Bike Boy."

"XXXX Restaurant" is a showcase for Viva, ------'s most durable and interesting Superstar ("Lonesome Cowboys," "Lions Love"). It opens with her submerged in a ---tub, à deux, and talking like crazy, while her tubmate absently fondles her **** and endeavors to get down to the nitty-******.

Cut to a restaurant, where Viva is a ---less waitress, clad only in an X-string and desultorily serving a number of individuals attired in a like manner. She is still talking. She says sculpture is dead, and there have been no playwrights since Shakespeare. She discusses the merits of a clitoral ****** vs. a vaginal ******. She reminisces about a horny priest, Lesbian nuns, being stoned and her mental breakdown.

Taylor Mead mumbles a little, plays harmonica and sings like a masculine Tiny XXX. Or maybe it's the other way around. Meanwhile, Viva continues talking. At the end, I had an insight: "XXXX Restaurant" proves you can sleep with your eyes open. Whether you're a critic or a newspaper.

WHAT MOVIE AM I IN?
October 29, 1973

If you can imagine English actor Roger Moore, the blue-eyed, sandy-haired, Etonian-accented, sinfully urbane former James Bond, in the role of a ruthless half-Sicilian Mafia thug, you are not going to have any trouble at all with "Street People," which is currently at one of the many St. Francis theaters.

And the scene where the chickens put on the lipstick probably won't bother you, either.

Moore, Stacy Keach and a variety of other criminals star in this "Godfather" rip-off about multi-million-dollar heroin shipments, crosses (religious), double-crosses (not religious) and other staples of the motion picture industry's lunatic fringe.

But before you go rushing off to see it, a word of warning. The picture you want is in the St. Francis theater reached by entering the main Market Street turnstile, then bearing briskly left until you get to an area that requires snowshoes in order to navigate through the flotsam and jetsam deposited on the floor for posterity by an entire generation of movie buffs.

This may sound obvious to you, but appearances are bereaving. Upon entering the theater, I found to my dismay that the picture had already started. Being unfamiliar with the street people and never being quite sure what St. Francis theater I'm in, I peered intently at the screen for some clue. Up pops Roger Moore. Hmmm, no street person him, I thought. Then Stacy Keach, looking as though he had just crawled out of the bath. Hmmm, I thought, him no street person, either.

Egad. Perhaps I am in the wrong theater. At that moment, a man two rows in front of me, wearing a Giants baseball cap, unleashed a massive expectoration on the floor to his right. OK, I said, now we're getting somewhere. A street person if ever I heard one.

I settled back, content in the knowledge that, even if I were in the wrong film, I could always do an interview with this chap. No sooner, however, had I unstuck my feet from the floor for a more comfortable angle than a man in front of me, another late arrival, turned around and, in a discreet whisper, asked if I knew what picture this was. I replied I didn't, but if enough of us got together and worked up a petition, I bet that we could force the management to turn over its records in the matter.

Snapping that he wasn't even registered to vote, he then leaned forward and addressed the same question to the drooling ptyalist in front of us who, by this time, had unleashed such a cloud of spittle on the surrounding terrain that one could extinguish a cigarette simply by hurling it into the air.

The rainmaker swallowed, turned around and confirmed that we were, indeed, watching "Street People."

Life is a cabaret.

Train Robbers With a Moral
February 10, 1973

If you were a normal, semi-sane individual, what would you do if confronted with the following dilemma?

You are riding through the Old West with your trusty band of loyal desperadoes, including Ann-Margret, Rod Taylor, Bobby Vinton and Ben Johnson. You are in pursuit of half a million dollars in gold.

You are riding along, jaunty-jolly, and you come to a pond—quite round, about 50 feet in diameter, maybe four feet deep. The area surrounding the pond is dry, flat land. With a little irrigation, a golf course.

In the pond, for all you know, are sharks, alligators and snakes. If you canter around the pond, on the other hand, you will lose up to 30 seconds of time. What do you do?

Naturally, you ride smack through the middle of the pond, thereby exposing yourself to crocodile-bites, your horse to athlete's foot and your boots to mold. In the process, you ruin local fishing for three days and leave such tracks on the other side they could be followed by a cross-eyed papoose. And, of course, you save 30 seconds. But that is not why you ride through that pond. You ride through the pond because it's there. And because you're John Wayne. And John Wayne rides through any damn pond that gets in his way. Pond, he seems to say, I spit on you. And your uncle, too.

That is the moral of "The Train Robbers."

The High Points of Scaramouche
April 3, 1976

The common female chest has many functions.

Children are often nurtured by it, adult males periodically gaze at it, the brassiere industry was built on it, North Beach's Broadway is suckled by it and Lloyd's of London occasionally insures notable specimens.

But never in living memory has a female chest, comely or otherwise, provided the only justification for attendance at a motion picture. With the arrival of "The Loves and Times of Scaramouche," however, that landmark has been reached. Ursula Andress, the Swiss sexpot, takes a bath near the end of the film, during which ablution her entire bosom may be observed by the naked eye.

Women, of course, may find this of less than riveting interest, but our great Constitution was written to carefully protect the rights of minority groups, namely men, and some men may be interested in this particular bosom.

It is a nice, two-toned bosom, each of the two parallel members being round at the hilt and pointy at the end. It is one of God's bosoms, being unaltered by foreign chemicals or synthetic substances, and it looks like a very sincere bosom.

Still, this particular bosom, outstanding as it may be, is on screen for only a minute or less, and that is not a very good reason for attending a movie 90 times that duration, even for those who respect a well-turned bosom.

The rest of the picture addresses itself to Michael Sarrazin, an actor impersonating the title role in what purports to be a breezy comedy-adventure set in Napoleon's 18th century France. Unfortunately, it is neither comedic nor adventurous. But it is breezy.

Which brings us to another part of the anatomy.

WORMS WEREN'T PROMISED A ROSE GARDEN
August 27, 1976

It had to happen. Rats had their day in "Food of the Gods." Bugs ran amok in "The Bug." Now it's the worm's turn.

"Squirm" is the most distinguished worm film of 1976. Set on the Georgia coast during an electrical storm late last year, "Squirm" tells the story of 27 million worms and the difficulties they face when power lines, snapped by powerful winds, shoot current into the contemporary worm cities that lie just below the surface of the ground.

The worms do what they have to do, which is to creep out of the ground and eat all the people for 50 miles around. This does not resolve the problem of electricity crackling into the earth, of course, but the worms resolve this dilemma by moving into the now-empty houses, having the cable-TV hooked up and enrolling their tiny worm children in the local bait shops.

"Squirm" was written and directed by Jeff Lieberman, who did all the painstaking research necessary at the Circle "O" Worm Ranch in

Pleasanton, but has denied in interviews that he is into worm-lib. There is substantial evidence that he is being too modest.

For one thing, the previously all-but-ignored Worm Extras Guild has a field day in "Squirm," with better than 200 of its members being flown out from Los Angeles to Georgia to take key roles as stuntworms, stand-in worms and, as they are known in the trade, "atmosphere worms."

Still other of the slimy little creatures worked on sound effects, rushing pell-mell about on sheets of tin in order to create the patter of tiny worm feet. But this probably won't be enough for some people. There are always going to be those who claim that this is token wormism, that only three percent of the worms employed were Spanish-speaking, that more than 26 million of the little devils were scab-worms and, from the Society for Decent Wormism, that all the worms used in "Squirm" were bisexual.

True enough, perhaps, but, in my mind, irrelevant. We are talking here about progress, not about solutions. There are hundreds of worm-ghettos spread across this great nation and a lot of talent is going to waste. Sure, "Squirm" is not the whole worm story, but what is? *Huckleberry Finn? Trout Fishing in America?* I think not.

Give worms a chance. Get plenty of rest, eat right and put some of them in your coffee. I think you'll be surprised.

The $25,000 Answer

October 8, 1976

A few months ago, Tom Laughlin, the star, director and producer of "Billy Jack" and "The Trial of Billy Jack," announced a nifty contest.

Entitled "Billy Jack vs. the Critics," Laughlin offered prizes ranging from $25,000 cash to 200 bicycles (unassembled) for 300-word essays on the subject: "Why are movie critics out of touch with the audiences?"

Laughlin's innovative contention is that what critics like and what audiences like are not always identical. "Why the enormous difference between the responses of critics and the audience they are supposedly reviewing for?" he asks bluntly, going on to reveal that a review is only an opinion, that critics are telling more about themselves than that about which they're writing, and that critics, like some emperors he knows, "wear no clothes."

My kind of contest. The only problem was that I had seen neither "BJ" nor "The Trial of BJ" and thus could not fully appreciate what it was Laughlin was talking about. I did once know a critic in Springfield, Ill., who often wore no clothes, but that's another story.

I waited breathlessly for Laughlin's next film. Finally, it is here: "The Master Gunfighter," a story of mass exterminations in early California. "The Master Gunfighter" is the third installment in a cinematic revolution envisaged by Laughlin, who states: "The basic thrust of everything we've done at Billy Jack has been to break strangleholds over the production, distribution, exhibition and reception of films."

My kind of thrust.

And so here's my essay, bearing in mind that, according to the contest rules, "neatness and originality count."

WHY ARE MOVIE CRITICS OUT OF TOUCH WITH THE AUDIENCES

(A) The first thing to acknowledge, Tom, as you point out, is that movie critics are not even qualified to comment on a film like "The Master Gunfighter."

Movie critics know only how to deal with such matters as acting, directing, script, photography, editing and the intellect behind a given film. Yet those considerations are moot for judging "The Master Gunfighter." Like the Russ Meyer films, your picture can be validly assessed only by trained specialists in abnormal psychology, anti-social behavior and close students of the McGuffey Reader. Moreover, you are absolutely correct when you state that "... anything popular (has) great significance for those who take the time to investigate the reasons behind its popularity." Unfortunately, movie critics lack the necessary masochistic tendencies to pursue this line of thought.

(B) Another reason movie critics are out of touch with audiences is that they try to avoid them whenever possible. If you ever had to spend time with an audience, you would certainly understand this. Audiences see films in theaters. Theaters each day pour several hundred gallons of a specially blended mixture of bubble-gum, Coca Cola concentrate and Lepage's mucilage on the floor.

Tom, have you ever spent two hours watching a film with your feet in the air?

(C) Another thing about being in touch with a theater audience—and I was for "The Master Gunfighter"—is that they make it very hard to follow what's going on; feeling, as they do, that your film is not so much to be watched as discussed, translated into foreign tongues and advised ("Look out behind you, Master Gunfighter!"). This is, indeed, fun, but not very helpful.

Well, Tom, that's my 300 words and I look forward to receiving my $25,000. Oh yes, one more thought. In your open letter, you ask why critics are so out of touch "with audiences they are paid to review for?" Hey, Tom, that one's easy. Critics are paid to review for the publications they work for, not the half-wits who go to your movies.

Respectfully, John Wasserman.

UNDER THE TUTU
October 7, 1977

All right, kids, what do we now know about Valentino that we didn't know before director Ken Russell got his teeth into Rudolf Nureyev's tutu?

We know that Nureyev, who has the title role, may be a heckuva hoofer but can't act his way out of the Gulag Archipelago.

We know that costars Michelle Phillips and Leslie Caron go down in very unchic-like flames with him.

We still don't know if Valentino was homosexual, heterosexual, bisexual or merely shy, despite the recurrent mutterings in the film about "pansies," "powder-puffs" and "walk-in closets."

We do know he is never actually seen fondling a male person, although he does engage in a little light ballroom dancing with Anthony Dowell (as Vaslav Nijinsky). But they never kiss or anything.

And we also know that he does fondle female persons, although he doesn't seem very enthusiastic about that, either.

Perhaps he's a nascent latent.

Ken Russell, the director, is merely blatant. The only thing latent in him is restraint.

"Valentino" is a docudrama about the short but action-packed life of Rudolph Valentino, the silent screen's greatest Latin Lover. Valentino, who departed this mortal dance floor in 1926 (at the tender age of 31) is traced, via flashbacks, from gigolo to superstar to flower-strewn bier through the eyes of the women—lovers, admirers, agents and other strangers—who adored him. Why they adored him—in Nureyev's hands, a man of little charm, warmth or substance—we do not know. It makes no never mind to Ken Russell. His fascination with cultural my-thology ("Liztomania," "Tommy," "Mahler," etc.) is well documented, and as long as there are legends, Russell will be around to exaggerate them. He is not interested in the truth—if it exists—but rather in recre-ating the aura of the legend. I can hardly wait for his next two tributes: "Abzuggery" and "Rebozomania." Except for the striking visual images and evocations of the bizarre for which Russell is justly renowned, "Valentino" is not worth discussing with a straight face.

The idea of casting the greatest ballet superstar since Nijinsky as the silver screen's greatest fox-trotter doubtlessly looked terrific on paper but, unfortunately, they put it on film. Under Russell's direction, Nureyev is hopeless. Rather than providing the impression of a magnetic but manipulated cruiser on the street of dreams, Nureyev is a caricature. His glower of smoldering passion is a chuckle, and he comes alive only when dancing. And, frankly, Fred Astaire he's not. As a Russian portray-ing an Italian, he sounds like he's doing Boris Karloff impressions. The logic carries on. Leslie Caron, the lovely French actress who will ever-more play "The Song From Moulin Rouge" on my heartstrings, is turned by Russell into a shrill, melodramatic Russian harridan.

Michelle Phillips, once a Mama and a Papa, whose performance may be even worse than that of Nureyev, portrays another Russian, yet. *Do svedanya.*

Oh yes, for the history books: Russell, when he is not concentrating on the sadistic and grotesque, which is rarely, manages to divest of their duds not only Phillips and Penny Milford (an actress Valentino beds in order to prove his manhood) but—lordy, lordy—Nureyev himself.

To see young women stark naked in the movies is not unusual, nor is it to see male ballet dancers with pouches the size of pregnant kangaroos. But the male member? Without even a scarf? In movies?

Yet there it is, Rudy *au naturel,* penis poised phlegmatically, his eyes darting about smolderingly, seeking the nearest orifice that is not a doughnut.

Well, I can't swear that this is the most celebrated organ to be unveiled in the history of motion pictures but, weenie-wise, name me another.

A MEDITATIVE REVIEW
March 24, 1977

Time spent watching movies can be very refreshing.

Sometimes, this is because you can see a terrific movie.

Other times, this is because you are afforded the opportunity to rest, to think, to contemplate the meaning of life, far from the hustle and bustle of the outside world—like lying under a hot towel in a barbershop for an hour and a half. You can get a lot of thinking done with the right movies, and "Mr. Billion" is the right movie.

"Mr. Billion" stars Jackie Gleason, Valerie Perrine, Slim Pickens and Terence Hill (he's a German-born star of Italian "spaghetti" Westerns—sort of a latter-day *Luftwaffe* Clint Eastwood) in the moronic tale of the travails of a poor Italian auto mechanic who abruptly inherits control of a multi-billion dollar American conglomerate.

I leaned back in the warm and comfy screening room as my mind turned to some major issues of our time.

I wondered if "Jonathan Kaplan," the name credited with directing and co-writing "Mr. Billion," was a pseudonym for Little Billy Osmond.

I restfully pondered the question: Can a motion picture be directed over the telephone? By hand-signals? While buried alive? From behind bars?

I dreamily thought of the Writers Guild of America, and its admission standards. Is a bumper-sticker that says "eat it" enough?

I mused in my reverie about Valerie Perrine and her shirt. She keeps it on in "Mr. Billion," yet it is common knowledge that she can act only with it off ("Slaughterhouse Five," "Lenny"). Has she sustained some grotesque hickey?

I dozed lazily while "Jonathan Kaplan" showed us wipe-cuts. Wipe-cuts are a sophisticated film technique which prolongs the transition from one scene to another. There are at least 25 different types of wipe-cuts in "Mr. Billion." This is very interesting. The last time wipe-cuts were used in a major film was 1955.

I awoke refreshed, stretched, headed for the nearest telephone and rang up the Atascadero State Hospital for the Criminally Insane. "I'd like to report an escape," I said matter-of-factly. "Says his name is 'Jonathan Kaplan.' Strange-looking fellow. Walks on all fours. Obviously schizophrenic. Thinks he's a movie director."

"I see. And you're the producer...?"

ANOTHER AIRPORT CATASTROPHE
March 26, 1977

It has come to my attention that Jennings Lang, the executive producer of "Airport '77," has announced his intention of presenting a new "Airport" catastrophe every year for the next two decades.

The first "Airport," a faithful adaptation of Arthur Haley's bestseller, was a perfectly respectable disaster film. The second—"Airport 1975"—was billed as a sequel and was—in the same sense that "Jesus Christ Superstar" was a sequel to the Old Testament.

Now comes "Airport '77," which was "inspired" by Haley's book. I will tell you what was inspiring about the original "Airport": The grosses were inspiring, is what was inspiring.

The first of this trilogy of tinsel dealt with a disaster on the ground. The second dealt with a disaster in the air. This poses an interesting problem: What's left? You've got your earth, you've got your sky. Where else does an airplane crash? Exactly.

Underwater.

Thus, "Airport '77" or, "Please Do Not Urinate In The Pool When

The Director Is Swimming."

And not to worry that there's no airport in "Airport '77." At least they've got the year right. At this point, we'll take what we can get. "Airport 1975" was released in 1974.

Jack Lemmon, Lee Grant, Brenda Vaccaro, Joseph Cotten, Olivia de Haviland, Darren McGavin, Christopher Lee, Robert Hooks, former Actor's Workshop stalwarts Monte Markham and Tom Rosqui and, in teenie-weenie roles, Jimmy Stewart and George Kennedy, star in an utterly ludicrous story about a hijacking by Markham and two other hooligans of a customized and treasure-laden Boeing 747 owned by multi-millionaire industrialist Jimmy Stewart in his teenie-weenie role.

Fortunately, the misdeed is thwarted. Unfortunately, it is thwarted because the enormous aircraft sideswipes an off-shore oil drilling platform in the Caribbean. Fortunately, it just skips along the water like a pebble until it comes bobbing to a halt in mid-ocean.

Unfortunately, it then sinks. Fortunately, the water is only 26 feet deep. Unfortunately, the 747 is only 25 feet tall. "This plane," Darren McGavin shouts in alarm, peering out the window at a school of fishies swimming by, "was never built to withstand this much outside pressure!"

Small wonder. Very few planes are built to fly underwater.

I know this because I called the Boeing Aircraft Corporation in Seattle after seeing "Airport '77." I wanted to ask a couple of technical questions, like when were they going to put out a contract on Mr. Jennings Lang.

"Hello," said a nice man in the public relations department. "Hello," I said. "I just saw the movie 'Airport '77' and I'd like to ask you a couple of technical questions."

"We had nothing to do with it!" he cried piteously. I would commend a similar course of action to the reader.

Spotting the Problems of a Dog's Life

August 4, 1977

"Arf."

"Woof."

"Bark."

"Rowf."

"Grrr."

"Yip."

"Yap."

"Meow."

That is a review of "For the Love of Benji" for its natural audience: namely, dogs.

"For the Love of Benji," which nuzzled its cute little floppy-eared way into town, is a sequel to the highly successful "Benji Goes to College" of a few years back. They were going to call it "Benji II: The Heretic," but Joe Camp, the writer-director, nixed the idea. "Derivative," he snorted.

"For the Love of Benji" is the story of a cute little floppy-eared mutt named Benji, its two cute little floppy-eared owners, Sally and Billy, their cute little fat-eared guardian, Mabel, and how some criminals are going to use Benji's cute little left paw to rule the world.

Since the last canine movie I saw was "Dog Day Afternoon," and I didn't understand it at all, I took my dog Spot along to the critic's screening for consultation.

Spot said "arf" when the credits said "A family film by Joe Camp." It reminded him of his own family, and his 3,900 illegitimate brothers and sisters.

Spot said "woof" when it was explained that Benji was one-third German shepherd, one-third Russian wolfhound and one-third Belgian endive. Spot thought that was cute.

Spot said "bark" when Benji got separated from his family and ran around looking dejected.

Spot said "rowf" when the bad guys stole Benji away and Benji looked frightened.

Spot said "grrr" when Benji escaped.

Spot said "yip" when Benji was recaptured.

Spot said "yap" when Benji escaped again.

Spot said "meow" when Benji saved cute little floppy-eared Sally from the threat of death.

Spot is a very stupid dog.

A VERY GRIM FAIRY TALE
April 24, 1978

"Daddy, daddy," little Mary Beth squealed as the family gathered around the cackling warmth of the fireplace, "tell us again about movies that suck!" "Yes, yes!" chorused little Billy and little Tommy.

I looked wearily at my wife, Tacit. She said nothing. "OK, kids," I said, "but only if you'll promise to go out and trash that Nativity Scene on Mr. Dingle's lawn before you go to bed."

"We will, daddy, we will!" the little nippers cried.

"Well, all right. A long, long time ago," I began, "daddy went to see 'I Want To Hold Your Hand,' 'The Silver Bears' and 'Rabbit Test'...."

"How long ago, daddy," little Billy cried, "how long ago? Ten thousand years?"

"Friday, little Billy," I replied, "and don't interrupt daddy again, or daddy will break both your little wooden legs."

"Now Wassy," my lovely wife said soothingly, "the youngster didn't mean anything. And anyway, I'm sure you'll feel better when you get a job."

"You're right, honey," I said. "Anyway, kids, daddy drove all the way over to Stonestown and guess what?"

Little Tommy's eyes lit up and his cheeks glowed. "Did it suck, daddy," he cried, "did it, huh, did it?"

"It sure did, you little moppet," I said, tousling his little hair.

"Oh, *goody*," cried little Mary Beth.

"Anyway," I continued, "'I Want To Hold Your Hand' is set in 1964 and is about some teenagers from New Jersey who go to New York to see the Beatles, who are about to make their first American appearance on Ed Sullivan's show."

"Are the Beatles in the movie, daddy, huh?" little Billy cried. "Is Ed Sullivan?"

"No, little Billy, the Beatles aren't in the movie except on old film and videotape, and Ed Sullivan is dead."

"Oh, daddy," cried little Tommy, his eyes glistening, "I didn't even know he was sick."

I looked wearily at Tacit. "There are no straight men left," I sighed. She said nothing.

"Are there any stars in the movie?" little Mary Beth cried. "Is it funny? Is it clever?"

"No, no and no," I replied.

"Oh, goody," little Billy cried. "Can we go?"

"Wait 'til you hear about 'The Silver Bears,'" I cautioned gently. "'The Silver Bears' has a wonderful cast—Michael Caine, Tom Smothers, Martin Balsam, Louis Jourdan, Stephane Audran, David Warner, Cybill Shepherd, Jay Leno—and it's about international high-finance swindles, adapted from Paul Erdman's novel and full of double-crosses and unexpected twists."

"Is it funny?" little Tommy cried. "Is it clever, exciting, suspenseful? Is there any bare ass?"

"No, little Tommy," I replied, "no, no, no and no."

"Oh, s—," said little Mary Beth, crestfallen.

"Mary Beth!" my lovely wife Tacit cried. "If you say that word again, you're going straight to bed without a whipping."

"All right," I remonstrated, "everybody calm down. You still haven't heard about 'Rabbit Test.'"

"Is that the hilarious comedy directed by Joan Rivers and starring Billy Crystal about the first pregnant man and featuring brief appearances by Paul Lynde, George Gobel, Imogene Coca, Roosevelt Grier, Tom Posten, Jimmie Walker, Sheree North, Bobby Camp, Peter Marshall, Roddy McDowell, Don Adams and Charles Pierce?" little Billy cried.

"No," I replied. "It's not hilarious."

"But is it a slightly off-color, crude, witless, labored, ineptly directed 84-minute turkey?" little Billy persisted.

I looked wearily at Tacit, my lovely wife. "You can't fool children these days," I sighed.

"Still, they keep trying," she replied.

HIM AND HER EQUAL SHE AND IT

May 12, 1978

She was the most famous woman in the world.

He was a peasant, a pirate, a shark. What he couldn't buy with money he stole with charm.

Fortunately, there was nothing he couldn't buy with money. If charm were Wheat Thins, he couldn't have catered Sandy Duncan's bat mitzvah.

She had short dark hair and was married to an American President who would be assassinated in office.

He had short white hair and was married to Camilla Sparv.

"Camilla Sparv" was an anagram that still hasn't been cracked.

She's doomed husband had short brown hair and a short white brother who had short brown hair and was United States Attorney General.

He was Greek and talked funny.

She was American and had an English accent.

He owned ships and airlines and banks and souls.

She was built like a brick Parthenon.

They met in a movie called "The Greek Tycoon."

Jacqueline Bisset was she.

Anthony Quinn was he.

Raf Vallone was he's brother and rival. Edward Albert was he's son, who would be killed in an airplane crash.

Charles Durning was he's enemy, the man who became Attorney General after she's husband was slain and his short white brother ran for President.

James Franciscus was she's husband, the President.

Marilu Tolo was he's long-time mistress, a tempestuous Greek actress with the euphonious name of Sophia Metalas.

How callous.

He particularly likes Marilu because she was the only actress in the film willing to bare her teeth and other vital organs for the camera.

He was crude, rude, ruthless, spoilt, foul-mouthed, unfaithful, volatile, noisy, demanding, erratic, vulgar, insensitive, worth $500 million and a good dancer. She was widowed, unemployed and a good dancer.

They were married. "A match made in Arthur Murray's!" trumpeted the press. They settled down in 27 different homes, one $5-million yacht and a makeshift island. They drew up a contract.

"Ees old Grick custom," he said, fondling her bazooms. "I am getting ten rolls in the hay eech month weeth you, you are getting six hundred thousand a year mad money, unleemited charge accounts and $10 million for eech year we are married."

"Those are my kind of customs," she said. "And tell me again the part about how I'm more famous than Indira Gandhi, Golda Meir and Ann-Margret put together."

She was now the most uniquely famous woman in the world.

He was a peasant, a pirate, a shark and given one year to live. He went down to the waterfront and watched the sunset. Alone. One of the richest men in the world, married to the most uniquely famous woman in the world. Alone, dancing in the golden shadows with the village peasants as twilight fades into darkness.

Which just goes to show. If you don't have your health, you don't have bananas.

A Very Short Review
February 27, 1970

"The Female Animal," a sex film, is now at the Golden Gate Penthouse. If it were a horse, it would be a mare. If a pig, a sow. In this case, it's a bitch.

6

The Screening Room

The theme [was] described by the Film Festival program
as a 'surreal American fantasy,' which strikes me
as redundant to the second power.
JLW

The morning of the 1975 Academy Awards, John appeared on the television show "A.M. America" to predict the Oscars, along with Roger Ebert of the Chicago Sun Times *and Susan Stark of the* Detroit Free Press. *They were introduced as "three of the nation's most distinguished motion picture critics."*

San Francisco was a serious movie town. There were the annual International Film Festival, filmmaking programs at San Francisco State College and the San Francisco Art Institute, and a proliferation of art-film theaters. Independent companies, too, were locating in the area, along with directors Francis Ford Coppola and George Lucas.

John spent a great deal of time on movie sets. He was George C. Scott's stand-in on "Petulia" in 1967, and Clint Eastwood's on "The Enforcer" in 1976. The mock high point of his career was a walk-on in "C.C. and Company," a motorcycle film. Tongue in cheek, he reviewed his own performance.

In 1969 the actress Viva, in town for a premiere at the Film Festival, told reporters she had gone to John's apartment for a late-night interview and ended up fleeing in terror. He gave her a "fishy" joint, "interrogated" her ("He asked my real name, my age ..."), made suggestive comments ("I don't think you have such a laughable body") and had her convinced (she claimed) that he was the Zodiac Killer, a serial murderer who was then at large. The Berkeley Barb *reported John's side: Viva became paranoid after smoking a joint of Acapulco Gold he offered as a conscientious host, and misinterpreted his reporter-like questions and polite comments. "The strangest thing is that she didn't behave like a lunatic, she only said things that were loony," John said.*

When speaking to groups of students, John insisted a critic's primary function was to help make economic decisions, not be the ultimate arbiter of taste. "Everyone should read at the start of a review, even if it's not printed there, 'In my opinion, which is more informed than most and less informed than some.' Because that's what it is," he told Frances Moffat's class in 1975.

Clint Eastwood, the top box office draw in the world, was a friend of John's and one of the regular guests at his annual "Media and the Arts" class. John pressed all of his show biz friends into service at one time or another. The two men shared a love of jazz, and Eastwood attended many of John's parties, where he sat under the piano when the room was too crowded.

"John could be a tough reviewer but was one of the few in San Francisco that you felt really liked *film," Eastwood says. "He went to find something instead of going there predisposed to whatever the fad was at the moment. He was one of the few around who tried to constantly expand his knowledge of the industry. He never assumed he knew it all."*

Screenings for critics usually took place at nine in the morning. Publicist Claire Harrison recalls that John would enter the lobby dressed in black, with his reporter's notepad, an extra-large coffee and a bag of buttermilk doughnuts. He would take his seat on the aisle, light a cigarette, and the film would roll. The critics usually didn't talk to each other but sometimes they talked to the film. San Mateo Times *writer Barbara Bladen once woke at the conclusion of a Jerry Lewis film to find John crying out in frustration and throwing his notepad at the screen.*

Woody Allen was John's favorite filmmaker. Their friendship began on the San Francisco set of "Take the Money and Run" in 1968, and they kept in touch through letters and visits in California and New York. When John's 1973 review of "Sleeper" appeared, Allen wrote, "After all these years, you, my analyst, and a very beautiful girl who doesn't let me touch her, remain the three most important opinions to me."

BIRTH OF A STAR
October 29, 1970

A star is born.

John Wasserman, formerly known as a pop music and drama writer for this newspaper, makes his motion picture debut in "C.C. and Company," a motorcycle gang satire.

As it was when Gary Cooper flashed on the screen in "Wings," as it was when Marilyn Monroe seared the celluloid in "The Asphalt Jungle," as it was when Dustin Hoffman won our hearts in "The Graduate," yes, such is Wasserman's impact in "C.C. and Company."

Whether he is grinning powerfully at Joe Namath or barking out dialogue like "Over at counter 11B," Wasserman's 10 seconds on screen have stunning impact. Even beyond this, however, is Wasserman the Actor.

There are many ways to read the line, "Yes, Sir?" It could, for example, be posed as a question. It could ring with joy or drip with sarcasm. Wasserman, rather, chooses to interpret "Yes, Sir?" as an unequivocal statement, a probing challenge of the NOW. One would have to search deeply through the motion picture industry to find another grocery-store clerk of this stature....

Namath, while no actor, has an easy presence and droll humor which stand him in good stead; Ann-Margret does what little is required with finesse. The screenplay is by Roger Smith, Miss Margret's husband,

and manages to get the scenes from one location to another. "C.C. and Company" cannot possibly be taken seriously but it has style and John Wasserman. That is no little accomplishment.

Rip Van Allen

December 21, 1973

Woody Allen's new film, "Sleeper," is not only the funniest film of the year but takes one more giant step towards establishing Woody incontestably as the most brilliant comic mind of the century.

That is a strong statement, of course, and subject to endless disputation. But Woody has mastered every outlet of comedy, from stand-up monologues to acting, directing and writing for stage and screen, through prose and pratfalls.

"Sleeper," which co-stars the lovely actress and comedienne Diane Keaton, is the fourth film Woody has written, directed and starred in. It is also the most successful as a motion picture. It is not only as funny as the best of those which preceded it (probably "Bananas") but is also cohesive, consistently focused (the story, in addition to the camera) and merciless in making fun of contemporary fads and pretensions.

The plot is a classic vehicle in which to comment on the current state of affairs: life in America in the year 2173. Woody, as Miles Monroe, clarinet player and former part-owner of the Happy Carrot Health Food Store in Greenwich Village, finds himself being thawed out 200 years hence after being subjected to cryosurgery by mistake after he went into the hospital for an ulcer.

No sooner is he removed from aluminum foil and revived (immediately wailing that "I'm 2,000 months behind in my rent") than he finds himself involved in a 1984-style Big Brother society and the inevitable underground revolutionary movement. From there, "Sleeper" turns into one long chase, culminating with Woody and the revolutionaries capturing the Dictator's nose and destroying it. I would describe why they have only his nose except that such things regularly happen in Woody's films and are more disfigured than enhanced by written explanation.

The temptation to describe scenes and quote lines is overpowering; I will submit:

Woody's physical and visual comedy, homage to Chaplin and the Marx Brothers, which includes his awakening from 200 years of inactivity and attempting to walk; his identification of ancient artifacts for puzzled anthropologists ("This is a picture of Billy Graham...he knew God personally...in fact, they were romantically linked for a while"—"This is Norman Mailer, a great writer...he donated his ego to the Harvard Medical School"); his impersonation of a robot (with glasses...?); his rendering unconscious a policeman with blue cheese, a scene in which Woody and Diane Keaton portray, respectively, Blanche DuBois and Stanley Kowalski; and the unadorned stand-up comedy lines: "It's hard to believe you haven't had sex in 200 years," says a friend. "204 if you count my marriage," replies Woody.

Additionally, "Sleeper" is the most politically active film Woody's made, although all the political comments are for laughs first, significance last. Woody wants to make people laugh, simply. If political jokes will do it, it will be done; if it takes a gay interior designer or a Jewish tailor, that also will be done. No discrimination.

Actually, though, there is one "meaningful" line in the film I will assign to Woody's philosophy. "What do you believe in?" he is asked at the end of the film by an earnest revolutionary. "Sex and death," Miles Monroe Allen replies. I suspect that flirts with the truth.

SOME KIND OF FUN
December 26, 1973

Who ever would have thought that Dirty Harry Callahan, scourge of hooligans and his police superiors alike, would wind up as a bleeding-heart liberal locked in mortal combat with a group of self-appointed vigilante-executioner cops?

No one, that's who. Nonetheless, with a little poetic license, that's what Clint Eastwood's doing in "Magnum Force"—a continuation of, if not sequel to, his very successful "Dirty Harry."

Harry, adventure-lovers out there may recall, was a tough, saturnine and thoroughly invincible San Francisco cop who held equal contempt for the law-breaking slime he pursued on the streets, the desk-jockey police brass who impeded his progress with little irritants like the Bill of Rights, and the fuzzy minded nincompoops of the courts who sentence mad dog nun-rapers to two days in traffic court. Suspended.

Nonetheless, Harry persevered, driven by that deep, if too rare, inner satisfaction of blowing a man's head several cubits off his neck.

Fortunately, Harry never did this to the innocent; only the guilty. Harry, like Eastwood's classic Man With No Name, only killed rotten folks. And who cares about them?

And now comes "Magnum Force" to continue Harry's one-man gang-bang of lawlessness and disorder. "Magnum Force" refers, of course, to a magnum handgun. They come mostly in the .357 and .44 varieties. They are very macho in handgun circles. Harry packs a .44. It is powerful enough to stun a building.

Our story opens in the usual manner. Harry is being subjected to petty harassment by his lieutenant, who has assigned him to a pinball machine stake-out. "Next," Harry snarls sarcastically, "you'll have me on the kitty-litter detail."

"I don't think that's funny, Harry," snaps the lieutenant, "and the boys on the Vice Squad won't think it's funny, either."

Then, abruptly, a gigantic mystery begins to unfold. Dozens of San Francisco mobsters (remember, this is fiction) are suddenly slaughtered by a man or men wearing police uniforms and riding police motorcycles. Visions of the Brazilian police murder-gangs, who killed crooks without benefit of trial, begin to dance in the head. Is it Harry? The lieutenant (Hal Holbrook)? Davey Rosenberg?

No one knows, including us, for the killers wear dark glasses. Anyway, there's the mystery for you. Harry is promptly taken off pinball machines (after killing two of them and permanently crippling the right flipper of another), put back on homicide and eventually wraps the whole thing up; expending only 6,914 bullets from his trusty .44 in the process.

As you can see, "Magnum Force" is kind of fun. Not to be taken seriously (either as a mystery film or a Disgusting Violent Film), but boasting plenty of action, some imaginative and effective staging of chase and battle scenes and the always delightful presence of the imperturbable Eastwood. Director Ted Post seems competent if not unduly concerned with the credulity of anyone whose IQ exceeds 75. The other folks, including a number of recognizable San Franciscans, do their jobs.

Mystics, Soothsayers and Lunatics

December 10, 1976

As surely as "All the President's Men" was intent on glorifying print journalism, "Network" has set out to destroy television.

This surreal black comedy, directed by Sidney Lumet from an original story and screenplay by Paddy Chayevsky, is the most brutal satire of network television ever filmed.

William Holden, Faye Dunaway, Peter Finch and Robert Duvall portray, respectively, a network news boss, its ambitious head of programming, its news anchorman and the quietly hysterical executive of a communications conglomerate that has taken over the network.

The premise of "Network" is perfectly reasonable: that the men who monitor the corporate red and black ink—in other words, the creative directors—will do virtually anything for ratings, including murder, and that the potential for evil inherent in their almost unchecked power is terrifying.

The vehicle for this viewpoint is triggered by the on-the-air crackup of anchorman Finch, who, following notice of his termination as a result of low ratings, blandly announces to a watching nation that he will commit suicide on his last show, a week hence.

This most un-Cronkite-like behavior sets into motion an Alice-in-Wonderland chain of events culminating in the Nightly News being turned into a circus of mystics, soothsayers and lunatics—the water of public discrimination rising to its own level.

Lumet's direction is crisp and professional, and all performances are vivid (among the smaller roles, Laureen Hobbs is memorable in the flashy part of a "radical" who quickly adapts to a reality where The Struggle is not for the rights of man, but for the right of foreign syndication) but, ultimately, the picture is Chayevsky's, warts and all.

First, he knows his subject, having begun hacking his way through the TV jungles back in the '50s at the beginning of one of the most distinguished careers in American play writing. Second, he wastes little effort in satirizing the medium's content, concentrating instead on power and savagely mocking those who determine how that power shall be expended.

And third, almost alone among film writers who are not also directors, Chayevsky fights for and maintains artistic control of his mordantly angry scripts. He is a rare winner in the writer's perennial guerrilla warfare with those who produce his work. At worst, this can lead to undisciplined self-indulgence; at best, it means that the system of sterilization by committee is, at least in his case, stymied in favor of the integrity of one man's vision.

Indeed, the shortcoming of "Network" is that it is too blatantly angry, contemptuous, savage, merciless. Everything is spelled out; nothing is left for one's own perception or discovery. Yet, for the most part, it works. There are a dozen different segments of exceptional theater and extraordinary parody: funny, articulate, scary and, unfortunately, accurate. If the dung heaped by "Network" is too often applied with a shovel rather than a teaspoon, we can excuse the excess as one born of passion, not the condescension that characterizes the medium in question.

TAXICAB FROM HELL
March 3, 1976

It may be only coincidence, but it seems that more than a fair share of the most vital and dominating film roles of recent months involve individuals in emotional straits ranging from mild desperation to full-blown madness.

Jack Nicholson in "Cuckoo's Nest," Al Pacino in "Dog Day Afternoon," Ben Gazzara in "The Killing of a Chinese Bookie," Giancarlo Giannini in "Swept Away" and "Seven Beauties," even Ryan O'Neal in "Barry Lyndon" have been, in differing degrees, both fascinating and repelling in their traumas.

Now we have Robert De Niro in "Taxi Driver," a new film directed by Martin Scorsese. And if the best films reflect the society from which they spring, then, as suspected, we are all going quite mad. Patty Hearst is not the only possible victim of extenuating circumstances.

De Niro, who will probably win the Best Actor Academy Award next year for this portrayal, is a lonely, rootless, neurotic Vietnam veteran whose job as a night-driving cabby exposes him to the quirky ugliness of derelicts, pimps, whores and violence that only Fun City can properly provide. He despises the milieu, yet clearly needs it as a vent for his hostility and fear.

His only touch with humanity, other than occasional monosyllabic exchanges with fellow drivers at an all-night cafe, is with two girls who could hardly be more dissimilar—Cybill Shepherd, type-cast as a beautiful, vacuous, aloof woman who dabbles in presidential primary campaigns; and Jodie Foster, a 12-year-old actress cast as a 12-year-old whore and a likely candidate to surpass Tatum O'Neal in the precocity sweepstakes.

De Niro keeps a diary into which, initially, he disgorges his hatreds; has insomnia and headaches and is clearly, almost from the first moment, heading for a spectacular doom. His performance is the showcase, but those of Peter Boyle (a fellow cabby), Miss Foster, Harvey Keitel as her pimp and a dozen others are indelible.

Scorsese, the director of "Mean Streets" and "Alice Doesn't Live Here Anymore," has done something fairly unusual with "Taxi Driver" (which, incidentally, is billed portentously as "a film by Martin Scorsese," although he neither produced nor wrote it; functions filled, respectively, by Michael and Julia Phillips, and Paul Shrader).

He has created a drama, a piece of theater, of blazing brilliance, and a statement, a commentary, of equally blazing pretensions.

"Taxi Driver" is riveting from beginning to end, superlative in its seedy, gutter atmosphere, awesome in the flair of a dozen different sequences and terrifying in a climactic scene of human carnage next to which Sam Peckinpah's work appears positively pastoral.

Yet its almost trick ending, an intentional anti-climax, is so "ironic" that it changes the film's entire thrust and, in trying to Make Us Think, compromises that which has gone before. Up to that point, the sledgehammer soundtrack and brutally repetitious evocation of New York City's human sewage is, if intrusive, not violating.

Then—well, you can see for yourself.

HOT ROBOTS AND ANTHROPOIDS
May 25, 1977

With the opening of "Star Wars," writer-director George Lucas makes a spectacular return to the screen. It is the most visually awesome such work to appear since "2001—A Space Odyssey," yet is intriguingly human in its scope and boundaries.

The major science-fiction films of the last few years—the Russian "Solaris," the French "Hu-Man," the English "Man Who Fell to Earth," as well as "2001," have all been exceptional, but all have displayed pretensions of one kind or another, generally cosmic.

"Star Wars" is not without content, but reaches as well for an area as embraceable by children or teenagers as by us older folks. With the opening declaration—"A long time ago in a galaxy far, far away"—it stakes out its turf: It will be a wonderful adventure, a fairytale, a contemporary "Star Trek" that will whisk us on the magic carpet of our imagination and Lucas' vision to a time and space where spaceships that exceed the speed of light are flown by anthropoids, where slavers deal in hot robots and where chess games are played with mini-monsters instead of rooks and pawns.

The only audible preaching by Lucas—in a whisper, to be sure—suggests that man is man and creatures are creatures, and it doesn't really matter how far forward or back you go to check it out. Here, God is The Force, feelings defeat the calculation, good conquers evil—but not without sacrifice—and love will keep us together.

Like that.

The story is an old one, even here on earth. As he did in "THX 1138" (1971), Lucas sets his story in a milieu of rebellion by the oppressed against Authority, in this case, the Galactic Empire. Princess Leia (Carrie Fisher) has obtained the structural plans of the Death Star, the Empire's chief instrument of terror, and with the help of an idealistic youth, Luke Skywalker (Mark Hamill), a lovably smug mercenary, Han Solo (Harrison Ford), and Ben (Obi-Wan) Kenobi, last of the noble Jedi Knights (Alec Guinness), sets about trying to save her galaxy from destruction.

In this context, Lucas creates a universe that combines the breathtaking visual wonder of "2001" with the bloodless battles of "Flash

Gordon" and a droll mischievous sense of humor reminiscent of Woody Allen's "Sleeper." The humans are human. "You can play with your friend only when the chores are done," Luke Skywalker's uncle admonishes. Spaceships are beat-up and dirty (the nearest garage is light-years away?), accuracy in the laser-beam gunfights is sensationally bad and the non-human characters—two co-starring robots, the golden See-Three-Pio and cute little Artoo-Detoo (who all but steals the picture), plus the wonderful Chewbacca the Wookie, the Sand People, the Jawas and the most delightful set of weirdos ever seen in the corner saloon—fulfill our wildest dreams.

The actors, while being generally upstaged by Wookies and Jawas, are fine (the cadaverous Peter Cushing, as the evil Grand Moff Tarkin, and David Prowse, as the ominous masked Lord Darth Vader, also have major roles) but inevitably, the star of "Star Wars" is special effects.

The shooting schedule of the $8.5 million production was a relatively brief 12 weeks in locations like Tunisia, Guatemala and Death Valley, but the special effects work took a year and a half. Every dollar and every hour are on screen, and if "Star Wars" doesn't garner at least half a dozen Academy Award nominations, I will eat my Wookie.

In addition to being a superbly crafted film, "Star Wars" is that rarest of creatures: the work of art with universal (excuse the pun) appeal. There is in all of us the child who dreams of magical beings and fantastical adventures. On a street level, "Rocky" fulfilled that need last year. "Star Wars" takes us beyond the heavens.

DIVINE INSPIRATION

January 26, 1979

"The Neon Woman," which swaggered into the Alcazar Theater on Wednesday night, has something for everyone: vulgarity, degradation, dirty words, heterosexuality, homosexuality, transsexuality, skin, curves, muscles, righteousness, prayer, bad taste, racism, sexism, fatism, deaf-muteism and an utter lack of significance.

If that ain't enough to revive theater in America, I surely do not know what am.

"The Neon Woman" is a "de facto" vehicle for a corpulent gentleman who calls himself Divine and is pleased to dress in women's clothing and bosoms. While just another pretty face to the straight world,
Divine is semi-legendary amongst the fringes of gay folks, kinkos and
those who covet the outrageous—all of whom were out in force for
Wednesday's official opening.

The comedy is set in 1961 in Baltimore, where Flash Storm (Divine) owns and operates a strip joint called the Neon Woman. Her
charges include Kitty LaRue (Sweet William Edgar), a cynical drag-
queen; Countess Bryn Mawr (Sally Train), an uppity college grad working for "the experience"; Connie (Valrie Riseley), a brassy, embittered
veteran; Kim (Katie LaBourdette), a Marilyn Monroe dumb blonde who
alternately moues and moos; Joni Belinda (Maria Duval), the deaf-mute,
and Laura (Hope Stansbury), Flash's innocent virgin daughter who
evolves into no less than an alcoholic, heroin addict and necrophiliac
under her mother's watchful eye.

Also present are the club's manager, Speed Gonzalez (George
Patterson), its grotesque janitor (William Duff Griffin) and two sin-
smiters: Matt the District Attorney (Andrew Potter) and a United States
Senator from Maryland (also Duff-Griffin).

The plot of "The Neon Woman" is, to put it generously, skeletal,
but, like some sort of combination of the recent "Movie Movie" and
Michael McClure's one-act "gargoyle cartoons," it hardly matters. So
brisk is the pace, so broad the parody, so quirky the individuals and
theatrical the production that there is not time—or desire—to reflect on
the lack of meaning of it all.

Although the script has genuinely comic moments, it also has
those bereft of wit or cleverness, but the caricatures are so endearing and
expert, and the spirit so utterly without pretension, that almost nothing
ever actually falls on its face—it just stumbles momentarily and then
goes crashing headlong on through the underbrush of social satire. Even
the fact that it sort of falls apart at the end has little impact. Divine's
spectacularly sleazy curtain calls become the climax.

I cannot number myself among Divine's supplicants, but she certainly has a lock on the Mae West tradition, and Patterson, Duff-Griffin,
Potter, Stansbury and Riseley are all appropriately hysterical. And sometimes funny, too.

But I must save my admiration for Sweet William, whose Kitty is a virtuoso display of bitchiness; for Duval, because she is simply wonderful to gaze upon when one tires of Divine's begowned whiskey barrel; for Train, for the same reason and her comic timing; and for La Bourdette, whose go-with-the-flow vacuity is as perfectly defined as any characterization present.

"The Neon Woman" is a burlesque show about a burlesque show, an engaging romp somewhere to the left of conventional theater and to the right of Honeysuckle Divine (no relation, I sincerely hope).

If you are easily offended, by all means go. Life gets harder all the time.

7

The Plot Thickens

How to Read a Critic: The Performer's Handbook
1) Don't read anything written about you.
2) If you must read your notices, have them pre-screened. Read
only the positive ones. Neither positive nor negative is likely
to tell you anything valuable, but the positive is more fun.
3) If nothing positive is written, note that the people
are the only true critics.
JLW

*John's early aspirations as an actor were squelched at age 14. During a dress
rehearsal of a production at Lick Wilmerding High School in San Francisco,
he recited his three lines in the wrong order and was ridiculed by the principal
and dropped from the cast. He came home saying, "I'm never going back
there," and switched schools, to Tamalpais High in Mill Valley, a few blocks*

from home. Thereafter he directed his considerable showmanship to doing voice-overs and stints as a television talk show host, movie stand-in, radio disk jockey and, once, a circus clown. He greatly admired our uncle, playwright Dale Wasserman ("Man of La Mancha," "One Flew Over the Cuckoo's Nest") and had a lifelong fascination for actresses.

In 1962, before the Chronicle *job materialized, he bought a share in a new improvisational comedy group, The Committee, headed by Alan and Jessica Myerson from the fabulously successful Second City in Chicago, spawning ground of Mike Nichols and Elaine May. When The Committee opened in April 1963, John was in place as part-time bartender, assisting Michael Stepanian, a law student and former hungry i bouncer. "John was a lively, happy presence," Alan Myerson says, "the guy who was always there when we needed him."*

The Committee was the first political theater in San Francisco with a popular base and the first performing group to espouse and support the Free Speech Movement before the major teach-ins. Myerson helped form the Artists Liberation Front, a consortium of arts groups and artists. When Michael McClure's "The Beard" was banned from further performances at A.C.T. The Committee produced it.

There was ample material for satire during those years—censorship, the sexual revolution, black power, psychedelic drugs, the women's movement, U.S. Government policy in Vietnam and the Haight-Ashbury scene. The Committee became a gathering place for performers and activists. Along with Enrico's sidewalk cafe and the hungry i, it was John's North Beach living room.

Paine Knickerbocker, the senior drama critic, was schooled in legitimate theater, while John was open to new directions and experiments. Nevertheless, they became close friends. Knick reminded John of his father—graceful, intellectual, grounded in his sense of himself—with the difference that while Knick and John disagreed on many things, their arguments were without rancor, whereas Lou could not tolerate opposition from his son. Both men urged John to finish college, read the classics, drive more carefully, drink and smoke less, with an equal lack of success. Knick's wife Nancy spruced up John's grooming; she bought him a tuxedo so he wouldn't have to continue renting one for openings. The Knickerbocker kids, Peggy and Tony, rounded out this surrogate family group.

As formal as his name, Knickerbocker dressed nattily even in the newsroom. John strode to his desk in rumpled clothes and unshined Hush

Puppies with a stack of take-out cups of coffee, which he downed cold. Knick sat at a desk, while John slung one leg over his typewriter table and slouched.

John was never a theater connoisseur in the sense that he became a connoisseur of comedy, and he seemed unashamed to admit gaps in his knowledge. Committeeman Scott Beach remembers him running into The Committee one night at seven to ask if anybody knew the plot of Edward Albee's "Tiny Alice" because he was supposed to write about it that night.

Knickerbocker retired in 1974 and John was not named to replace him. Many in the theater community missed John's reviews, according to Steve Silver, "Beach Blanket Babylon" producer. "He was the intelligent guardian. He understood the big picture, that his job was not only doing critiques but being supportive of theater."

Michael McClure, whose post-Absurdist plays took beatings from local critics even after he received an Obie for "The Beard," reflects that he probably would have continued writing plays if John had continued as a theater critic. "His response was open and natural and vivid and intellective without being smug or academic," he says. "He had the ebullience himself and the spirit that he didn't have to fear what people thought or felt or did."

"He would follow things along to the point that they were taken over by more liberal mainstream critics, then sort of let them go," John Lion, former director of the Magic Theatre, remembers. "When something had moved along, he would deal with the next thing. He was always interested in the next new thing."

GRRRRRRK!
May 10, 1970

Michael McClure has written a play called "The Authentic Radio Life of Bruce Conner and Snoutburbler." Many people have asked, "What is a snoutburbler?"

"It's sort of like Robin is to Batman," McClure explained recently. "When Bruce Conner says 'Shagarayoth'"—a McClure acronym for Solomon, Hercules, Arthur Rimbaud, Ganymede, Albrecht Durer,

Yeesus Christ, Oscar Bumblefoot, Teddy Roosevelt and Hades—"he turns into SuperConner. But unfortunately, he meets his nemesis, AntiConner, from the Universe of Reverse Matter, and his cohorts, the Paranoids; and he and Snoutburbler fight crime together."

Michael McClure is not known for double-talk. He is not a stand-up comedian of professional confusion like Professor Irwin Corey or Norm Crosby. In fact, much of his poetry and his best-known play, "The Beard," are notable, rather, for their passion, bluntness, nasty words and—periodically—contrived inarticulateness, i.e., a "meat poem" might be titled "GrrrRRK!"

But, in the last year or so, McClure has taken a swing into a new form, the "gargoyle cartoon," and his preceding description of a snoutburbler is quite consistent.

Gargoyle cartoons (the name was coined by McClure's wife Joanna) are short, mad, whimsical, funny, incisive one-acts which are quite unlike anything in the 37-year-old poet's previous output. McClure has been giving the premiere rights to most of them (there are 11 written, seven have been produced) to the Magic Theatre company of Berkeley, with notable success. Now, for the first time, a San Francisco production of five gargoyle cartoons is in the offing and McClure is very high about it.

"The Magic Theatre is really getting together," he said. "I think they're the best group in the Bay Area now; certainly for doing my plays." The five gargoyles, lumped under the title of "The Brutal Brontosaurus" (a sequel to another such evening, entitled "The Charbroiled Chinchilla") will have their official opening on Wednesday at the Village, 901 Columbus Avenue.

"We're reviving two that were done in Berkeley," he continued, "'Spider Rabbit' and 'The Meatball,' and adding three new ones—'Apple Glove,' 'The Shell' and 'The Authentic Radio Life of Bruce Conner and Snoutburbler.' John Lion is directing and, as usual, he is contributing very heavily to the plays. There's no doubt I write director's plays. What they really are is five short universes in the shape of comedies. They're nuevo-Ibsen social dramas about worms, ogres, giant flowers, meatballs and snakes."

McClure smiled at his florid word games. "These plays are new things for me. As a poet, you keep pursuing a vision until it's burned out, and then you have to find a new foundation...that part of you you've never let blossom before."

McClure says he will write no more gargoyle cartoons. "I think that was just a flash. Eleven plays, all first-drafts, and then the tank sprayed out. All of my plays have been like 'The Beard,' in that they're image flashes I get, usually when I first get up in the morning. Then I write what I've seen and heard."

The Magic Theatre will bring over its fine regular company, including Kathy Harper and Kathy Mallory (who will star in Evalyn Stanley's sexy lobby display), Christopher Brooks and Peggy Browne.

McClure's current activities include a book-length essay on poetry and biology ("It's about the nature of man as an animal, not just as a human creature"), a just-published new book of poetry for Evergreen entitled *Star*, a just-published novel entitled *The Mad Cub*, a novel for the fall entitled *The Adept* and a screenplay—"St. Nicholas."

Jim Morrison, best known as the leader of the Doors and exposer-of-self on stage in Tucson, is McClure's collaborator on "St. Nicholas."

"We've been pursuing it off and on for about a year and a half," he continued. "Jim describes it as sort of an alchemical version of 'The Treasure of the Sierra Madre.' I haven't come up with a better one. It's an adventure. We should be finished within a month. Jim is one of the best new American poets. His new book, *The Lords and the New Creatures*, is really fine."

But that's still in the future. "The Brutal Brontosaurus" is at hand. McClure is looking forward to it. Lion and the Magic Theatre usually tell him more about his cartoons than he knew when he finished writing them. He mulled the upcoming event, which will likely be the best showcase for his dramatic work yet seen in San Francisco, and assumed a wry smile of pleasure.

"Do you think people can take five different head trips in one night?"

A Night in Clod's House
June 27, 1975

The role and function of the producer of popular entertainment is one rarely appreciated in full by the public.

Oh, sure, everybody's heard of Billy Graham, and those wonderful fund-raising crusades he puts on with George Beverly Shea and the Billy Joe Bobby Jack Billy Singers.

But how many people know about Hal Zeiger?

And it is the Hal Zeigers of this world who are the adventurers, the pioneers and innovators who tread those unexplored pathways of success eschewed by the more conservative likes of Bernie Kornfeld, Glenn W. Turner and Emir de Hory.

It is the Hal Zeigers who show us not where we have been, but where we are being taken.

Perhaps one small vignette in the career of this extraordinary man will be illuminating. When Hal came to San Francisco, he didn't come the easy way, he didn't bring a sure thing like "Under the Yum Yum Tree" or "Pajama Tops." No, he started out at the top, with the big one. He determined to present "Jesus Christ Superstar."

Not a challenge, you say? Hear me out. First of all, "Jesus Christ Superstar" is not a play at all. It is a phonograph record performed live.

But that's not all. "Jesus Christ Superstar" is not only a phonograph record, it is a lousy phonograph record. Although adapted from a runaway bestseller called "The Bible," it is somewhat confused in the story line, and has added some songs, notably "The Nazareth Rag," which aren't even in the original.

The story, as well as I could follow it on Tuesday night, when it opened at the Orpheum:

Jesus Christ, a sometime carpenter and son of God, has a pal named Judas Iscariot. They hang around the local Gethsemane Fried Chicken on Saturday nights, ogle passing maidens and talk about religion.

Then, one day, Jesus is approached by a local resident, Norman, to heal his pet fish. "This poor fish hasn't walked since birth," Norman says, moaning softly. "And none of the fish doctors will give us an appointment because we don't belong to Blue Cross."

Jesus looks kindly at the man and gently removes the tiny fish from its tiny wheelchair. "How long has this tiny fish been a cripple?" Jesus asks soothingly. "Three years, your Lordship," comes the piteous reply.

"Well, Norman, I have news for you," Jesus says, quietly, gently stroking the small creature. "This fish isn't crippled at all. This is a dead fish. And you, Norman, are a real dummy."

"Oooooooohhhh," goes the assembled multitude, attired in the traditional pre-Christian raiment of reinforced athletic supporters and heavy twine. "We didn't know that...."

So there was Hal Zeiger: Stuck with a real turkey, no big names and a budget of $1.89. This calls for some ingenuity.

First, he conceived a startling, perhaps even revolutionary ad campaign: "And Now the Real Thing! Live! On Stage! First Time in San Francisco—The Complete Production—Fully Staged and Costumed. Company of 50—Including Full Orchestra and Choir."

Now, that may not sound too creative to you, but what if I should tell you that it's not the first time in San Francisco? What if I should reveal that on Tuesday, March 28, 1972, another fully staged and costumed and semi-live production of "Jesus Christ Superstar" opened at the very same Orpheum Theater?

Give up?

OK, then what if I should confide that the "full orchestra" numbers 14 pieces and the full cast, 20. And then what if I should ask you to add 14 and 20 and see if you get 50?

But still, Hal Zeiger was not through. One final slashing burst of derring-do was called for: Keep the critics away. Critics were not invited to opening night. They were not given tickets. The company's representatives would not speak with them.

And frankly, I was hurt. Because I couldn't believe that Hal Zeiger was trying to discourage my attendance merely because he had a total fiasco on his hands. So I bought my ticket for "Jesus Christ Superstar." And, by golly, Hal Zeiger *does* have a total fiasco on his hands.

Now do you appreciate Hal Zeiger?

NANCY DREW AND THE COCKETTES

February 4, 1974

London

When one thinks of English theater, one thinks of the National Theatre, the Royal Shakespeare Company, the Old Vic. Classics of traditional repertory and contemporary play writing.

But, for the last six months, one of the hits of the London stage has been "The Rocky Horror Show," a satirical musical less reminiscent of Shakespeare than a combination of "Hair," "American Graffiti" and the Nancy Drew Mysteries—presented by the Cockettes.

The influences of the show's writers must remain a mystery, since there is no program ("They haven't arrived yet," an usher explained cheerily, as if a half-year wait for delivery were standard), but it would be quite astonishing if "The Rocky Horror Show" evolved entirely without reference to above-mentioned institutions.

From "Hair," we find hobnobbing with the audience before the show formally begins, acrobatic leaping up and down ladders, elevated sets, splashy signs ("Acme Demolition Co." is ubiquitous), scanty costumes and even communal fondling.

The "influence" of "American Graffiti" is not so much imposed as shared, for England's 1950s and early '60s teenagers had their own largely home-grown Mods and Rockers who differed culturally from our own mainly in that, while we rolled up Luckies in our T-shirt sleeves, they used Players.

Nancy Drew (one may substitute here any of the classic melodramas, e.g. "A Girl Goes Bad," or "Showdown at Posey Gulch") dictates the plot and playing style of the hero and heroine who are, not coincidentally, presented in American accents by English persons.

Finally, more dominant than any other reference is the Cockettes; for the biggest role in "The Rocky Horror Show" is that of Frank, a bisexual transsexual transvestite who hails from the planet Transsexual in the galaxy of Transylvania. Frank, a bull transsexual, if there is such a thing, affects net stockings, tight-fitting Merry Widow corsets, ample make-up, an occasional whip and the slightly out-of-breath, high dudgeon camping best executed by Paul Lynde on "The Hollywood Squares" and "The Paul Lynde Show."

Beyond Frank's sexual ambiguity, there is throughout "The Rocky Horror Show" a near-obsession with sexual roles, virginity, seduction and related matters.

Finally, leaving no stone unturned, "The Rocky Horror Show" also parodies classic horror films like "Frankenstein" and "Dracula."

The plot revolves around Brad and Jane, a clean-cut young couple who, while driving on a dark and stormy night in a deserted country-side, have a flat tire. "Oh gosh," wails Jane, "whatever shall we do?" Brad squares his shoulders, drops his voice an octave and reassures her. "Never mind, Jane," he says. "We'll get help from that castle we passed down the road a few miles."

A narrator appears and, reading from a dusty tome, comments in sepulchral tones: "They had found a solution to their plight...." He pauses dramatically and slowly raises his eyes to the audience. "Or, had they...?"

With solutions like this, Brad and Jane don't need plights. For the castle is inhabited by Frank, his grotesque, hunchbacked manservant Riff-Raff, two freaky girls named Magenta and Columbia, and Rocky himself, a skinny blonde lad who has been created by Frank and Riff-Raff for their deviant pleasures. Brad's sole defense to these weirdos is his voice, which reminds one of the nonpareil announcer of "Laugh-In," Gary Owens. "Hi," Brad repeats endlessly, extending his hand, "I'm Brad Majors!"

Apparently aware that a little of this, no matter how skillfully executed, goes a long way, the creators of "The Rocky Horror Show" have produced just a little—an hour and 25 minutes, with a dozen or so songs and a jolly, unsophisticated score combining rock and jazz.

The show I saw was sold out to a young and tittering audience. It would appear to be in for a long run. It is testimony to the anarchistic flavor of "The Rocky Horror Show" that I'm not at all sure whether the lobby signs—"Best Musical of the Year by the *Evening Standard* Drama Awards and *Play and Players*"—are authentic or merely one more instance of amiable parody. The King's Road Theater is the scene of the crime.

Don't Let 'Em Change Your Name, Honey
July 11, 1975

One of these days, someone from New York is going to see Nancy
Bleiweiss in "Beach Blanket Babylon Goes Bananas," present his card,
take her to dinner at Ernie's, produce a pen and a piece of paper covered
with dollar signs and lots of numbers, and we are never going to see her
again.

Except when she is on the Johnny Carson show (for the 58th time)
and casually mentions that she was discovered in San Francisco.

"Beach Blanket Babylon Goes Bananas," the spiritual heir, if not
sequel, to "Beach Blanket Babylon," is a very funny comedy revue—
again, built on nostalgia—with some highly talented musicians, singers
and hoofers, bright and imaginative costumes, backdrops and props, and
a producer-director-designer, Steve Silver, who is little short of a genius.

But as was true with the original, which played at the old Village-
Olympus, it is Nancy Bleiweiss's (and don't let 'em change your name,
honey) show. Possessed of an operatic-quality voice, next to which, by
comparison, a chameleon is drab and lifeless; and the largest eyes, per
square inch of face, in the entire world (again, by comparison, Carol
Channing squints), Miss Bleiweiss has proceeded to take these two magnificent natural resources, combine them with what can only be an
equally God-given sense of the nonsensical, and produce on stage a
singer-actress-impressionist-parodist-comedienne the likes of which I
have never seen.

The show opens with a quartet of musicians, dressed, logically
enough, as sheep, playing, "Yes, We Have No Bananas," followed by the
appearance of the mad Planter's Peanuts Peanut singing "Stardust,"
followed by three lads in Bermuda shorts rendering "Twilight Time,"
followed by two mobile M&Ms who join "Stardust," followed by three
young ladies who break into "Stairway To The Stars," followed by the
first grand entrance of Miss Bleiweiss (her every entrance is a grand
entrance), attired in a pink prom gown, covered with stars, a wand and a
mammoth, diaphanous pink crown—yes, it must be said, the Fairy
Godmother—and singing "California Here I Come."

Fugazi Hall, the 678 Green Street location of "Bananas," jammed
to the rafters, simply (on a Wednesday night, yet) erupted.

And that was the pattern of the no-intermission, 95 minutes show: nine singers appearing and reappearing in different vestments, singing songs of the Old West and the New West, with each switch of focus highlighted by a spectacular Bleiweiss entrance, each time with a new hat almost beyond description and attaining maximum altitude of fully five feet. An amazing lady.

The balance of the cast comprises Tony Michaels, Jim Reiter, Fran Moitoza, Glenda Glayzer, Roberta Bleiweiss, Lynn Brown, Philip Tobus, Bill Kendall and Kirk Frederick, all of whom are fine but each of whom must inevitably labor in Nancy Bleiweiss's encompassing shadow.

Nancy Bleiweiss was indeed on a star track. She signed with TV's "Laugh-In" but after six months married, went into the travel business and retired from the theater. "Beach Blanket Babylon" is the longest-running revue in America.

8

The San Francisco Sound

[Bill] Graham himself, when asked about his off-camera role in "Fillmore,"
merely adopts one of the distinctive Graham expressions—combining
tolerance for the unenlightened, affection for the self-deluded,
and the pacific knowledge that truth is truth, and the
Great Amplifier in the Sky understands completely.
("Fillmore Bill in the Movies," *Saturday Review of the Arts*)
JLW

*John celebrated his twenty-seventh birthday, August 13, 1965, at a new
club, the Matrix, reviewing the debut of the Jefferson Airplane. The same
week, Country Joe and the Fish opened in the East Bay, and the Warlocks,
soon to be renamed the Grateful Dead, were playing cover tunes in bars on the
Peninsula. John was the first person Marty Balin asked to manage Jefferson*

Airplane, but he turned him down, saying they were going to be a lot bigger than he could handle.

John's friendship with rock producer Bill Graham—"tough guy, hard case, screamer"—dated from 1964, when Graham managed the San Francisco Mime Troupe. He would come to the Chronicle to hustle publicity and John took a liking to him, lending him his phone, or better, the Rev. Lester Kinsolving's. John couldn't stand the pompous religion editor and liked to hide his telephone, but it was even more fun to loan it to Graham, who clung to it like a pit bull. The friendship was cemented in 1965 when John appeared as a defense witness in the trial of Mime Troupe director R.G. (Ronny) Davis, who was charged with defying a San Francisco Recreation and Parks Commission ban on performances of "Il Candelaio," a salty commedia dell'arte farce. Following Davis's conviction, Graham mounted the Mime Troupe Appeal Party—his first rock production.

Ralph J. Gleason, the Chronicle's pop music and jazz critic, became the chief interpreter and champion of the new rock scene. In 1970 he gave up his column, "On the Town," to work for Rolling Stone, the magazine he had founded with Jann Wenner. Bill German, recognizing John's talent as a music critic—largely developed through assignments Gleason threw him over the years, as well as guest gigs on Time and LIFE magazines (John reviewed the first Monterey Pop Festival for Time)—awarded him the column and charge of the pop music department.

As John and Graham—both thin-skinned, competitive and highly energetic—grew in power and prestige, they clashed frequently. John used more ink on Graham, and broke more phones hanging up on him, than on anyone else. The sound of screaming and slamming phones became so disconcerting that Carole Vernier, columnist Herb Caen's aide-de-camp, glued quilting all over John's phone.

The two men turned backstage at Winterland into a Ping-Pong battle zone, recalls rock critic Joel Selvin, who was John's assistant. "They'd stand six feet back from the table and slam the ball at each other while 50 people stood around watching. Those matches were legendary."

Winterland and Fillmore West were Graham's main venues for rock concerts on the West Coast. In 1973 John publicly criticized festival (non-reserved) seating at Winterland and incurred Graham's ire, which was an easy thing to do. In 1974 he crossed Graham again with a surveillance of ticketing practices at Winterland after Rock Scully, manager of the Grateful

Dead, told Selvin that bands were being shorted. When Graham found out about the stake-out, he threatened John with bodily harm and a law suit, and banned him from his offices and concerts. Zohn Artman, Graham's diplomatic lieutenant, smoothed things over and the ban was soon lifted. The ticket-practice exposé, revealing that houses were indeed oversold and underreported, was not published. "Bill managed to convince John there was no story," Selvin says.

Paul Kantner of Jefferson Airplane/Starship characterizes John's and Graham's relationship as "love-hate, big brother-little brother," with the roles constantly changing back and forth. They shared a love of guitar and were frustrated musicians. Both sat in with bands (John on congas, Graham on cow bell) and had to be kicked off the stage more than once, Kantner says. John wrote many positive columns about Graham as well as magazine features and was part of the producer's circle of intimates.

"I admired John because he never pandered, he always said exactly what he felt," says Jerry Garcia, the Grateful Dead's guitarist. "A lot of times he disagreed with other people just from a critical point of view; I always liked him because he took his own tack."

Bill Graham refused to be interviewed for this book, citing without elaboration "many negative memories" and "disappointments" concerning John. He died the night of October 25, 1991, with Melissa Gold and pilot Steve Kahn, when their low-flying helicopter smashed into an electrical tower in a rainstorm. A memorial concert took place 26 years almost to the day after the event that launched Graham's rock music career—the Mime Troupe Appeal Party.

LOOKING BACK AT A ROCK LANDMARK
November 12, 1975

Insofar as the world of San Francisco rock and roll is concerned, everything began between Aug. 13 and Dec. 10, 1965.

In that period, the Matrix and Jefferson Airplane were born, Bill Graham and Chet Helms let out their first squall, the Fillmore Auditorium and the Avalon Ballroom came into being and some groups name of Grateful Dead, Big Brother and the Holding Company, Quicksilver Messenger Service and Charlatans were introduced to a world that didn't know what it was waiting for, but realized that it had found it.

On Aug. 13 of that year, Jefferson Airplane and the Matrix made simultaneous debuts at 3138 Fillmore. On Dec. 10, Bill Graham gave his first "dance-concert" at 1802 Geary. In the next few months came the Trips Festival, with Stewart Brand, Ken Kesey and his frolicking rascals; and Graham gave his first non-benefit at the Fillmore, something called "The Batman Dance and Film Festival."

Since the Airplane (now Starship) is, as unlikely as it may seem, at the peak of its career, and since last Thursday marked the tenth anniversary of Bill Graham's first show, it might be interesting and amusing to look back at those days of innocence and yearning.

Everybody at the *Chronicle* was hip to the Airplane from the start, for two of their retinue, Bill Thompson (now their manager) and Gary Blackman (still a friend) were copyboys at the newspaper....

I earnestly observed, in a story on Aug. 20, 1965, that it was an "oddly named" group and boldly predicted that "it is entirely possible that this will be the new direction of contemporary American pop music." Looking back at that quote, which would appear prescient, I cannot for the life of me understand how I could have foreseen that. Bill Thompson probably told me. He still does....

While on the subject of me, it is also a fact that Airplane founder Marty Balin asked me early on if I would like to manage them. I demurred, not because I questioned their future, but because I questioned mine. Still do....

Marty then chose a man named Matthew Katz, who pronounced his last name "Cates." Only a year earlier, of course, the Republican Party had chosen a man named Barry Goldwater....

On Oct. 8, 1967, Captain Charles Barca and the San Francisco police department closed the Matrix during an engagement by Big Brother because the band was "disturbing the peace." Captain Barca was planning to arrest the entire band....

When the Avalon got a new dance permit on Aug. 9, 1967, the *Chronicle* reported: "They (Helms and Bob Cohen) showed up at the hearing armed with two lawyers, more than 100 letters attesting to their probity and good character, and more than 50 hippie supporters"....

On April 21, 1966, a *Chronicle* editorial supporting Bill Graham in his fight for a dance permit noted that "numerous witnesses" had reported that "participants in the revels are peaceful and well-behaved, though they have long hair, and some wear beards, and few adhere to fashions approved by *Esquire, Vogue* or the *Gentleman Tailor.*"

On April 23, 1966, a 14-year-old, arrested at the Fillmore, asked his captor for an explanation. "I'm arresting you," came the reply, "for being under 18 and for being in attendance at a public dance."

The first concert Graham ever produced, the Nov. 6 affair on Howard Street to benefit the Mime Troupe, listed the following performers: Jefferson Airplane, comedians Ullett and Hendra (then playing the hungry i), Lawrence Ferlinghetti, Sandy Bull, pianist Jeanne Brechan, the Fugs, Sam Hanks, Jim Smith and "others who care."

Oh yes, there was another act listed by Graham among the performers committed for that night: The Family Dog.

Bill thought it was a poodle act.

JANIS JOPLIN TURNS 'EM LOOSE
July 15, 1970

"I haven't had so much fun since the first year with Big Brother," Janis Joplin hollered before she went on stage Sunday night at the Santa Clara County Fairgrounds.

"I told the band that if they quit, I'm going to kill 'em, man. I'll tell you why I love them...we were in Kansas City, playing to half an audience of 12-year-olds and they weren't givin' us NOTHIN'. And this band SMOKED, man, they ROCKED! You'll hear, man, I'm gonna turn 'em loose for one number by themselves."

Janis was about three feet off the ground and didn't come down until 10 songs and an hour and five minutes later. And then only two feet of the three. She calls the new band, which was put together four months ago, Janis Joplin's Full-Tilt Boogie ("What else?" commented *Rolling Stone*'s Ben Fong-Torres). It comprises piano, organ, bass, drums and guitar, four Canadians and an American, no horns, all lovin' and kissin'. Guitarist John Till and pianist Richard Bell ("Who is currently charming them across the country," Janis drawled, "including the chick singer") are both veterans of the Ronnie Hawkins band; bassist Brad Campbell used to be with the Paupers, organist Ken Pearson may be heard on the new Jesse Winchester album and drummer Clark Pierson, the sole Yankee, was with Linn County. Till and Campbell were with the Kozmic Blues band.

Janis has had trouble getting it together since she left Big Brother and the Holding Company almost two years ago. And since she is unquestionably the most dynamic female performer in rock music, troubles for Janis are troubles for us all. The new band is news—she has just come off the debut national tour—and the news is good. Full-Tilt Boogie is just that—a driving, full, tight organization with roots from everywhere in American music, right back to James P. Johnson and the boogie-woogie. When they did their own number, they did smoke. Each is an accomplished soloist. Guitarist Till and pianist Bell are sensational, the total sound is an integrated no-gaps blast.

I asked Janis if she could describe the sounds in visual terms. She snorted. "Man, I don't think about it in terms of pictures, I think about it in terms of kicks in the ass."

A vision of feathers, velvet, beads, chains and bracelets, Janis whomped her way through golden oldies like "Summertime," "Try a Little Bit Harder," "Tell Mama," "Get It While You Can" and "Ball and Chain," interspersing those with newer material like "Move Over," her own composition. "I write," she said later, "every time something happens to me that's heavy enough." "Move Over" is, if it need be said, about a man.

She jumped and stomped and flailed and wailed, throwing herself into the songs with an abandon unshared by any other girl singer currently performing. The Who's Roger Daltry could be compared, I suppose, or Joe Cocker. But there's a crucial difference—Janis is, I think, controlled by the music and the lyrics; it is the reverse with Daltry and Cocker. Janis is more comparable to the late flamenco dancer Carmen Amaya than to another singer.

LOSING CONTROL

April 30, 1971

Bill Graham likes to be in control, to hold the trump card, to know what skeleton lies in which closet.

Nor does he like to be pushed around in any way, shape or form. He will unhesitatingly cut off his nose to spite his face if either feature offends his sense of propriety.

These qualities are the factors which led to his abandonment of rock concert production yesterday morning. For he is fast losing control—control of prices, of booking, of musical quality, and of audiences.

I would not be particularly surprised, incidentally, if his plans change as they have before. But I would be even less surprised if this time he carried through with his announced intentions.

The real difference now is that groups big enough to pack a relatively small auditorium (2,500–3,500 seats) are getting too big to hire at the relatively low prices ($3 to $3.50 here, $3.50 to $5.50 in New York) Graham has tenaciously held to for years.

Sure, he can book them into the Civic Auditorium or the Oakland Coliseum Arena, but that's not Fillmore West, that's not home, that's not what rock and roll means to Bill Graham.

So he's losing control. Financial demands bring on yelling matches, agents oblige him to accept "B" and "C" flunky groups in order to get "A" superstar.

It is a seller's market, and the groups—not the producers—are selling.

It used to be that Graham could book anybody—anybody but the Beatles, the Stones, or Dylan—into Fillmore West and still make a buck. That is no longer true.

Elton John, who played the 150-seat Troubadour Club here for pennies less than a year ago, will play the 8,000-seat Civic Auditorium next week for an hour or so and take home some $20,000.

Bill Graham feels he is no longer a creative force, but a mechanic. And with a net worth that approximates one million he probably doesn't need the money.

Rattlesnake in Slow Motion

October 11, 1972

I'm not sure whether the Grateful Dead is or are back in town, but whatever the case, dearie, it's time to haul out them rock and roll cliches.

Bill Graham has long been fond of saying that, when they're on, the Dead is the world's greatest rock and roll band. He was at least half right on Monday night at Winterland—the Dead was on. They played for nearly two hours, took 30 minutes off to regroup, then returned for another 120 minutes. Being a mere mortal (Dead buffs are not mere mortals), I vacated the sweltering premises after the first half of the four-hour extravaganza, but I can only assume they got better. True to Dead precedent, the evening was anything but normal, even for Winterland. The only thing that didn't happen was a repeat of the mass freak-out which marked their last stay at Winterland.

Otherwise, business as usual. The evening raised in the neighborhood of $10,000 for the band's roadies (so that they might buy a house, and what other band jumps to mind for giving benefits so that their roadies might buy a house?) and a touch football game was played on the Winterland floor until 3:15 a.m. It was suitably entitled The Toilet Bowl. The trophy—engraved, of course—need hardly be further described. Graham's home team lost to the roadies, 36-18. He is appealing the outcome. On the basis that he lost.

The evening started appropriately enough: A girl, in disarray and not quite herself, was curled up on the Winterland basement parking lot floor, taking comfort from her attentive beau. This in itself is not of great moment, but they were occupying Bill Graham's parking stall. When the Dead play, apparently, nothing is sacred. Then into the hall, full but not jammed, where Graham associate Jerry Pompili smiled and cooed, "Don't drink anything you haven't opened yourself."

On the stage itself, Noelle Barton, the Dead's house dancer, was doing her rope trick—the rope being her body—and Jerry Garcia regarded his court with a beatific combination of sleepy contentment and total, unwavering concentration. Heavy Water, which has been doing the Winterland gigs of late, flashed its kaleidoscopic light show overhead, the stage was crammed with a motley ranging from the Jefferson Airplane's David Frieberg to Gay Talese, author of *Honor Thy Father,* and strange Day-Glo painted beasties roamed unfettered through the night. Some celebrants popped off a string of firecrackers, others teetered merrily in the highest reaches of the upper balconies, bothered neither by acrophobia nor a healthy concern for their own well-being.

It was, then, vintage Dead, and unfettered by reserved-seat formality of their four Berkeley Community Theater concerts in late August, Monday night brought their total attendance to some 18,000 in the last seven weeks. They probably could do it again in the next seven.

As for those threatened cliches, well, the band hit 'em all. Lead guitarist Garcia, rhythm guitarist Bob Weir, bassist Phil Lesh, drummer Bill Kreutzmann and new kid piano player Keith Godchaux shook, rattled, rocked and rolled, they boogied and smoked and cooked and trucked, they got it on and got it off, mellowed out and laid back, uptight and outasite, whatever that means, and so on and so forth. They moved, is what the Dead did, and not just from point A to point B.

The set—or first half of it—began kind of easy, with the country-rock sound that has predominantly identified their music of the post-"Viola Lee Blues" period. Garcia and Weir split the vocal chores pretty much down the line, integrating their singing flawlessly with the instrumental work, ambling through such as "The Streets of Laredo" like your basic old cow hands. Godchaux's rolling piano, with the feel, if not the technique, of honky-tonk, beautifully complemented matters (as in, How come they never had a piano before?) and his wife, the lovely Mrs. Godchaux, bobbed in now and again to warble a few notes herself.

The crowd, as always, went mildly berserk at every opportunity, throwing their hands into the air like thousands of tiny shrimp waggling in a wading pool.

But it was on the last tune, lasting 20, even 30 minutes, that the Dead outdid itself. It began as an irresistible, underplayed, non-Rolling Stones rocker, striking like a rattlesnake in slow motion; moved into an extremely complex section of Garcia and Weir entwining each other in molten guitar lines, rolled back and forth from ensemble to solo to duet, dissolved into an area that was almost Pink Floyd, then broke out with long, sweeping lines by Garcia, riding the rhythm section like BART to the end; no crash except from the audience.

TIM LEARY IS NO MARTYR

September 30, 1970

In May of 1968, I interviewed two homosexuals in regard to a film entitled "The Queen."

During the conversation, I asked what was, in retrospect, a particularly naive and stupid question concerning the incidence of drug usage in the homosexual community. It was pointed out that the gay society is, within itself, exactly the same as the so-called normal society. There are drug users and super-straights, poets and killers, artists and laborers, marriage and divorce.

This is also true of the pop music hip-youth community, but one wouldn't know it sometimes when listening to the prophets. Two recent incidents bring the issue to mind—the death of Jimi Hendrix and the escape of Timothy Leary.

Leary is a despicable man; if for no other reason than his years-long advocacy of the use of hallucinogenic drugs—something that even habitual users generally refrain from doing publicly. There is no way to measure the damage caused directly or indirectly by Leary to those who have heeded his messianic exhortations without the control or maturity to handle the results. Even the consumption of booze, accepted by society, is not promoted by any responsible person.

Yet because of the stupidity of the law and an insane sentence handed down in Leary's Texas case (10 years for two ounces of grass), this man—the same one who gave a speech at the First Unitarian Church here in the early '60s praising the California penal system—has become a false martyr, an escaped "political prisoner."

His exit from the California Men's Colony near San Luis Obispo inspired the Jefferson Airplane's Paul Kantner to dedicate a set to Leary during the group's recent Fillmore West appearance. My negative reaction in print to Kantner's dedication inspired an unsigned letter which said, among other things: "Brother Tim has become a hero all over again, and on a higher level—that of the dedicated enemy of the pigs, the true revolutionary, guided as Che said, by a great feeling of love."

Ralph J. Gleason, in his column of last Sunday, did not congratulate Leary on his escape but did suggest that "One does not have to approve of Leary's desperate escape act to have some appreciation of the despair which brought him to it."

Although it is fascinating to find that a "dedicated enemy of the pigs" is guided "by a great feeling of love," it is even more interesting to ponder the "despair" which motivated Leary. Is this, then, a despair not shared by other caged men and women? Is it somehow a special despair, an elevated emotion, thanks to his sanctified crime?

Leary was a political prisoner of the magnitude of Granny Goose. Political prisoners exist in this country. Leary was not one of them. The enforcement of dubious laws does not create political prisoners like instant coffee. Leary was harassed. That much seems certain. And nobody asked for it with more determination.

Gleason also found significance in the death of Jimi Hendrix, which he called suicide although there is no evidence to support that conclusion. He comments that "Audiences in our mass media world devour their heroes and Jimi Hendrix was one of these. The terrible pressures unleashed by that carnivorous drive force performers into twisted, perverted parodies sometimes of real life and it is deeply sad and all the more regrettable that some of them succumb to those pressures."

It is unquestionably sad that Jimi Hendrix died, perhaps because he somehow succumbed "to those pressures," more likely because he simply, unknowingly, took too many sleeping pills. Such an accident is not without precedent.

But a lot of people don't succumb. Others are destroyed by pressures which have nothing to do with playing a guitar uniquely well. Sweden, which does not devour its heroes, is well known to have a higher suicide rate than ours. And they don't even suffer from any of the ills (destructive capitalism, economic and military imperialism) of which the United States is so regularly, and sometimes accurately, accused.

Jimi Hendrix was a man first, a superstar second. Like other men, he was fallible but he was also manipulated by pressures he himself courted. Even if he did commit suicide, would that make his death more tragic or more "significant" (except musically) than that of Ernest Hemingway or Joe Blow? Otis Redding died nearly three years ago, "... a victim in his own way," Gleason says, "of the terrible rigors of the entertainment business."

Otis Redding died in an airplane crash. If he was a victim of anything, it was the plane or pilot. Unless one figures that the Middle East hijack victims were martyrs to tourism or that a pedestrian fatality was killed by his feet.

All actions have reasons. Everyone is the product of heredity and environment, but we all are also responsible for our own actions. We have to look deeper than commercial pressures for the cause. I am tired of the facile reasoning which holds that musicians in particular and the young in general are somehow uniquely anointed and/or crucified.

"WHEN YOU'RE STONED, YOU'RE NOT FREE"
February 17, 1971

"Now, it doesn't matter what I say," Country Joe McDonald said with a small smile. "I say, 'Gimme an F,' they give me an F. I say 'Gimme an I,' they give me a U. I say 'Gimme an S,' they give me a C...."

Country Joe sighed with both fatalism and amusement at the monster he has created, the famous "Fish Cheer" which has, in slightly altered form, landed him in the pokey at least twice for being a "lewd, lascivious and wanton person." Aside and apart from legal expenses and the fact that he is banned by the National Association of Civic Auditoriums (both for his cheerleading activities and "for defiling the name of the President"), Joe has gotten considerable mileage from the Fish Cheer and "Fixin' To Die Rag."

It is poetic that the song should have been so important in his life (it was the highlight of his acclaimed solo performance at Woodstock) for it is a microcosm of Joe's work—droll, satiric, melodically and lyrically uncluttered, gentle yet forceful. McDonald—like Frank Zappa, Nick Gravenites and John Lennon—is a unique personality in the sensationally bland world of rock music. Now, with Country Joe and the Fish but a year-old memory, he is carving a new career that is extraordinary in its scope and ubiquitous in its presence.

McDonald, who was born in Washington, D.C., reared in El Monte, California, and trained as a trombonist, is now in his late 20s and, like the more thoughtful of his contemporaries, going through some changes. He now rejects a "political person" label while also saying that "The Fish are 90 percent responsible for the political statements that are heard in rock today.

"I'm not a dogmatic person, you see, and you have to be rigid to be political in that sense. A dialectic doesn't interest me at all. I make music and I'm a humanist. Bertolt Brecht was not political; he was a writer who chose to use his talents in a political way. Sometimes I use my talents in a political way, sometimes not. Freedom is an act of discretion and I make choices...sometimes based on concepts of art, sometimes on money, sometimes on morals. I keep changing my mind as I get disillusioned. I just stopped using drugs. About a year ago I decided not to take any heavy psychedelics anymore, but I was smoking grass and hash. Now I'm through."

I asked him why. There was a long, long pause. He looked at his wife, actress Robin Menken, then thought about it some more. Finally he spoke.

"Our baby, Seven, was choking one night. It's something that happens to babies. I was stoned. I did what had to be done, it worked out all right. But later, I could hardly even remember what happened. I don't want that to happen again.

"I just came out of a period of wanting to escape, but now I want to control myself and have the freedom to do whatever it is I want to do. When you're stoned you're not free. A lot of people are going to find this inconsistent, because I've been an advocate of drugs for several years now. But I've changed my mind. And it's not because I've become spiritual. I've just changed my mind. It's a pragmatic decision. At this point in my life, it's important for me to take care of business as efficiently as possible, and to conserve my energies."

WHEN THE MUSIC FINALLY STOPPED
July 5, 1971

Fillmore West finally closed last night, but the San Francisco Sound—that mystical product which includes geography, chronology and lifestyle as well as music—had its Fillmore closing on Friday and Saturday nights when the Grateful Dead, Hot Tuna, the New Riders of the Purple Sage, Quicksilver Messenger Service and Yogi Phlegm (the original Sons of Champlin) played their final sets for Bill Graham at the venerable Market and Van Ness ballroom.

Only Jefferson Airplane was missing (Marty Balin has left the group he founded and Grace Slick has been bedeviled by minor ailments of late), but the musical guts of the band—lead guitarist Jorma Kaukonen and the surpassing bassist Jack Casady—were present as the leaders of Hot Tuna.

The Dead played Friday, and needless to say, dominated the evening. The house had been sold out for a week and people started lining up seven hours before the doors were opened, not for tickets but to assure a close proximity to their beloveds.

The Rowan Brothers opened the program, augmented by the ubiquitous Jerry Garcia (Garcia was to play guitar and pedal steel guitar from 8:30 p.m. to nearly 3 a.m. with only three breaks along the way). The New Riders—with Garcia on pedal steel, Bill Kreutzmann on drums and Marmaduke offering up some gentle vocals for your dancing and listening pleasure—followed with silky smooth country rock and their large contingent of admiring howlers in full disarray, shouting and hooting, an embarrassment of wretches, love and affection and dope measured by decibels and stripped throats.

Then, at 11:15 p.m., Bill Graham took the microphone, as he is wont to do. "After all the (bleep) that's gone down over the years," he intoned, "I'm very grateful to them and consider them friends...The Grateful Dead!"

The crowd erupted, the Dead's psychedelic amplifiers began spitting, one of the Heavy Water light show girls started moving in a Westernized version of T'ai Chi Ch'uan, a mini-flame thrower behind the musicians split the darkness, Garcia, now on conventional electric guitar, embraced the room with a molten solo and the band—the group that many think is the world's greatest rock and roll band—began a three-hour set interrupted only by one intermission.

They did "Me and Bobby McGee" and a smashing "Good Lovin'," and demonstrated a musicianship attained by few groups in the short history of rock.

Saturday evening, for me, belonged to Hot Tuna, which had graciously consented to take second billing to Quicksilver.

Kaukonen, Casady, Papa John Creach (the nonpareil fiddler) and drummer Sammy Piazza played a two-hour set which ranged from the pure, tingling blues of "Rock Me Baby" to the old folkie "Know You

Rider" to the hoe-down of "Never Happen No More" to the wildly exciting "Three Weeks on the Road," a tune on the upcoming new Airplane album which evolved from the written song to a 15-minute jam session among Kaukonen, Casady and Papa John.

The Tuna vibes were similar to the Dead's—bodies in the crowd bobbing as if each were undergoing individual and personalized earthquakes, a phenomenal blonde dancer named Renea on stage—a fifth member of the group—the smiles and the joy, the carillon-bells sound of Jorma, the soaring violin of Papa John and the earth-rending bass of the unflappable Casady, a separate amplifier-speaker system for each string; notes as powerful and assertive as their author is quiet and slim.

It was our music at its very best.

9

The Search for
the Music of the Seventies

The music ... was so loud that it challenges
descriptions. It wasn't heard in the ear;
it was jammed into the body like sausage into casing.

JLW (ON THE WHO)

*After Fillmore West closed in 1971, John lost much of his enthusiasm for
rock music. He still had his favorite performers—Eric Clapton, the Rolling
Stones, The Who—but the spirit of the '60s had all but evaporated with the
deaths of Jimi and Janis, and the halls were too vast, the crowds unruly, and
the volume an assault. He left most of the rock reviewing to Joel Selvin, whom
he hired in late 1972. Joel was his third assistant, after Dennis Hunt, a
film specialist—now a staff writer on the* Los Angeles Times*—and Jon*

Hendricks, the great jazz singer, who tended to sit in with the musicians he was reviewing.

John maintained an interest in the rock scene in part because disco, punk, mascara rock and other '70s permutations were possible material for satire. Was Wassy, as some thought, over the hill? Record producer Jim Dunbar, Jr., who says John was his mentor when he was a teenager, says no. "Even when we disagreed about music John was willing to listen. He asked questions. And he was there. Some writers won't touch new groups until they're already performing in big halls. He'd be there at their first San Francisco club performance and his review, even if it was a slam, meant someone was paying attention."

John had fun with Rolling Stone's *much-touted search for a music to define the new decade. It inspired one of his favorite columns, "'Natural' Music of the Seventies," which like all of the selections in this chapter deftly balances fact and fiction.*

He loved it when people took his satire seriously. "If a small percentage of the people don't believe that what you are writing is literally true, then you have been too broad," he told Alan Farley. "I try to avoid the obvious wink at the reader. Deadpan as possible and let the ludicrousness of the circumstances be the clue rather than giving you an elbow in the ribs and saying, 'Look how clever I am.' Because a writer doesn't ever want to appear trying to be clever. I may be furiously trying to be clever but I don't want anybody to know that."

A SEARCH FOR THE MUSIC OF THE SEVENTIES
September 1, 1975

It is common knowledge that there are, today, two major ongoing inquiries that have captured the imagination of an entire nation. The rummaging around for Patty Hearst and the search for the Music of the Seventies.

The former quest is, of course, in the capable hands of the Federal Bureau of Investigation. The latter duty falls to us authorities of the music industry. Until very recently, the success of these pursuits has been approximately equal. Or, to put it another way, a wild goose could fall on your head by comparison.

The problem is, of course, that simple rock and roll has been voted out as the Music of the Seventies. It was the Music of the Sixties, which are past. Yet each decade must have its own Music. Otherwise, how is one to know to what one is listening?

The search for the Music of the Seventies began on March 12, 1973, when *Rolling Stone* announced that the decade had changed. Since then, us music authorities have been frantically casting about. Some said the Music of the Seventies has been hiding in a clothes hamper on a farm in Pennsylvania. Others claimed that the Music of the Seventies was pregnant by a Chinese high-jumper. Still others suggested that the Music of the Seventies was trying to obtain a Texas distributorship for Coors beer. These theories have been discounted, however, because they are so silly. As have the nominations of:

A) SOFT ROCK: Soft Rock had a fling as the Music of the Seventies until it was discovered that Soft Rock was just a quiet version of Loud Rock.

B) BISEXUAL MASCARA ROCK: Again, there was a rush to apply Bisexual Mascara Rock, a fusion of two exciting schools of music, until it was discovered that its inventor, David Bowie, was pregnant by a Chinese high-jumper. Since that theory had already been dismissed, it was dropped like a hot (pink) lipstick.

C) Once these two major competitors were found out, the candidates rushed forth like flies to anointment:

Alice Cooper proposed S&M Rock and was promptly beaten to within an inch of his life by a Fender Telecaster. He loved it and they were subsequently wed....

Johnny Cash advanced God and Country Rock until he smoked a joint the size of a salami, was converted to Rastafarianism by Bob Marley and took a co-op apartment in Trenchtown....

Kate Smith made a bid for Puck Rock but unfortunately fell through the ice at the Philadelphia Flyers' hockey rink in the middle of "America the Beautiful," froze solid and was sold as an ice cube for a Tequila Sunrise, mixed in the new White House pool, to commemorate the First Lady's admission to *Women's Wear Daily* that it is okay with her if her daughter marries a collie....

139

Nor was that the end of it. Rock of the Humpbacked Whale was given a total media blitz by Clive Davis, but the subsequent Arista release was a stiff, despite the presence of famed studio percussionist Jim Gordon on blubber. The artist, as it turned out, was a camel who could swim.

John Denver, not surprisingly, also gave it a shot with Rockies Rock but, despite astounding sales toted up in the various goat ghettos surrounding Boulder, it never got a foothold below 9,000 feet.

Last, but not least, was the Osmond Brothers' Church of Jesus Christ of Latter Day Saints Rock, which attracted considerable attention for several days, until it was discovered that it was getting airplay only in their tabernacle markets and among Morons.

So there it stood, a decade without a Music, until three days ago, when I received in the mail a record that I honestly believe—and I know I'm putting my reputation on the line here—is at long last, the final breakthrough: The Music of the Seventies.

It is, simply, Womb Rock.

"NATURAL" MUSIC OF THE SEVENTIES
September 3, 1975

Out of the blue and without fanfare, it appeared in a bundle of new releases from Capitol: "Dr. Hajime Murooka's 'Lullaby From the Womb.'"

Quivering with anticipation, I gingerly removed the soiled disc from its Pamper, swabbed it clean, sprinkled some talcum powder on it, rushed for the phonograph, turned it up to "boogie" and sat back breathlessly.

Frankly, friends, I could not believe my ears.

"Lullaby From the Womb" is no less than six tunes recorded by an eight-millimeter microphone "near the head of the fetus in a woman eight months pregnant," plus six more cuts collectively entitled "Familiar Music for the Baby's Environment."

And, if Capitol Records is right—and it is said the company has sunk upwards of $37 in the project—they may well have a runaway hit single on their hands: a tune which, in the words of Bill Graham (who is even now trying to book a pregnant Trident waitress as opening act for Elton John next month), "looks like a real sleeper ...."

That tune is cut three, side one: "Sounds of the Main Artery and Veins of the Mother." Already, the prestigious *Gavin Report* reports that "Mama's Main Veins" (as it is being called on KSAN) is No. 37 with a sponge on the Blue Cross charts, while no less than KSFO music director Elma Greer has dubbed it, with an eye on burgeoning sales, "Rock-a-Buy."

But we are getting ahead of ourselves, for the story behind "Lullaby From the Womb" is a startling one. Only through a combination of the pioneering research done by Dr. Murooka, and the foresight—and yes, courage—of Capitol Records, did this historic recording ever get out of the maternity ward.

"I had spent a long time looking for a 'natural' method to put a newborn baby to sleep," Dr. Murooka has been quoted as saying, after he found that parents often deeply resented his previous method, which was to sock baby in the jaw.

"And it occurred to me that a recording of the mother's body could serve a similarly useful function." Dr. Marooka had, you see, made an astounding deduction, one that will surely rank historically with the discovery of running water: "That crying babies may sometimes just be homesick for the familiar prenatal environment of their mothers' wombs."

Thus, "by playing a recording of the steady pulsating of blood rushing through the mother's aorta as it passes by the uterus, together with the smoother, more even sound of the pulsating umbilical cord, Dr. Murooka achieved outstanding success in his tests."

To wit: "Of the 403 sobbing babies who listened to the tape, every single one stopped crying." Especially after Dr. Murooka removed the burning cigarette from their tiny bodies. Furthermore, 161 of the 403 dozed off to sleep "in an average of 41 seconds" and 29 actually ordered the album.

So now, only one final question remains: Will Capitol Records' great gamble pay off? Not only will they have to reimburse Dr. Murooka for his teenie-weenie microphone and the Telefunken tape recorder, not to mention rental of a pregnant woman, but tremendous legal complexities lie ahead—especially if the album is as big a hit as now seems likely.

First of all, what is the going royalty rate for a uterus? Indeed, can a uterus even join the Musician's Union? What of the aorta? Or the veins? Will they have to be content with sideman's scale? And what of the womb itself? Will it be paid as a recording studio?

And what, God forbid, if Dr. Murooka tries to stiff the misshapen young woman who actually composed "Mama's Main Veins?"

What, alackaday, if he should reveal that "Lullaby From the Womb" is, in fact, a live recording of a choo-choo train?

THE SUPERSTAR OF GLITTER ROCK
October 11, 1974

Walked into the Cow for the Elton John show on Wednesday night around 8:30 and was greeted by the deafening ministrations of English rock singer Kiki Dee and her band of merry ranksters.

Sidled through 14,500 screaming adherents to the side of the stage. No redress.

Gosh, I said to myself, I don't have to take this. My ears are finely tuned instruments, sensitive to the most subtle nuance of harmonics, dietetic octaves and counterparts. I can walk and chew gum at the same time.

Miss Dee concluded activities with "I Got the Music in Me," her big hit, and departed. A master of ceremonies took the microphone. "Hey, guys and gals, can you get behind intermission?" he howled. "Solid. Like, there's peanuts, popcorn and places where you can tinkle, you dig it?"

I folded my notebook and headed for the exit. Bill Graham blocked my path. "I am a journalist," I announced, "not a masochist."

"You can't leave," he implored. "Elton won't perform if you're not here!"

"Nonsense," I retorted. "Try to get control of yourself, Bill." I slapped his face, hoping that he would come to his senses.

We fell to the floor, grappling like animals. He got a stranglehold on my Flair felt-tip pen and ran backstage, your correspondent in hot pursuit. We were separated by security guards.

OK, I said, after he stuffed cotton candy in my ears and I licked his boots for five or ten minutes. All right. I'll stay. You know where to send the check.

Best decision I've made in '74. Elton John came on at 9:22 and scurried off two hours and three minutes later. In the interim, he produced the finest rock and roll show to appear in these parts since, at the very least, the Stones in June of '72. It is now clear, if qualified, that Elton and his fellows (guitarist Davey Johnstone, bassist Dee Murray, drummer Nigel Olsson and new kid Ray Cooper on percussion) comprise the top rock act in the world.

As is true of the Stones, The Who and, say, Led Zeppelin, the John company can cook as vehemently as any band in the field. Moreover, Elton's sense of theatrics and show biz, while matched for flamboyance by some, is the most tasteful of all the glitter rockers.

But the diminutive and clinquant ornament from England has two hole-cards: songwriting collaborator Bernie Taupin, a genius and the least confined lyricist in pop music, and Elton himself as composer-arranger. Their songs, both in lyric content and musical fertility, are the most interesting, substantial and flexible to emerge from any major group since the Beatles.

The performance itself did full justice to the material. Elton has mastered all the blues vocal techniques without sounding like anybody in particular (e.g. Joe Cocker-Ray Charles), sings beautifully, plays piano like a demon and leads a group both tight and skilled.

The theatrics are, of course, just a bonus, yet cannot be ignored. My dear, Elton was outrageous. The entire stage (including the monitor-speakers!) was upholstered in deep red carpet, accented by white rugs and mirrors; the piano was demurely attired in spangles (on the sides) and more red carpet (the better to dance on) and Elton himself was a symphony of feathers, fur (fur-lined eyeglasses, etc.), Dracula capes (in gold and silver), domed hats, tuck-and-rolled bell bottoms and a jumpsuit with holes of such magnitude as to suggest a previous assault by Mothra.

The final touch: During the show, I was asked by one of Elton's aides if I'd like something to slake my thirst. I acquiesced. He produced a dark green bottle and poured. The shape was familiar. Is that, by any chance, Dom Perignon? He nodded gravely. I did not ask the year.

143

OPEN LETTER TO LILY TOMLIN

February 13, 1976

Dear Lily,

How are you? Well, enough about you.

No, just kidding, ha ha. Actually I am writing because I saw a very strange thing on Wednesday night and I thought I'd better tell you about it. I don't know if you have copyrighted characters like Edith Ann and Ernestine, but if you have, I think you may have ground for a hefty lawsuit.

Have you heard of Patti Smith? Well, she is a new comedienne who opened at the Boarding House on Wednesday night. I know that "imitation is the sincerest form of flattery," but I think this Patti Smith has gone too far. She is doing your act.

Not all of it, actually, but quite a lot. The backbone of her show is an imitation of your character Sister Boogie Woman. Oh, this Patti Smith also does more conventional impressions—you know, Mick Jagger, Bob Dylan, Richard Nixon, Tarzan—but they are "real people." Sister Boogie Woman is your invention.

Well, anyway, I'll tell you what happened on Wednesday night and you can judge for yourself. It was the damnedest thing I ever saw.

The show opened with another comedy act (I think that's too much comedy for one show, but then, it's not my club) called "The Noel Redding Band," which does imitations of a 1966 high-school rock group. They weren't funny at all.

Then came Patti Smith. Some people have compared her to Brigitte Bardot, physical-wise, but she plays that down and immediately assumes the characteristics of Sister Boogie Woman: face contorted, string hair cut with pinking shears, angular and gangly, dressed in boots, dungarees, a T-shirt, an over-blouse and a black-leather jacket. Then she started throwing herself about and yelling, but I couldn't understand a word she said, partly because she is unintelligible and partly because her back-up group was so loud that I couldn't have understood her if she were Henry Higgins.

Sometimes she would throw her arms in the air, sometimes she would punch at flies buzzing around her head, sometimes she would swing herself around, as if her skivvies didn't fit, and all the time she was ranting and raving and carrying on as if possessed. Just like you-know-who.

Then she really started to "get down." She got down on her knees and started creeping toward one of the guitarists, who had also "got down." Then she "got up" and went over to the electric piano, which she grabbed, and started pivoting her pelvis back and forth in a yoga exercise. The piano player was really surprised, but kept playing, even though she tried to get it away from him.

Then she went back to the microphone and started howling again and—get this—a lot of people in the audience howled right back at her. This was, as far as I can tell, traditional call-response of the evangelical church (again, Sister Boogie Woman).

Then she fell to the stage, placed one hand on the right side of her nose, one hand on the left side of her nose, bent very close to the floor and blew her nose. Lily, I was sitting all the way in the back of the room and I could hear that familiar refrain. Fortunately, the band had quieted down at that point.

Then she wiped her fingers on the floor, got up, wiped her hands on her T-shirt, shrieked again for a few moments and spit on the floor. Boy, night club stages sure take a beating.

Now, I know what you're thinking. This will never hold up in court because Sister Boogie Woman never blows her nose on the floor. True enough, but, on the other hand, Patti Smith never made me laugh, either. So it all balances out.

Frankly, I don't expect that you are going to file suit in this matter, even though you may agree that Patti Smith is a copy-cat. For it is clear that this is not a well person we're dealing with. Candidly, Lily, it was the most pathetic thing I've ever witnessed. Just pathetic.

Perhaps you will join me, however, as co-despondent in a suit I myself am planning to file. Against the audience. For cultural genocide.

It's not Patti Smith's fault.

She was just following orders.

PUNKED ON BY THE SEX PISTOLS
January 16, 1978

"Oh, how disappointing!" my escort wailed as we cruised past the be-draggled line on the rain-soaked sidewalk outside the Winterland Arena, "nobody's punked out."

Her eyes, barely visible through a cloud of mascara, misted over woefully as she peered in vain for like-minded souls waiting for the West Coast debut of England's notorious Sex Pistols.

The bone in her nose—a chicken femur, she had pointed out earlier—trembled slightly as she fretfully ran her ring-laden hands through her orange and green crew-cut.

"They all look so...*normal*," she said uncomprehendingly, "like they were going to see the Grateful Dead or something...."

She turned her head away, just as I thought I saw a tear trying vainly to force its way over the dam of mascara blocking its path. "There, there," I cooed, gently stroking her handcuffs. "I'm sure it will all be better inside. I'll bet there will be lots of 12-year-olds there."

It was 8:45 Saturday night and we were now inside—high, as it were, in the stage-right balcony of the jammed 5,500 seat auditorium, looking almost straight down on the equipment-cluttered stage and the seething mass of adolescent humanity clawing to get closer, valiantly striving for a ritual mass-suffocation.

The little blue Nuns—perfect for both meat and fish—had just departed and the Avengers were coming up. An Avengers representative approached the microphone. "F— you," he said amiably to the audience. "F— you, too," he barked to the straining middle-fingers being extended to him from the front row. "F— you all!" he cried triumphantly, leaving the stage to the Avengers and a chorus of obscenities and flying fruit.

The Avengers, a New York punk-rock band, began the second assault of the evening. Foodstuffs continued to rain through the air. "All right!" cried my Punkette, hurling one of her six-inch spike-heeled shoes at the guitarist. "Now we're punking!!"

Only momentarily stunned by the blow, the guitarist was helped back to his feet and continued to play the single chord in his repertoire. The half-dozen people in the front wearing crash helmets looked smugly in our direction. A fight broke out between a black-helmeted punk and a quadriplegic.

The Avengers completed their set to a chorus of boos. "That means they liked them," my Punkette explained radiantly, hurling her other shoe in approbation. The crowd in front was so tightly packed that if one itched, 80 scratched. They swayed back and forth like a multi-directional tide, like a herd of dominoes headed for the cliff.

"Hey," the Avengers spokesman howled, returning to the microphone, "you people stink. San Francisco stinks. This rain stinks. F— you! F— you all!"

Bill Graham, under whose auspices the recital was being held, walked up to the microphone and informed the Avengers spokesman that his presence was no longer required. The Avengers spokesman questioned Graham's perception of the situation. Graham's arms shot out like pistons, catching his silver-tongued adversary in the chest and propelling him a half-dozen steps backwards. More words were exchanged. Another push. Yet more words. A final thrust.

The stage was again empty. "You can't talk like that here," Graham said later. I don't think he knew exactly what he meant. It was somewhat like hiring a bodyguard and then berating him when he slugs someone.

A girl suddenly appeared from the audience at the front of the stage. She had been passed along, hand to hand, like a dish of mashed potatoes on a bridge over troubled waters. Security men hustled her out.

"Hey," someone nearby said, giddy with anticipation, "that's only the beginning of the violence tonight!"

The road crew set up for the Sex Pistols. More people were passed up to the stage and zipped from sight. The stage was the only exit for those up close. Once you got in, there was no other way out.

The guy with the black helmet was thrown out. I went down to the stage, handing my remaining supply of banana cream pies frosted with ground glass to my associate, who was busily sharpening her razor blades.

"They bit off much more than they can chew," a veteran stagehand said dryly, nodding to the crowd up front. More bodies were sucked from the quicksand, most of them barely able to walk. "Oh, God," a girl gasped as she was trundled past the mixing board, "they just pushed me and pushed me...."

At 10 o'clock, lead singer Johnny Rotten, bassist Sid Vicious, drummer Paul Cook and guitarist Steve Jones slunk onto the stage.

"They were real pleasant young men," the stage-hand remarked, referring to a Sex Pistol visit to Graham's office the day before. "I'm not real crazy about their audience, though."

Vicious warmed up with a couple of locked-knee, two-legged, pogo-stick leaps. The guitarist, wearing a red jacket and spurs, expectorated into the delirious crowd. Johnny Rotten, in leathers, just stared straight ahead, as if undergoing an eyesight test at his pre-induction physical. Vicious removed his leather jacket. His left arm was bandaged. Probably an abortive suicide attempt.

All were wearing safety pins—no doubt in case of accidental dismemberment.

The barrage from the audience began in earnest—flashbulb cubes, grapefruit, empty half-pint whiskey bottles, smuggled past the search parties at the door.

Ice, clothes, hairbrushes, empty crumpled paper cups, paper cups full of soda and ice. The concession stands did land office business on Saturday night at Winterland.

The music crashed through the rain of debris, a banshee cry of hostility and rage and hypnotic repetition, the same song over and over again; only the titles changed to protect Warner Brothers, the Sex Pistols' record label.

Graham kneeled behind the bandstand, then joined the prowling crew in grabbing the garbage and snuffing the smoke bombs. "I feel like a linebacker," he said.

The Sex Pistols were no doubt saying horrid things, irreverent, rebellious things, but I can't say for sure, 'cause I couldn't understand a word of it.

Sid Vicious spat on some people. They spat back. The rites of saliva. He kicked out at a blonde kid. The blonde kid made as if to try to climb out of the crowd to get Sid Vicious. The security men crouched in readiness. Johnny Rotten appeared comatose. He seemed not to notice the melee. A used sanitary napkin arrived.

"Never again," Graham said, "never again. And that's off the record."

A roll of paper towels flew over the drummer's head, draping itself over his tom-toms. He looked at it blandly, took it in hand, wiped his forehead, blew his nose and tossed it aside.

A blonde girl in the front row, crushed against a sound monitor, no more than 17, angelic face, empty eyes, looked about to pass out. I pointed her out to Graham. He alerted the forward ranks of security. I kept an eye on her 'til the end. She never fainted. At the party backstage, after it was over, she was there. She wasn't smiling.

A young man, clean-cut, handsome, was fighting to get to the stage. He was the twentieth person who was pulled through the band during the set and led away. But he was different. It looked like he was trying to get at the Sex Pistols, not get away from the pressure.

He was grabbed and pulled toward the back, not gently. Graham looked at him and told his men to lighten up. The kid was shaking, having a seizure of some kind. They sat him down on an empty equipment box. The kid's eyes were unseeing, he couldn't talk. Two stagehands sat next to him, trying to find out what was wrong, trying to soothe him, their arms around his shoulders. The kid just sat there, a nice-looking kid, not responding. Every few seconds, his arms and hands would start shaking, then stop. Another kid appeared with a stethoscope. I tried not to stare.

Eventually, he was led gently down the backstage ramp and out of sight. I don't know what happened to him.

10

Blues to Bossa Nova

Bill Evans is 46 years old. His piano is as God intended.
His associates play instruments that can function without the
cooperation of the Pacific Gas and Electric Company. And
Evans wears neither mascara nor boa constrictors. He merely plays the
piano with a graceful power, beauty, skill and deceptive simplicity…
hunched over the piano in his identifying arc, so still a glass of water
could balance on the back of his neck….
JLW

*John was turned on to jazz when he was 14 by one track, "All the Things
You Are," on a Hampton Hawes Trio album. Many years later, Hawes
played in his living room, as did Cal Tjader, Oscar Peterson, Bill Evans,
Toots Thielemans and virtually all of San Francisco's best, including John
Handy, Denny Zeitlin, Eddie Duran, Mario Suraci and John Rae.*

He identified closely with the struggles of jazz musicians and worked hard to promote their music, which he loved for its intelligence, sophistication, emotion and spontaneity. As in other areas, his strength was not scholarship but curiosity, "big ears" and passion. He rarely panned a jazz artist, although he had troubles with Miles Davis in the late '60s and early '70s. John couldn't understand Davis's work in the avant-garde. He asked Oakland producer Mary Ann Pollar, the founder of Rainbow Sign and a friend of the trumpet player's, "Why is Miles doing this?"

"It was not so much jazz but what you could loosely call 'black music,'" Pollar says. "I'd say to John, don't say it isn't going on; say 'this is what I hear.'" John's reviews, damning with faint praise or clearly puzzled, finally pushed the volatile Davis too far. On Oct. 19, 1970, after reading a column describing his latest performance in the Bay Area as "{A} seething, intense set, one theme blending into another without fanfare. Variations of time and tempo, but the sound eventually becomes repetitious. Miles spurts and blurts and soars and runs, bass rumbles...." Davis sent John the following telegram:

> Don't ever mention my name again in a column, in a whisper, in a conversation, on music or just plain in any form because your head leans toward your white brothers and everything that goes with it, including attitude, long hair blonde chicks, you have no idea whatsoever of how a black man plays music in 1970 of the rhythms of 1970 or the vibes of 1970 or the attitude of 1970 or the dress of 1970 It is such a shame because you missed something but then again everybody couldn't be born black....

"We kidded John that Miles had friends in the Mafia, hit men," Peter Breinig, a Chronicle photographer who frequently accompanied John on jazz assignments, says. "He was astonished about the telegram and didn't take the hit man joke well. It was typical of Miles to send him that telegram. After he spouted off, both of them retreated into their shells."

Davis was one of very few jazz performers John alienated. When singer/guitarist Kenny Rankin was going through troubled years—drug use, misbehavior ("I was a jerk for awhile, a real jerk," Rankin says)—John reported the behavior without devastating the singer. "He focused on the things that would best serve my ends, without me knowing it," says Rankin, *whose music John once described as "like a Black Russian...sweet like moon-light, searing like a straight shot."*

"If he saw something valuable in an artist that needed to be nurtured, he was there to nurture it," singer Carol Sloane says. "He didn't encourage crap and he could recognize it a mile away. But he saw lots of good and hoped that with his little help, and their own sense of dedication to their work, they might get there. He didn't lie, he never lied. That's why we loved him."

"He was a nurturer, he was a commentator, he was a source of reflection," Rankin says. "He was a lot of things to a lot of musicians in this city. A real sadness, a heaviness came over the entire musical community the day he died."

KHAN AND HANDY CAST A SPELL
March 29, 1971

They started at midnight and played one raga for an hour and 10 minutes without interruption or pause. It was hypnotizing, mesmerizing, ethereal and mystifying; peaceful, restful, enthralling and exciting beyond description.

Alto saxophonist John Handy and Indian sarod master Ali Akbar Khan appeared together in concert at the Harding Theater on Friday night. It was a profoundly moving experience.

Khan and his tabla player, Zakir Hussain, walked stolidly in and perched on a slightly elevated and rug-covered platform. Handy plopped on a short stool to the side. Khan tuned the sarod, then the drones; Handy fiddled with his reed...a problem which was to bug him again although nobody else could hear anything wrong. Hussain shook some sort of talcum powder or resin in small piles to the right and left of his drums, the drones started and Khan picked a short, simple theme which Handy then gently blew back to him. The drones—tamboura and another I did not recognize—whined, Khan started to improvise and Hussain sat immobile, his hands at his side. The music carried through absolute stillness and Khan played each note as if it were an entire symphony in itself...never letting one go unembellished unless in the middle of a run.

Handy took an equal share, unable to match the bending, wavering flexibility of the sarod but seeking parity with quick flutter notes and shimmering runs. Sometimes he seemed to follow Khan's musical ideas; sometimes his radiant tone seemed not so much inspired by a theme as a feeling, a sharing of will.

At 12:15 a.m., Hussain started. His right hand, on the smaller drum, a tap dancer; his left a snorting bull. He had been nodding his head for the first 15 minutes; now he showed elation. His left hand—at 4-4, 6-8 and God knows what other times—was bump-bump, scrunch...his right cracking and flashing accents and one-handed rolls. It propelled and enveloped the music in a trance. Hussain, who is 19 and the son of Alla Rakha, was to keep this up 55 minutes—broken only by milli-second dabs at the flanking pools of powder.

The pattern was not disturbed. Drones droning, Hussain flying, Khan soloing, then a nod to Handy, then a duo restatement of the theme. Then three things happened. John started smiling as Khan handed the solo work back to him. It was a wry smile, an awed smile, a what-am-I-doing-here smile. I would bet that he would have given a year of his life in trade for not having to breathe while playing. Khan's hands took no breaths.

Khan now played faster, runs and strums that are difficult to explain because they are to fine guitar technique as is a mastery of the French horn to playing slide-whistle. The audience, for the first time, could no longer restrain its applause.

Hussain had made a switch, too. From playing straight rhythm, he joined the soloing himself, exchanging choruses first with Khan, then Handy. Khan would play a complicated figure, Hussain would mirror it on the drums. It was both complementary and competitive, a demonstration of creativity and technique that has no Western counterpart.

Handy was first hesitant to play the game. He had met Hussain only minutes before they went on Friday night, although he had practiced extensively with Khan. He shook his head after the Khan-Hussain exchanges, a rueful smile on his face—a hesitancy to enter the fray. But then he did, whirling and inspired, playing as well as he has in 20 years of dogged dedication.

At 1:10 it was over. Four hundred people exploded. Seventy minutes without a break, yet there was no listener fatigue, only euphoria. That doesn't happen very often.

Johnny, age eight, in 1946, conversing with Mother's puppet "Donkeyskin." Her father, Gus Leland, carved the hooves. Photo by Marjo.

The Wasserman family in 1943: Caroline, Lou, Johnny, me and Richey.
Collection of Caroline Wasserman.

Me, Johnny and Richey in 1946.
Photo by Marjo.

John and me in 1956. Collection of Agnes Leland.

At home in Mill Valley, circa 1956. John's favorite spot was next to the hi-fi in the living room. He played his percussion instruments to Cal Tjader records at first; years later, he sat in on congas with the Grateful Dead, Jefferson Airplane, Toots Thielemans, John Handy and Oscar Peterson. Collection of Caroline Wasserman.

Publicity photos taken for the Brebner Casting Agency in 1956, when John still entertained the idea of being an actor. The pose in Navy uniform is ironic: he had joined the Navy right out of high school and been rejected—on the eve of departure—because of his asthma history. Collection of Emily Romaine of Moulin Studios.

John and his college girlfriend, Elaine Hamilton, at a Tau Kappa Epsilon party, Whitman College, circa 1957. Photo by Roberge, Walla Walla.

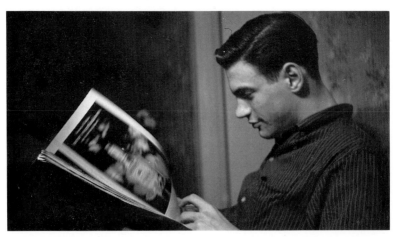

John, age 17, as a young member of the Chronicle *copy desk staff.* Photo by Michael Kelly.

John and his Swedish fiancée, Monica Hedin, whom he first befriended in Stockholm in 1959, in San Francisco on October 25, 1965. Monica, who had recently begun work at the Swedish Consulate in New York, found John self-confident and sophisticated in San Francisco, but ill at ease and even gauche in New York. She remembers he wore white socks, and her friends thought he was cheap. Their brief engagement was broken off after a fight over the regular-sized frozen peas John bought for dinner. Hurt and puzzled, he asked his best friend, Mike Kelly, "If she wanted petit peas, why didn't she just say so?" Chronicle *photo by Art Frisch.*

John and drama critic Paine Knickerbocker arriving at a theater opening on October 21, 1964, with Nancy Knickerbocker (partially hidden) and a young woman, probably John's date. Nancy bought John his first tuxedo. Chronicle *photo by Bill Young.*

Actress Ulla Bergryd ("Eve" in John Huston's "The Bible"), John, Charlie Stanyan and his wife Mary, fashion editor at the San Francisco Examiner, *at the opening of the play "Hostile Witness," October 10, 1966. John met Bergryd when she came to the* Chronicle *on a publicity tour.* Chronicle *photo by Joe Rosenthal.*

Interviewing Lassie, March 26, 1971. Collection of the *Chronicle* Archives.

John with his trusty Royal in the Chronicle *newsroom, 1966. He felt completely at home there—so much so that when he was caught for speeding not long after he was hired, he told the CHP to send the ticket to him care of the* Chronicle. *"Look wise guy," the cop said, "I want your home address," but John insisted the* Chronicle *was the proper place, and pulled out his employee card to prove it.* Chronicle *photo by Bill Young.*

John in 1970 at home on California Street, a second-story apartment next door to a church. He owned state-of-the-art hi-fi equipment and thousands of records, and liked to place his visitors squarely in front of his huge speakers to listen to selected cuts from his favorite albums at top volume. Photo by John Chang McCurdy.

Elton John at the Houston Space Center promoting his record "Rocket Man," 1972. Bob Levinson, founder of Levinson Associates and Elton's publicist, arranged the junket. From left: Levinson, John (in dark glasses), John Breckenridge of Levinson's staff, Apollo 15 astronaut Al Worden, Elton, two unidentified band members and post-Apollo astronaut Gordon Fullerton. Photo by Ed Caraeff.

John and rock producer Bill Graham circa 1975. Paul Kantner describes their relationship as "adversarial, enjoyably so—love-hate, big brother-little brother, positions changing rapidly." Photo by Jim Marshall.

*Playing congas with Benny Goodman at Herb Caen's 60th
birthday party. John organized much of the event. He ordered
hand-calligraphed invitations from Ward Dunham, arranged
for Goodman to play and for a record to be cut. He obtained
permission from his friend Charles Schulz to use a drawing of
Snoopy playing the clarinet on the album cover and made sure
each guest got a copy.* Photo by Lani Mein.

The Now Society

By WILLIAM HAMILTON

2-15

I suppose marrying John Wasserman is in keeping with Governor Brown's lowered expectations thing.

William Hamilton featured John in a number of his "Now Society" cartoons, and also named a character in his play "Save Grand Central" after him. John frequently put in-jokes addressed to Hamilton in his column. When this cartoon appeared on Feb. 15, 1978, John fired off a telegram: AM NOT AMUSED STOP MY ATTORNEY WILL BE CONTACTING YOURS INSTANTER STOP ACTION BEING FILED DEMANDING $1 MILLION FOR HOLDING UP TO PUBLIC RIDICULE, AGGRAVATED HUMILIATION, HUMILIATING AGGRAVATION, SLANDER, LIABLE, INVASION OF PRIVACY AND RESTRAINT OF TRADE STOP GOVERNOR BROWN AGREES TO TESTIFY AS LACK-OF-CHARACTER WITNESS STOP ASKING $1.95 REAL DAMAGES, $9.98 PUNITIVE DAMAGES AND $999,988.07 MAD MONEY STOP IF I DON'T RECEIVE THE ORIGINAL WITHIN SEVEN (7) DAYS AM PREPARED TO VERIFY YOUR VICIOUS BASEBALL BAT ATTACK ON LITTLE ARTIE MITCHELL WAS UNPROVOKED AND WHEN HE WAS ASLEEP...."
The last thrust referred to an incident at a party of John's not long before, when Artie Mitchell broke Hamilton's drawing thumb in a fracas. Collection of William Hamilton.

With Ann Getty at a dinner party she and her husband Gordon hosted for Governor Jerry Brown on June 13, 1978. John once told her, "You and I are the only two people in San Francisco who know how to throw a party." One night at the Gettys' he danced with prima ballerina Natalia Makarova. Photo © 1978 Peter Stein.

With Joan Baez at the same dinner. "We let all the barriers down," Baez said of her friendship with John. "There was an enormous amount of wisecracking. He couldn't get too close to sadness, that was evident. He would be kind to me always when I was sad, always with a sort of bravado—my sadness had a complaining quality of 'poor me,' and he would defend me against the world, saying, 'Who do those bastards think they are?'" Photo © 1978 Peter Stein.

In Moscow, 1978, at Time *Bureau Chief Marsh Clark's flat. John journeyed to the Soviet Union that summer with Joan Baez and translator Grace Warnecke. In spite of his constant drinking, John was a hit with the Russians he met. He managed to produce a thoughtful four-part series on the adventure for the* Chronicle, *which included an interview with André Sakharov and his wife.* Photo © Grace Warnecke.

A Glowing Sun Ra

April 26, 1971

"What the hell is this?" a woman muttered as the third set at the University of California Jazz Festival started on Friday night.

What it was, was Sun Ra, a mystery man of jazz, who is a legend to those who know of him and a what-the-hell-is-this to those who don't. I first heard of Sun Ra maybe 15 years ago but I never heard anything that really formed an image in my mind—unless it was an image of blur. In 1964, I ran into an extraordinary conga drummer named Leah Ananda. Ananda, a figure of some mystique himself and a self-described master of Hatha Yoga, had recorded with Sun Ra in a small group and talked about him with the air of a tamboura player for Ali Akbar Khan.

About all I knew of Ananda—who has since vanished—was that he could live without eating food, could control the rate of his heart-beat and played a single untunable conga with a dishtowel over the head. The first two items were his assertions; the latter my own observation. To this day, I have never seen another master drummer play a drum covered by a dishtowel. Nor do I really understand Sun Ra.

Ra and his Astro-Infinity-Intergalactic-Space Arkestra appeared about 11 p.m. and, suddenly, what had been an unconventional evening (the Last Poets, followed by the Alice Coltrane group with Archie Shepp and Jimmy Garrison) turned into pure surrealism. White stagehands and black musicians scurried around setting up, the black men dressed in purple and red satin capes and tunics, their heads covered by shining metal helmets, refugees from a science-fiction film of the '30s where everyone was named Gar and Kelk and Taun. I lost count of the drummers, but there were at least two with conventional sets, four hand-drummers and one man who played a giant African drum with sticks while standing on a chair. In addition, there was a full complement of horns, several chant-singers, two or more dancers, various gongs, several strobe light boxes, a large round ball with an interior light source and, finally, the great man himself with three or four electric and amplified keyboard instruments at his disposal.

The performance went upward from there. It opened with a cacophony of squawks, squeaks and bleats from the horns, anarchy in sound, then abrupt silence as a single spot focused on Ra and the glowing red ball lurking at his feet. It would not be very helpful to say that he began playing; rather he turned the electric piano into a grunting, growling Creature from the Black Lagoon, running his hands up and down the keyboard, slamming clusters of emotion as the giant screen behind him showed first projections of the heavens, then switched to photographs of African tribesmen.

A dancer appeared, holding large stars in each hand and whirling like a dervish in front of the band, then others shot across the night, capes and bodies whirling as demons. There was a pause, the near-capacity crowd exploded, then the drums took over, the brass marched off, reappeared in the lower part of the audience, the singers started, and it came to me: I was watching a jazz opera, perhaps the first jazz opera, or maybe the greatest jazz opera.

For, as The Who's "Tommy"—an opera spiritually if not technically—was and continues to be the ultimate rock statement of its kind, so does Sun Ra's Astro-Infinity Arkestra tell an amazing story unified from beginning to end: the progress of the black man, and so all men, from a highly delineated tribal life to a cosmic consciousness. It's fantastic theater—the Metropolitan Opera should ever present such theater— thrilling, bizarre, transfixing, musically and rhythmically satisfying.

GILBERTO'S BURNISHED GRACE
May 14, 1976

On Wednesday night at about 10:55 p.m. at Keystone Korner, tenor saxophonist Stan Getz introduced the reclusive Brazilian musical giant João Gilberto as "To my mind, the most original singer of our time."

The statement is so broad that it defies acquiescence or dispute, but those who were present for what followed would not likely quibble with this much: João Gilberto is surely among the most engaging, magical, thoroughly riveting performers of this or any other time. In a set of just 35 minutes, he transformed a hot, sweating, funky night club into a temple of charm, warmth, beauty, longing and sadness with a small, reluctant voice and small, buoyant chords from a burnished guitar.

If anything ever gave credence to the adage that people will listen more attentively to one who speaks softly, it was Gilberto's first set Wednesday. Barely audible, even though his mouth was no more than two inches from the microphone, he sang "Aguas de Marco," "Wave" and five other Brazilian songs to a motionless silence one simply does not encounter in such houses of revelry.

He sang with eyes burned shut and droplets of sweat clinging unmolested to his face, unwilling to part of their own accord, while Getz watched transfixed, joining no more than half the songs, perched high on a stool. So absorbed was the capacity audience that it even eschewed, for once, the mandatory ritual of breaking into hysterical cries and shrieks at the end of every solo within every song.

He spoke not at all, not one word which wasn't sung in Portuguese (although he is not entirely unfamiliar with English), and scurried on and off the stage like a rabbit raiding a vegetable garden in broad daylight.

Backstage, before he went on to join the Getz quartet, Gilberto was mildly accosted by an admirer, who professed a decade-long admiration for his work. The Brazilian's eyes blinked in astonishment and he looked momentarily at the floor, apparently convinced that some ghastly mistake had been made, some confusion, a mistaken identification, perhaps. Later, when Getz so effusively brought him to the stage, I'm certain that Gilberto had no idea who the tenor saxophonist was talking about.

Gilberto is, as I said above, a reclusive, elusive figure. Once the husband of Astrud Gilberto and now married to another singer, he last appeared in San Francisco in 1964 and last performed anywhere in public more than three years ago. It was only his friendship with Getz, with whom he has been living recently on the East Coast, that allowed this extraordinary engagement to take place.

There may be no single music that perfectly expresses the heartbeat and metabolism of the human animal, but there is nothing more closely allied than bossa nova, and no exponent of that music superior to João Gilberto.

WHO WILL TAKE HIS PLACE?

April 17, 1974

Baby Laurence, the great jazz tap-dancer, died of cancer at 53 in New York City a few days ago.

With him died part of what is, ironically, a dying art. The layman would call it tap-dancing. Baby called it "jazz tap-percussion."

Baby Laurence was considered the living master of jazz tap-percussion. I saw him for the first time less than a year ago at the Newport Jazz Festival in New York, performing on a clear, sultry afternoon in Central Park with a group of his near-peers including Buster Brown, John T. McPhee and Chuck Green. They were accompanied by organist Milt Buckner and drummer Jo Jones and they opened a whole new world to me.

I had read over the years of the jazz tap-dancers, most lucidly described by Whitney Balliett in *The New Yorker,* but had never had the opportunity to see these heirs of Bill Robinson and other men who could control their feet like Art Tatum could handle a piano.

They were, by their own insistence, at least as much musicians as dancers. The tap-dancing of Fred Astaire and Gene Kelly was a vehicle for movement; the music of Baby Laurence was sound, tone, rhythm and even, extraordinarily, melody.

Baby Laurence was a man of somber mein and ebullient body, generally dressed in black, his face impassive in repose, his carriage that of an aging Baptist minister. But his body at work was a thing of beauty and a joy forever: a graceful, soaring, weightless mass, arms crooning harmony to legs, feet moving with the uncharted swiftness of a hummingbird, toe in counterpoint to heel, flashing across the splintery boards as if he were a flat rock skimming a still lake.

The jazz tap-dancers identify with instrumentalists. Thus, Buster Brown took his inspiration from Coleman Hawkins and Baby's buoyant introduction of himself included "The sound of the greatest musicians who ever graced the music world: Mr. Charlie Parker combined with Mr. Max Roach."

It was not an idle comment. Baby had grace, and could do a buck-and-wing if so inspired. But that was not the essence of his art. With Buckner and Jones he completed a jazz trio. He soloed and improvised, produced rim shots and counter-rhythms, changed tempos with the certainty of a computerized metronome, held conversations with the drums and produced variations in tone that were simply astonishing.

Choreography would have been to Baby Laurence as written music to Erroll Garner: useless and, moreover, pointless.

Writing a column generally has little effect beyond entertaining members of the writer's immediate family, but Baby provided me with an opportunity to transcend that limited fate. The piece I wrote after seeing him work was read by Jimmy Lyons, head of the Monterey Jazz Festival. Lyons knew, of course, who Baby Laurence was but not that he was actively performing. He invited him to last fall's Festival.

Baby said okay, but more gigs would be needed to make the trip economically feasible. Jon Hendricks promptly hired him for "The Evolution of the Blues" at the Paul Masson "Vintage Sounds" concert series, and provided him with living quarters. Todd Barkan subsequently arranged a week at Keystone Korner.

So Baby Laurence came to San Francisco and I saw him again and so did a lot of people, for the first time. It was magic, and we were all a little richer.

Then he left and returned to New York, but it was nice to know that I'd had a part in it. For watching Baby Laurence dance was more than watching a genius at work. It was a bit of American history. It was a bit of American black culture which never spread with any impact beyond the confines of Harlem. It was the privilege of watching an endangered species with all its dignity and beauty still intact.

And now he's dead. Who will take his place?

ELECTRIC ZEITLIN

January 25, 1971

The new Denny Zeitlin-Jerry Hahn aggregation was astonishingly explosive the other evening at the Matrix. The group, which includes bassist Mel Graves and the phenomenal drummer George Marsh, has just been founded—an indirect result of the breaking up of the old Jerry

Hahn Brotherhood after losing its lead singer-organist.

Guitarist Hahn needs little introduction to the San Francisco rock-jazz audience. He played with the great John Handy Quintet of five years ago, was submerged in more modest groups and teaching for a while, then reappeared with the Brotherhood at Bay Area rock clubs a year or so ago. He is a musician of tremendous technical ability and original conceptions.

Pianist Zeitlin's underground reputation is national, his over-ground fame almost nonexistent. He first appeared in the middle '60s with a piano trio, an overwhelming technique, a splattering, distinctly non-commercial, non-George Shearing approach to the instrument, a Columbia recording contract and a hardy band of fans at the Trident in Sausalito. But Zeitlin shared his love of music with the study of medicine and psychiatry and, in effect, dropped out more than two years ago to pursue his profession and expand, with electricity, the limitations of keyboard instruments.

With the semi-disintegration of the Hahn Brotherhood and the long relationship of Graves and Marsh with both Hahn and Zeitlin, a pooling of resources was natural and that is what happened at the Matrix this weekend. The first set was a Hahn-led trio, the second a Zeitlin-led trio, the last a Hahn-Zeitlin Quartet. The club was standing-room-only and those present, by and large, knew they were witnessing a modest historic event.

Although Graves and Marsh have certain unusual percussion and electronic/hand effects, they play relatively conventional instruments. Zeitlin, however, appears to be testing equipment for both IBM and PG&E. He is playing, albeit with only two hands, an acoustic spinet piano (miked), and the following electrified keyboards, stacked like a multi-rank organ console—a Fender Rhodes piano, a Hohner clavinet and a Farfisa Professional organ. In addition, Zeitlin bobs like a freaked-out Korla Pandit to a melodica, various percussion instruments, an Effects Generator and what he is pleased to call The Doomsday Machine.

The effect combines the best of outer space and Oscar Peterson—swirling, blinding, transcendent sounds which are bound together like dogs in heat; sometimes shooting off like flares amok, sometimes playing straight, strong, swinging jazz lines with all the psychedelia of the Count Basie band. It is demanding, exhausting and, most of all, exciting music.

Back in Smoke-Filled Rooms

October 7, 1977

For those of you who have never heard of her, Carol Sloane has been known to the jazz world for some 15 years as one of the finest singers extant. In the '60s, she recorded a couple of albums for Columbia, played the Monterey Jazz Festival and occasionally filled in for Annie Ross when Lambert, Hendricks and Ross were setting the vocal world on fire. She was scheduled to play the Ghirardelli Square hungry i in 1969, but the Feds padlocked the joint the day of her opening and, coincidentally, she subsequently went into semi-retirement in Raleigh, N.C., working by day as a legal secretary and, on the odd weekend, singing at the Frog and Nightgown or performing for a lark in musical comedies.

A couple of years ago, she decided to go back to work in smoke-filled rooms on a regular basis, and has since released one album (just 2,000 copies pressed on her own label) and played several dates on the East Coast, sometimes backed by pianist Jimmy Rowles, a nonpareil vocal accompanist.

On Monday night, with a bare minimum of publicity, she played a special gig at the Mocambo, and those fortunate enough to hear of it were treated to a consummate display of the art of the singer.

Sloane was a superior singer in 1964, when I first heard her, but she is better now. Her voice has grown more warm, more rich and burnished (the only comparable instruments that come to mind are those owned by Sarah Vaughan and Cleo Laine) and her reading of lyrics has matured. Truly good singers inevitably get better with age, at least to the point of physical debilitation, and Carol is a long way from there. She now stands at the very pinnacle of jazz-pop singing. Comparisons are odious, but it must be said that only Vaughan, Laine, Ella Fitzgerald and Carmen McRae inhabit the same plateau. And an ordinary person needs oxygen at this elevation.

The first set opened with a number by accompanists Larry Vuckovich, piano; Al Obindinski, bass; and Clarence Beckton, drums; then Carol joined them for a classic set, including "While We're Young," "Autumn in New York," "In a Mellow Tone," Juan Tizol's rarely sung "Caravan," "I Didn't Know About You," and, for an encore, a delightful "As Time Goes By," complete with some funny asides of dialogue from "Casablanca."

In addition to the extraordinary voice, the most striking thing about Carol's singing is its utter effortlessness, poise and control. She was suffering from a cold on Monday, and nervous as the next director of the Office of Management and Budget, but sang with total assuredness, perfect intonation, quicksilver phrasing, fluid, economical scat choruses, irresistible momentum and exquisite, velvet texture. She toyed with melodies, with intervals, with shadings, dynamics and accents like the musician she is, yet never frivolously or for effect. Some songs were caressed, others cooked over a low flame; always with, rather than in front of, the accompanists.

To hear Carol sing is to sense perfection.

11

A Measure of Laughter

An entire audience of 3,000 souls is laughing uproariously at the comedian.
You join them. The comedian is obviously very funny.
An entire audience of 2,999 is laughing uproariously at the comedian.
You do not join them. The comedian is obviously not very funny.
Such is the transcendent power of one's own opinion.

JLW

Stand-up comedy is the riskiest business in show business. John loved it for its risk and because in his cosmos, music, laughter and telling the truth were the greatest goods.

San Francisco comedy in those years was nurtured by two men—Enrico Banducci and David Allen. Banducci presented Woody Allen, Bill Cosby, Professor Irwin Corey, Flip Wilson, Richard Pryor and many more great comedians at the hungry i, where David Allen—a man of tremendous girth, with gout and dark circles under his eyes, who collected Christmas lights as a hobby—was his manager. A few years after the i closed, Allen opened the Boarding House at 960 Bush.

"John and David Allen were like a team," Robin Williams says. "David would find these strange unique talents and John's reviews would get people in." Steve Martin, Martin Mull, Robert Klein, Williams and Lily Tomlin—a new generation of comics—got their jump-start there. John's customary seat by the light booth was dubbed "the Pope's Booth."

Steve Martin calls John "the catalyst for my career, which began in San Francisco." John spent years encouraging him personally (they used to play pool together) and praising his madcap comedy in print before the man in the white suit became a success. One night John took Clint Eastwood to Martin's show, saying, "This guy's going to be an immense star." John also predicted success for Billy Crystal, and for Jay Leno ten months before his first appearance on Johnny Carson's "Tonight" show—the official launching point of his career. In May 1992 he succeeded Carson as the show's host.

Henny Youngman, the King of the One-Liners, appeared at the Boarding House after a 30-year absence from San Francisco, and credited John's rave review with a revitalization of his brand of humor among young people. As thanks, he staged an impromptu performance in John's apartment, a large flat on the third floor of the Boarding House which, John said when he asked Gordon Pates for permission to move there, was "the only place in town I can play music at the proper volume."

John wrote often that no comedian was the best, but he had his favorites, among them Lily Tomlin. He wrote about her at least once a year. When her first one-woman show, "Appearing Nitely," came to San Francisco in 1978, she told him, "You've had a lot of faith in me and belief in me for a long time, and it's kind of like I want to show off for you, you know? When you come I want to say, 'See, you weren't wrong to have faith in me, I'm gonna do a really hot job here for you.'"

There was a saying among comedians: "When you come to San Francisco you get your Wasserman." Robin Williams flunked his first Wasserman—John criticized his over-reliance on scatology. Later he praised the young comic's unique creative gifts. "He was nurturing," Williams says. "Sometimes rough, but when I changed and grew up he noticed, and I started to get people into the show."

David Allen, like Banducci, was a poor businessman. In 1978 John

M.C.'ed a benefit to keep the Boarding House afloat. Steve Martin, Billy Crystal, Joan Baez, Martin Mull, Robin Williams, Loudon Wainwright III, Jimmy Buffett and Melissa Manchester were headliners.

Frank Kidder, co-founder of the San Francisco Comedy Competition, credits John with its initial inspiration. In 1971, John wrote a column on Don Rickles using a made-up laugh measurement called Laughs Per Minute (LPM) as a criterion for judging Rickles' effectiveness. He divided laughter into titters, chortles and guffaws. Kidder's first "round robin," in 1976, used LPM as a basis for judgment and was such a hit that later that year a second competition using more sophisticated criteria followed. The annual comedy event will celebrate its 17th anniversary in 1993.

A FUNNY BUSINESS
September 1, 1976

We all know how comedians start: as class clowns. And we all know where successful comedians finish: with fame and fortune. But what about the period in between?

On Sunday night at Joe Nobriga's Showcase, a night club at 900 Franklin that specializes in giving exposure to local singers, musicians and comedians, a small part of the answer surfaced at the First International Open Stand-Up Comedy Competition. Five comedians, all unknown to the public but the victors in preliminary trials which eliminated more than 200 of their colleagues, did 20-minute routines to a standing-room-only crowd of friends, family and aficionados of the burgeoning comedy scene.

They were competing for prizes of $100, $50 and $25, but more, for the kind of professional recognition and prestige that come rarely to those who do it for love.

There were no scouts for Carson or Merv Griffin in the audience, no emissaries from the city's big clubs. And none of the five—Bill Farley, Mitch Krug, Mark Miller, Bob Sarlatte or Robin Williams—is, in my estimation, yet ready to join the big leagues.

But they were the survivors, the finalists, and they made us laugh.

The show started about 9:40, after master of ceremonies José Simon explained the rules (points were awarded for stage presence, material, audience response, delivery, technique, audience rapport and presentation) and introduced impressionist Jim Giovanni for a guest set.

Giovanni, called by *Laff Maker* "the guy with the obvious talent-to-make-it," did not enter the competition (a form of comedic noblesse oblige) but started the house roaring with his version of Hamlet as played by George C. Scott, Groucho Marx and Tom Smothers. Giovanni is regarded with respect, if not awe. He has played the Great American Music Hall on several occasions.

The big time.

Then, in the hot, muggy, densely-packed room, a window outlined in flashing lights as their frame, the competitors went to work Each did 20 minutes, give or take 60 seconds (if they gave or took more than three minutes, they were disqualified), and each got laughs, but they had little else in common. They were short and tall, meek and assertive, confident and tentative, good looking and funny looking. They used, and did not use, props, voices, sound effects, their bodies, their audience, and their wits. They wore (and peeked at) watches on their wrists and in their socks. They were smooth and clumsy and hot. Each was bathed in sweat when he finished, each slumped in exhaustion from the heat and the pressure.

The television camera and microphone from KGO's "A.M." show lurked about, shooting everything that moved. The judges—Paul Krassner of *The New Realist, Chronicle* theater critic Bernie Weiner and Francine Foster—regarded their task with appropriate solemnity.

At five minutes to midnight, it was over. The audience had remained remarkably receptive through a long, stifling night. Competition co-founder Frank Kidder (a comedian who adopted his wife's last name for obvious reasons and who has been for years the driving force behind San Francisco's comedy workshops) and Bob Barry did a pantomime while the judges tallied their sheets.

Farley won. Williams, Sarlatte, Miller and Krug followed. Not the way I would have picked them, but OK. Except for Krug. A funny man. No way Krug finishes last.

Unless he happens to be Charles Krug and the judge is Robert Mondavi.

A funny business, comedy.

UNINHIBITED SLANDERS

May 24, 1971

In 1964–66, Lenny Bruce was wrapping up his life and career as the most important comedian of the decade. In the same period, Jack Shelley was Mayor of San Francisco.

The chances that they ever met, much less that they ever met on an informal ground of mutual respect, are remote. If Shelley had seen Bruce perform, the odds are that it would have been as a generalissimo of a vice squad raiding party, not as a fan.

On Saturday night, Warren Widener, the mayor of Berkeley, attended Richard Pryor's first show at Mandrake's. The club was already at standing room capacity when he arrived and Widener was lucky to grab a straight-back chair, without table, at the very back of the room. He was not there to see if Richard Pryor said anything naughty. He was there to enjoy himself, which he did, and to say hello backstage after the show.

That says a lot about the last five years, about Bruce, about Pryor, about Widener, about Berkeley and about the state of the union—at least hereabouts.

For Richard Pryor is, if anything, naughtier than Lenny Bruce. He employs our favorite four- and 12-letter words with astonishing facility and frequency. And his commentary on the police (without discrimination as to race, creed, color or condition of previous servitude), religion and the sexual proclivities of the current Administration contain an outrage factor perhaps superior even to that of the great Mr. Bruce.

And the mayor was laughing, for the same reason we laughed with Lenny—the material was funny. Any fool can assault the police, religion and politicians. Many do. Few are funny in the process. Fewer still are funny *and* trenchant. What separates the laugh-getter from the Richard Pryors and Lenny Bruces—and Redd Foxxes, and Irwin Coreys—is the capacity to make the listener investigate his own attitudes, to communicate insights as well as chortles.

And Bruce is the one who really opened it up, who first brought our most cherished hypocrisies into the light without also bringing along Sea & Ski. And Widener is a representative of what we can only hope is a new breed of political leader—a man who can find a city, or a country, worth working for while not also buying the myths of infallibility we have so long cultivated.

And the state of the nation? Well, Richard Pryor voiced the most extraordinary slanders without any real fear of Government reprisals. Sure, he can't do it on television; sure, many places wouldn't hire him. But similar material in Greece, Mexico, Pakistan, Hungary or France would almost certainly land him in prison.

Although Pryor is a lineal descendent of Lenny Bruce, he can more precisely be described as a combination of Bill Cosby's style and Redd Foxx's content. His specialty is telling stories of his youth and the similarity of technique with Cosby is sometimes profound. But Cosby's stories of childhood are universal—black, white and maybe Indonesian.

Not so Pryor's. His are black, and populated not by Fat Albert but by pimps, whores, cops, poverty, winos and the uninhibited performance of bodily functions ranging from sex to scatology.

It ranges from the frivolous—a commentary on white girls' use of strawberry-flavored "feminine hygiene deodorant"—to the less funny: "Cops is dangerous because they kill niggers 'accidentally.' I don't know how you shoot a nigger between the eyes six times accidentally...."

He is a master of voices—from the black street kids to the white matron—and has an excellent sense of the non-sequitur, as in the white evangelist "who touched a rock and turned it to stone," or the Buddhist who set himself afire, thinking that Americans would be sympathetic but finding that all they did was "ask for marshmallows."

Strangely enough, the best thing he did during the first show Saturday night was the least "funny" and the least blatant. It was a long piece on skid-row blacks (they could have been white), reminiscing, between swigs of Gallo Tokay, how they fought Jack Johnson and knew "that Jesus was a nigger 'cause they'd of shot a white man...."

It was, beneath the chuckles, a poignant and moving piece on our lost dreams. Another factor which separates Richard Pryor from the conventional.

COMEDY WITH A CORE

June 2, 1975

In the past, women stand-up comedians have been relegated to the status of second-class show biz citizens; at least by those of us who are paid to make our private idiosyncrasies public.

There has, in my own experience, simply never been a *substantial* woman comedian. Even the term "comedienne" has a faintly condescending connotation; as if one were to refer to a woman university professor as a "professorette."

The Carol Burnetts, the Lucille Balls and Phyllis Dillers are clowns and/or buffoons; both directly and indirectly reinforcing the traditional stereotypes of scatter-brained females while at the same time dealing with subject matter of surpassing, Bob Hopeian irrelevance.

That is the way it has been. There were no exceptions. It will never again be that way. Lily Tomlin is the exception. The barrier has been broken; a result of changing concepts in our society and the fact that Lily Tomlin is a genius, the most creative and innovative comic mind working today.

She is not the funniest. And *no one,* as I am pleased to repeat to the point of tedium, is the best.

But she is very funny, very good, and the most jolting force to come along in the field of stand-up comedy in 20 years (not coincidentally, the period subsequent to the emergence of Lenny Bruce).

Lily's innovations fall roughly in three areas. In the first instance, she depends for her material neither on the Woman's Burden nor matter of a topical nature, per se. Working on several levels—sometimes dazzlingly so—she reveals all of us through herself; stripping down to an inner core shared by everyone but acknowledged only rarely and reluctantly by most. That core is often dark, and anxiety-ridden, and unappetizing. But it's there, and to understand it is to be more human, in the good sense. As her newest character Sister Boogie Woman evangelically exhorts, "Don't try to be perfect! Try to be alive!"

The second level on which she parts company with most comedians is that she is willing to take chances to a unique degree. She invokes a disquieting tension by simply standing and staring at the audience. She delivers a three-minute montage of aphorisms and apparent non-sequiturs while lying supine on the stage, not even visible to all but the ringsiders.

"Have you noticed that bread-crumbs cost more than bread?"

"That the people who sell you a remedy for wax-buildup are the same people who sold you the wax?"

"The other day I bought a waste-basket and carried it home in a paper bag. When I got home I put the paper bag in the waste-basket."

She will remain dead silent for long seconds. Switch from one subject, character or voice to another without the vaguest trace of a connective sentence or pause for transitional purposes. Use her exceptional arsenal of impersonations in play against, rather than with, what she is saying (the dissonance, not harmony, of her character Edith Ann). And in general, defy every deified "law" of performing except to be present at the appointed place and hour.

Lastly, even that bulk of her material which is designed to provoke laughter is multi-layered. Every silver lining, if you look closely, has a cloud. Even the best comic satirist says something to be funny. Lily is funny in order to say something.

It's not for everyone. If you want to be simply Entertained, you might skip it. On the other hand, the Venetian Room audiences—not generally thought of as the hippest in history—were hugely appreciative at both the first show Thursday and the second show Friday; far more so than the equivalent during her engagement there three years ago.

For the record, the shows included some new Ernestine, The Sorority Girl, the World's Oldest Beauty Expert, Edith Ann, Sister Boogie Woman, Rich Lady/Poor Lady, a touch of the Tasteful Lady and the devastating routine about Bill Beasley. Although Friday night was a bit less manic than Thursday, Lily tends to rush too much on both the Sorority Girl and Sister Boogie Woman. The complaint is not one of aesthetics, but of intelligibility.

A psychic recently told Lily that she is a medium and that her now-famous characters are not acted inventions, but rather "possessions," à la "The Exorcist," except that the spirits are benign and she is in complete control of them.

Sheer nonsense, of course.

But don't think about it when you're watching her....

Nice To See You Chairs
May 24, 1976

Jay Leno, a virtual unknown who is at the Playboy Club through Saturday night, is simply the funniest comic to come along since the Robert Klein/Martin Mull/Steve Martin invasion two or three years ago, and in terms of pure laughs, the funniest man to play the club since it opened 10 years ago.

Plagued by an audience of, shall we say, modest size, Leno opened with some exceedingly amusing comments on the crowd ("I'm glad to welcome both of you to the Playboy Club tonight...and where did you chairs come from?") and then proceeded through nearly an hour of comment on television commercials, television newsreaders, Bunnies, singles bars, personalized license plates, drive-in movies, Elvis Presley, radio talk shows and the fanciful treatment of a male rape victim by female police officers.

Obviously, on the face of it, these topics are not unique to Leno (pronounced Len-o, not Lean-o), but his treatment is freshly irreverent, his perspective is of dumbfounded outrage and his mind is as quick as a brown fox. The temptation to repeat his lines is great; but I'll control myself for two reasons. First, I shouldn't ruin the surprise factor; second, they don't work in print.

The latter reason, of course, is true with almost all first-rate comedians, for the laughs come from timing, facial expressions, physical posturings, inflections and voices, and Leno, at 26, has it all down. Take my word for it. The kid's got it. Within 12 months, he'll be a national name.

Take My Review...Please
January 21, 1977

You could almost feel the audience waiting for the line and then, finally, about half-way into the 45-minute show, it came:

"Take my wife..." Henny Youngman said Tuesday night at the Boarding House.

The crowd was silent, quivering, barely breathing. Youngman paused for exactly, precisely, the right 2.7 seconds.

"Please...."

From the roar that went up, you would have thought the Surgeon General just declared marijuana to be helpful to your health.

Henny Youngman, the last and king of the one-liners, had returned to public performance in San Francisco for the first time in 30 years. And they loved him. Oh my, how they loved him. He got more laughs than he had jokes. Every punch-line hit, and some that weren't, did, too. In one five-minute segment, I counted 20 jokes—one every 15 seconds. The next five minutes, I counted 25 laughs—one every 12 seconds.

Then I resumed laughing myself. Henny Youngman is a funny man. Another triumph for David Allen, the Mad Booker of the Boarding House.

Before I saw the show, I got a bright idea. I'd write my review in Youngman's style:

"Henny Youngman opened Tuesday night at the Boarding House...
"Opened the doors early for the crowd waiting outside...
"Before they found out who was on the bill...."

Forget it. Only a masochist would try to compete with:

"They gave me a lovely dressing room...
"A nail...
"Played golf today...
"Broke 70...
"That's a lot of clubs to break....
"A doctor gave a man six months to live...
"Man couldn't pay his bill...
"Doctor gave him another six months...."

And so on.

Henny's jokes are like a bride's ensemble: some old, some new, some borrowed, some blue—and all corny. But he thinks "the kids," as he calls them (and they substantially outnumbered the over-35s on Tuesday) are ready for his old-fashioned, good-natured, non-"significant" humor, and he would appear to be right. They loved him—his contemporaries, his kids, his grandkids (he's 70), the waitresses, the ushers—everyone.

And it's not just that he's a nostalgic relic from a bygone time—so is Bob Hope, and Bob Hope isn't even faintly amusing.

For it's not only the timing, it's the attitude. Henny barely moves on stage, save to switch his ever-present violin (which he plays with triumphant ineptitude) from one hand to the other, from under one arm to under the other. But he's always, in effect, shaking his head dolefully, unable to quite fathom the ironies and vagaries of life.

At the end, he received two or three standing ovations and beamed effulgently at the howls of "More! More!" But he knows better, after 45 years on the stump. He left them laughing.

COMEDY AS JAZZ
March 6, 1978

In a conversation with Bill Cosby a couple of weeks ago, the comedian assessed his style by saying that "The forms I'm working with are very much like those of a jazz musician. I take a theme, I know the chords, I know the changes, so now it's a matter of how I want to play the solo."

On Saturday night at the Circle Star Theater, a sold-out first show audience was given a consummate demonstration of this technique. Cosby began his hour and 15 minute monologue with certain themes in mind, ranging from relatively short bits about going through airport security and finding a lizard on your neck to much longer stories having to do with aging, "natural" childbirth and the timeless irony of parents repeating actions that, as children, they condemned on the part of their own parents.

But, within those melodies, he improvised at such length and with such seamless digressions that I'm not even sure that the lizard-on-neck story, for example, was not itself entirely ad-libbed.

It grew out of a story about biscuits and the biscuit story grew out of a discussion of the Southern tradition of "sopping" and that was fathered by a bit with a man from Memphis who Cosby called to the stage and *that* emerged from Cosby's reaction to the habit of people who applaud when their home town is mentioned.

Was it all ad-libbed? Probably not, for that was surely not the first time Cosby had ever noticed the hometown syndrome. Was it all a set routine? Certainly not, for it presumes that Cosby waits each show for someone to applaud the mention of Memphis at a specific point in the monologue.

What it was, was improvisation. No musician plays a solo the ingredients of which he has never played before. What he does, and what Cosby does, is assemble the notes, the component parts, in a way unique to that moment. As a study in the art of comedy and performing, it was awesome. As laughs, it was side-splitting and tears-to-eyes. The man is a master.

"White Suits and Banjos" was John's last column.

White Suits and Banjos
February 26, 1979

Los Angeles

Today's challenging difficult quiz: What prematurely gray-haired comedian, dressed in a three-piece white suit, carrying a banjo, shimmying like his sister Kate, appeared here at the Sunset Strip's Comedy Store on Saturday night in front of an ecstatic audience and said, *"We're having some fun tonight!"* and *"Well, excuuuuuuse me!"*

If you guessed Martin Mull, Robert Klein, Richard Pryor, Lily Tomlin, Woody Allen, Bill Cosby, Henny Youngman or Joan Rivers, you are a moron.

The correct answer is, of course, Mark Phillips, a 25-year-old Nashville medical research scientist who won the first and probably last annual "Steve Martin Look-Alike, Act-Alike and Sound-Alike Contest" while conquering some 2,000 other pretenders to the throne of the hottest comedian in show business. Six regional winners of the SMLAAAASAC met in arrow-through-the-head competition to determine who is the greatest imitator of the most imitated comic of our time.

The evening began with a short statement by Carl Reiner, who will direct Steve's first motion picture, "The Jerk—A Wild and Crazy Movie." "I'm here for a very special purpose," Reiner began without a flicker of a smile. "We're about to start this film which Steve has written and plans to star in, but, frankly, I'm not that sure that we've got the best Steve Martin we can get. And if we can find a better Steve Martin here tonight, well, frankly, we'll drop him like a hot potato. Show business has no room for sentiment."

Reiner then called Steven to the stage, apologized for not having any film clips of "The Jerk" to show us but, after maneuvering Steve into position, went through some rehearsals for major scenes. "This one," Reiner explained, "is the big hitchhiking scene."

Steve stuck his thumb out.

Martin, himself dressed in a three-piece faded pink suit, then took the microphone—still a bit shaken by the emotional wringer he had just gone through—picked up a plug at the end of a microphone cord, announced "And now, I'd like to end my career" and stuck it in his mouth.

The contest itself was sensational. Although several of the contestants had performing experience of one kind or another, none was a working comedian, yet each brought much—appearance (all wore the obligatory white suits, several employed banjos and other props, all but one had grayish hair), facial expressions, physical bits, voice similarities, inflections, timing, accents—to his impression.

Their abilities were attested to by the toughest audience—Steve, his manager Bill McEuen and McEuen's wife, Alice. All giggled, grinned and guffawed continuously through the six 10-minute stints. Winner Phillips will appear with Steve on a network television show as his prize.

After it was over, all concerned repaired to a nearby restaurant for a Chinese dinner. Steve kissed a 14-year-old at her adjoining birthday party. Visions of three million sales for his "A Wild and Crazy Guy" album swam in the heads of the Warner Bros. Execs, who picked up the contest tab. David Allen, proprietor of the Boarding House, where Martin enjoyed his first major performing success, held forth with pronouncements of Steve's genius.

And the subject of all this sat quietly, as is his wont, in a corner— perhaps contemplating the strange experience of watching himself perform for a solid hour, without benefit of a mirror.

12

Show Business Is My Life

So much to cover, so few doilies.....
JLW

All his life, John lived by the clock and the calendar. He had a horror of boredom and passionately hated repeating himself. He was therefore perfectly suited to be an entertainment columnist. He had an extraordinary ability to entertain and was willing to try anything. His columns often read like Adventures with Wassy in the Weird, Wonderful World.

For John there were no half-measures; he gave his all, relishing the grand entrance and the grand gesture. His dramatic black attire, his dark apartment decorated in black and orange, the parties he orchestrated so carefully (to the point of instructing guests on the exact minute to arrive), his "Media and the Arts" class, the 1978 Bay Area Jazz Foundation gala he produced to benefit KJAZ Radio, starring Sarah Vaughan, Herbie Hancock,

Tony Bennett, Bill Evans and Boz Scaggs and featuring Clint Eastwood as
a guest M.C.—and most of all his stylish, lively column, were marks of a
Performer with a capital "P."

There are many Wasserman the Performer stories, one of the most
famous concerning the white suit that his girlfriend Charlene Spiller gave
him. John didn't like white—his only variation in public dress was all-
burgundy, or sometimes a red tie with his black suits—but he appreciated the
theatricality and humor of the gesture. So he bought expensive accessories, from
shoes to shirt, to go with the suit, and wore it twice. He arrived at Bill
Hamilton's birthday party in St. Helena in a limo and the suit exactly one-
half hour late, upstaging Herb Caen; and he put it on for TV host Jim
Dunbar's surprise birthday party for his wife Beth in the Napa Valley, then
deliberately fell backwards into the swimming pool, swam a lap and emerged
dripping and grinning. He took a few more plunges, eventually prompting
Jim to invite him testily to leave. John shivered so in the air-conditioned limo
that Charlene insisted he take off the suit, and he arrived home nearly naked.
The white suit was retired.

From the Hookers Ball to the Tattoo Ball, from the Ringling Bros. &
Barnum and Bailey Circus to Name That Tune, from a night train in
Argentina to an interview with Lassie, John made sure he was never bored.
His frequent tag line, "Show business is my life," was equal parts irony and
celebration.

MAY I PLEASE KISS A TIGER?

August 26, 1974

When I was a kid I envisioned, at various times, a career as a cowboy, an
Indian, a policeman, a fireman, a master criminal and a star of the circus.

Then I grew up, ho ho. I found out there were no cowboy gigs in
Mill Valley. I discovered that this is the wrong country in which to be
an Indian. It's not even that hot a job in India.

It turned out that policemen were underpaid, overworked, bum-
rapped for idiot decisions not of their making and occasionally used for

target practice. Firemen, I eventually realized, were crazy. Only a crazy person would rush into a burning building or climb any ladder more than six feet off the ground.

And it wasn't long before I realized I wasn't bright enough to be a master criminal.

But I still want to be in the circus. I hope Mr. Irvin Feld, President and Producer of the 104th edition of the Ringling Bros. & Barnum and Bailey Circus, will read this.

I cannot walk a tightrope. Sometimes I have trouble with a sidewalk. I can handle a teeter-totter but not a teeterboard. The closest I've ever been to a flying trapeze was when a friend once suggested that I "go take a flying...." That's silly, of course. Even Tito Gaona couldn't do that.

As for the animal kingdom, I packed it in after I taught my dog to "speak" and he said the same thing as my friend.

But, Mr. Feld, I can type like the wind and once beat Bill Graham in Ping-Pong. I realize that this isn't Center Ring stuff, but I would appreciate it if you would give it some thought, anyway. I saw your show on Wednesday night at the Oakland Coliseum Arena, along with 11,973 other kids, and not once was there any typing or Ping-Pong act. I'll let it go for now, but I was sort of envisioning a Ping-Pong game on the back of a moving elephant, using IBM Selectrics for paddles.

I guess that does sound a little far-fetched. But Mr. Feld, is it any more so than a man kissing a 400-pound Bengal tiger or people playing basketball on unicycles?

Closet Clown Opens the Door

August 30, 1974

Who says the power of the press is waning?

No sooner did I note in this space my desperate wish to run away to the circus than the office phone went "jingle-jangle-jingle."

Or was that my editor's spurs?

Well, no matter. It was the circus calling. "The pen is mightier than the sword," said the voice. "How'd you like to audition?" "Golly," I retorted, "I'd love to, but the *Chronicle* probably thinks I'm irreplaceable and would offer me vast amounts of cash to stay on here."

"Let's see," said the Managing Editor when I approached him for a counter-offer. "I can't promise this until I check with the Board of Directors but I think we can come up with three framed crank letters and a copyperson to lug your crap out of here."

"Oh, yeah?" I snarled. "Well, I've got news for you. That's not good enough. I'm leaving. And see how many freebies you get to opening night next year...."

What a relief. Eleven years is enough in the tension-packed, energy-exhausting business of telling other people what to do. I now could, finally, do what I was born to do: play Ping-Pong and type.

Off to the Cow Palace, where the circus is currently headquartered. I'm taken to Clown Alley and introduced to Swede, a Dane who has been with the circus since the Constitutional Convention and who is Clown Boss. He pales visibly under his white-face make-up, no small feat, and turns me over to Chico.

"Here's the buffoon they told us about," he sighed. "Clown," I corrected.

Chico sighed, too. He told me to take off my clothes. "Now just a minute here," I said. We were in a little cubicle in the livestock barn adjoining the arena. On one side were the horses. On the other side were women. One of my fellow clowns got up on a chair and peered over the wall to the next section. Good Lord, I breathed, a Peeping Clown! I spotted two teeterboarders practicing their vaults. Whoosh, up in the air. Amazing. They didn't even have a teeterboard.

Chico applied my make-up. "Do you want to be happy, sad or merely bland?" he inquired. "I dare to be great," I replied simply.

He described our first exercise. We were to go out on the floor, 20 minutes before the opening, and entertain the kiddies with rollicking good humor and deft pratfalls. I was now made-up: huge shoes, silly tie, funny hat, baggy pants and a shirt saying "Kick Me."

"But what about my FACE?" I cried. "Terrific as is," Chico said.

We headed for the floor. A little kid tried to pull my nose off. Sent him flying with one deft swing of my enormous shoe. "My God!" Chico howled, "that was Michu, the Smallest Person In The World!"

Off, obviously, on the wrong foot.

Chico and two other clowns did a music and dance act. I was to hold Chico's violin case. I dropped it. A little girl laughed uproariously. Hey, this is easy!

"If you ever upstage me like that again," Chico hissed in my ear, "I'll feed you to an elephant."

Sour grapes.

Then it was over. I retired to Clown Alley to remove my make-up. "Say," one of the press agents said, "you were TERRIFIC!" I blushed modestly. "When," he continued, "are you going to write about it?"

What! WRITE about it? I can't. I've quit the paper. "Oh," he said. "That's too bad. Well, I hear Clyde Beatty's coming to town next year...."

So that's it. How disillusioning. It was all a trick. They don't want a typing act at all. I already had the title, too. "Tremendous Typist Typifies Terrifying Trials and Tribulations of Tedious Tiresome Tendencies To Fall On His Ass."

I skulked out of Clown Alley, once again disguised as a dedicated journalist on a giant metropolitan daily. "Hey," a little kid called to his mother, "look at the funny-looking clown!"

Damn, I muttered to myself, where are those shoes...?

A Normal Hallow's Eve
November 4, 1974

Things started out normally enough: a seven-foot tall penis walked out on stage at Winterland, trailed by a scantily-clad young lady wearing pasties shaped like horizontal Eiffel Towers.

The judges looked at one another knowingly and scribbled notes on their pads. "A good penis," one commented. "Not a great penis, to be sure, but the best one we've got."

Gene Schoenfeld, M.D., also known as "Dr. Hip," regarded the couple with cool, professional detachment. "No social diseases apparent," he observed matter-of-factly.

Margo St. James, head of the hookers' defense organization, Coyote, was dressed as a nun. "What number are you," I inquired coolly, noting with favor the perky flair of her black-and-white caftan and the long string of dried garbanzo beans she fondled periodically.

"I'm a judge, you imbecile," she replied briskly.

"But," I said, aghast, "surely it must be against the law to impersonate a woman of the cloth."

"Only if you solicit money," she answered sweetly.

After 101 entrants, it finally came down to aforementioned organs, a Richard Nixon dummy and a motorcycle act. "I vote for the penis," one judge blurted. Schoenfeld, ever alert, whipped out his business card and handed it to the young man. "Call my office on Monday morning," he said gently. "Yours is not an uncommon insecurity."

The nun smiled.

Things started to get a bit kinky after that. We—your earnest correspondent, *Variety* writer Jim Harwood and a female person (to prove that we were heterosexual)—next made for Olympus, the new night club theater located on the premises of the old Village at 901 Columbus Avenue. Olympus was to have its gala opening the next night, with Charles Pierce and "Beach Blanket Babylon," but no self-respecting club-to-be could keep its doors shut on this Night of Nights.

We were escorted to a front-row table by a toga-clad lovely named Bill, ordered three sarsaparillas and surveyed the scene. The joint was packed: gays, straights and decline-to-state. Charles Pierce, on a busperson's holiday, swept out as Bette Davis. Claude Sacha swept out as Bette Midler. And Lori Shannon, real name unknown, swept out as Lori Shannon, a mammoth chap in platinum wig, double-chin, double-eyelids and double-ankles.

"My GOD," breathed the tuxedoed gentleman across the table, "they've NEVER been on the same STAGE at the same TIME before!"

The mind reeled. In a matter of seconds, they would fall grappling to the floor, hurling insults ("How'd you get the wig," Charles would snarl, "with a fill-up at the Shell station?") and the entire club would become a battleground of flying cans of Secret and other bizarre weaponry ("Deformed Woman Garroted With Own Falsies!" the newspaper headlines would scream).

No such luck. Linking arms, they danced across the stage singing "Tea For Two" with original obscene lyrics.

The costume parade on stage was seized with a momentary lull. Charles Pierce surveyed the scene. "Any more people coming out?"

he inquired. "I mean, costume-wise...?"

Next was No. 63 in the "Best Female" category, operating under the nom de plummage "Miss Hooker." Number 63 whipped off his top and reeled madly about the stage, his flawless breasts aglow in the spotlight.

"My goodness," I exclaimed to the tuxedoed gentleman across the table, "that is the most incredible silicone job I've ever seen! Who's his doctor?"

"That's a girl, you fool," he said.

"Well," I said, recovering swiftly, "that's not a bad costume, either."

Busloads of drag queens were zinging in and out of the club. Between groups, Charles and Bette Midler staged a contest to see who could touch his tongue to his nose. The tuxedoed gentleman leaned over the table conspiratorily, glancing from side to side before he spoke. "For GOD'S sake," he whispered, "don't DARE leave before the Golden Dildo bus arrives."

We left for Enrico's. Ward Dunham, the bartender and keeper of the peace, was busily thrashing a group of unseemly patrons. "They got out of line," he snarled, placing several of the smaller ones in the ice cream churn. I looked about. It was 2 a.m. Every freak in San Francisco lined Broadway. Ward had turned his attention to a 93-year-old woman, belaboring her with a bar-stool while Enrico himself yanked the wiring out of her electric wheelchair.

Another day, another dollar.

THE TATTOO BALL

April 3, 1978

The lady who calls herself Satana Starslick parades the lobby of Bimbo's 365 Club with statuesque composure, flashbulbs illuminating her pathway.

She is wearing a black, off-one-shoulder leotard top which sags under the weight of her abundant bosom and a black miniskirt slit to the waist. Much of the skin visible on her bared shoulder, arms, thigh and leg is tattooed with dragons, flowers and abstract expressionist meanderings in blues, blacks and reds. She moves with regal authority, like the tattoo queen she is.

Satana Starslick pauses periodically in her travels to dole dollops of discourse to a dozen diligent reporters.

"I am a tattoo artist," she announces. "I'm 22. I got my first tattoo when I was nine."

A reporter paled visibly. "What did your mother think of that?" I cried.

"Being tattooed?" Satana Starslick needled. "My mother has one on her sn—."

"The First Annual Tattoo Ball," a production of tattooist Lyle Tuttle in the great San Francisco tradition of wacko events, was held Friday night at Bimbo's for some 350 tattooers and tattooees; and as many again idle voyeurs. The tab was $7 ($1 cash refund if you could show a tattoo; the man with one on the outermost reach of his most private part mercifully declined). The entertainers included Nicholas Gravenites, Mark Naftalin, Anna Rizzo, Pee Wee Ellis, Rene LeBallister, Snooky Flowers & Smoke, George & the Superstars, belly dancer Khadija and Martha the Opera Singer, who was wearing a push-up bra, the better to lend proper curvature to the tattooed flower peeking out from deep within her cleavage.

"I also have a trellis on my leg," Martha allowed at a pre-induction physical and cocktail party, but she declined to reveal either the concealed herbiage or her Christian name. "Kurt Herbert Adler is not into tattoos," she conceded glumly.

Bobby Librarry was also present at the festivities. Miss Librarry, confided maestro Tuttle, "is The Fairy Godmother of the Tattoo Art Museum" and, at 84, perhaps the world's most venerable tattooed lady. Miss Librarry was perched in a chair as admirers, photographers and a man with a magnifying glass perused her now flaccid designs. She is a very old person, blind in one eye, deaf in one ear. I asked her when her tattooing was performed.

"I would never show you *all* of my tattoos," she said with prim rebuke.

I repeated my query in her other ear. "It was all done in a three-week period in 1918," she replied.

I wandered over to Khadija, who offers, according to her card,

"High Energy Belly Dance Instruction." Khadija is probably the most tattooed belly dancer this side of Istanbul. "It's a hobby with me," she said brightly, exhibiting shoulders beladen with Japanese flora. "I won 'Best On A Woman' at the 1977 Tattoo Convention in Reno. It gives my mother nightmares."

Khadija, who is a 10-year tattooee veteran at 29, said that 25 percent of her body is currently inscribed. "My goal is 100 percent within two years," she concluded, undulating off.

Back at Bimbo's, the party was bubbling as bikers, businessmen and gay blades, housewives, hookers and molls of every description vied for attention from the ubiquitous TV cameras and raucously cheered every raised skirt and lowered Levi's.

"For many people, tattoos are private," Tuttle observed benignly, "but it's a great medium for an extrovert and a great excuse to take your clothes off."

Off in a corner of the lounge, Satana Starslick tugged her leotard down to her waist and revealed heaving breasts tattooed from floor to ceiling. A thin gold ring pierced her right nipple.

"Uh, didn't that, uh, smart?" she was asked.

"No more than the ears," she replied coolly. "I have nine holes in each ear."

"Tattoo," advises the Oxford English Dictionary. *"To form permanent marks or designs upon the skin by puncturing it and inserting a pigment or pigments; practiced by various tribes of low civilizations and by individuals in civilized communities."*

THE TRAGEDY OF PEANUT VENDER

April 28 & 30, 1975

"Do we have to do the Bid-A-Note?" the portly lady with the warts inquired anxiously. "That's one thing I don't do good on."

She was told she wouldn't have to do the Bid-A-Note. "Good," she sighed to no one in particular. "I do good on all the other parts."

The portly lady with the warts was one of three women and seven men, including your faithful correspondent, holed up in the Becky Thatcher Room of the Mark Twain Hotel here last week, trying out for "Name That Tune."

It was the initial, tentative, guarded step on a trail which could lead, we were informed by the associate producer, to cash and prizes amounting to more than $15,000.

"Name That Tune" is the niftiest game on TV. On "Name That Tune," one may pit one's own sly and wizard-quick self against the creeps and degenerates who regularly walk away from the seven-tunes-in-30-seconds "Golden Medley" with umpteen thousand dollars, a re-conditioned King Midget and an almost-all-expenses-paid two week vacation for two in the Upper Volta.

I recall with a profound sense of warmth and well-being, for ex-ample, the time the woman set the all-time "Name That Tune" record by bringing the "Golden Medley" to its knees in a scant 17 seconds.

Yours truly, stop-watch at hand, was three ticks faster.

A cup of tea.

So, upon discovering that the show's talent scouts were taking their act on the road from Los Angeles for the first time, I quickly whipped off a telephone call to the Mark Twain, asked for "Name That Tune," identified myself as George "Peanut" Vender and made an ap-pointment for the tryouts.

It was 2 p.m. Thursday afternoon. I propelled my wheelchair jaunty-jolly through the lobby, zoomed up to the first Hollywood TV-type I saw and cooed "Love For Sale" to his knees.

Then I saw the sign, "Name That Tune," with an arrow pointing past the Tom Sawyer Room to the Becky Thatcher Room. I entered boldly, bounced down the steps and was immediately greeted by John Harlan, the associate producer—a tall, hale fellow with the booming, resonant voice of a game show announcer, which he is.

"WELCOME!" he boomed, shattering my contact lenses. "Do-you-understand-that-if-you-are-invited-to-the-studio-in-Los-Angeles-that-our-inviting-you-in-no-way-guarantees-your-appearance-on-any-of-said-programs-and-you-agree-to-appear-at-the-studio-at-your-own-expense-with-the-understanding-that-you-may-never-be-used-on-any-of-said-programs?"

"Of course," I answered, barely restraining my condescension. "Doesn't everybody...?"

Harlan gave me a second look. This is a fellow to watch, he was thinking.

"GOOD!" he resonated. "WHAT'S YOUR NAME?"

"George 'Peanut' Vender," I replied.

"SWELL!" he thundered. "MIND IF I CALL YOU GEORGE?"

He motioned me into the room, which was already occupied by a portable tape recorder, several long tables, a Polaroid camera, the portly lady with the warts, two slim young women, six nondescript men between 25 and 50, and one greasy-looking chap who was obviously the assistant manager of a pornographic movie theater in Campbell.

A cup of tea.

How would these amateurs compete with a professional—a man of music, of song, a person who has dedicated his life to melody, harmony and countertops; polyphony, medleys, overtures, syncopation, madrigals, sonatas, glees and mirths?

"HOW OLD ARE YOU?" John Harlan said. "Eighty-seven," I croaked, patting my gray hair with my right hand as I fondled with my left the bottle of Grecian Formula 16 secreted in my tattered bathrobe.

"OCCUPATION?" "Retired. Used to be an organ grinder. Hard work. Some of your big organs, like your Wurlitzers, would take weeks."

"HEY!" said John Harlan. "THAT'S TERRIFIC!"

It had worked. The disguise was perfect. I was in the "Name That Tune" Quiz. I looked around the Becky Thatcher Room at the poor unfortunates who would have to compete with me. The portly lady with the warts looked anxious. The pornographic movie house assistant manager wiped the sweat from his brow, then wiped the grease from his hand. The two young ladies looked slyly at each other. Frankly, I suspected a fix there. The six nondescript men just stared at the blank pages in front of them. On the pages, we would have to write the names of songs as they were played on the portable tape recorder—some for 15 or 20 seconds, others for as few as three or four seconds.

"IT'S A SPECIAL ABILITY TO BE ABLE TO NAME TUNES, AND I HOPE YOU HAVE IT," John Harlan thundered sonorously. And with that, he started the tape recorder. I immediately recognized Mozart's "Flute and Harp Concerto in C, K. 299," followed by "Missa Solemnis," "Stormy Monday Blues," "The Lord's Prayer" and "How Can I Miss You If You Won't Go Away?"

"Keep 'em coming!" cried the portly wart lady. The tunes went on: "The Star-Spangled Banner," "Gimme a Pigfoot (and a Bottle of Beer),' "Bachianas Brasileiras No. 5," "The Gettysburg Address," "Happy Birthday to You," "Auld Lang Syne," "Three Blind Mice" and "Chopsticks."

"What if I don't know how to spell it?" wailed the portly warts. I smiled inwardly. "I-t," I said, patronizingly.

"You couldn't play that one again, could you?" whined the pornographic assistant.

"HECK, NO!" boomed John Harlan, "BUT, HA HA, I SURE CAN'T BLAME YOU FOR ASKING...."

Then it was over. John Harlan gathered up our papers and left the room. The tension was unbearable. For the others. I simply fiddled with my fake hearing aid until I got the Giants and leaned back confidently.

Ten minutes later, John Harlan returned. Half of his face was ebullient, happy, congratulatory. The other half was sympathetic, sad, compassionate.

He looked at one of the men. "Steve, you didn't hit it too heavy," he said, his voice now lowered to a level more in keeping with the bad news. "You missed 'I Left My Heart in San Francisco.'" Steve cast his eyes downward, as the rest of us hooted and jeered and tried to kick him in the shins.

"Mrs. Portly Warts, you didn't do too well, either." Of course, Mrs. Portly Warts could have gotten 100 percent and she wouldn't have done too well, but that's another story.

Then his face turned sad on both sides. "I'm afraid you two girls didn't do well enough." They looked at each other and shrugged. "I just did it for the trip of the day, anyway," one said. "I don't even have a TV."

The last one to go was Mike, who is working on his Ph.D. at Cal. "Hey, Mike, you didn't do too well, either, but you're a good-looking guy and obviously very bright. We'll have to ask you to leave, though. Tough bananas."

"And the same to your mother," Mike said.

Finally, all had been dismissed except yours truly and three other men.

"Well, George 'Peanut,'" John Harlan said to me, bellowing into my hearing aid. "You got three right, and we like your sense of humor. You're the first one who ever wrote 'Happy Birthday to You' when we played 'God Bless America.' That was a good one! However, we'll have to ask you to roll your ancient buns out of here....."

"You fool!" I shouted, leaping out of my wheelchair, tearing off my hearing aid, rending the tattered bathrobe that covered my "WORLD FAMOUS MUSIC AUTHORITY" T-shirt, sprinkling some Grecian Formula 16 on my hair and breaking my "Gray Power" picket sign across my knee as though it were a matchstick. "Don't you know who I *am* ?"

John Harlan smiled softly. "Of course," he said. "But you're in the wrong room. 'Let's Make a Deal' is next door."

THE NIGHT TRAIN FROM B.A.

September 30, 1974

The train rattled and clattered through the night, en route from Buenos Aires, the largest city in South America, to Rosario, "the Chicago of Argentina."

Its cargo included singer Joan Baez, Manny Greenhill, her manager; Bernie Gelb, her road manager; and Victor Perera, a journalist and writer based at UC Santa Cruz, currently on assignment in Argentina and Chile for *The New York Times*.

It was Joan's first night away from "BA," as it is called, since her arrival a week earlier to begin a South American tour comprising stops in BA, Rosario and Caracas. It was her first Latin American tour and would be followed by stops in Ann Arbor, Denver and Vancouver and would conclude this Sunday at Stanford University's Frost Amphitheater. Its genesis was: an interest in South America, especially Chile, stemming from her work with Amnesty International; a tie-in with her last album, the Spanish-language "Gracias a la Vida"; and, put simply, to make some money. Her United States concerts of the past few years have been almost exclusively benefits.

The train was a put-put, consuming four hours to travel 150 miles or so. It was old, and wobbly, its movements labored, its attendants tired and inattentive, their uniforms soiled, the food they served running the gamut of taste sensations from warm porridge to cold porridge. Joan, Manny and Bernie had all been working assiduously on their Spanish but it was left to Victor, born in Guatemala, once an apprentice U.N. translator, also fluent in French, to interpret the subtleties.

We chugged through the outskirts of this mammoth city of more than eight million population, the grubby outskirts one passes in any city when leaving it by rail. The decision to go by train instead of plane had been made in order to see some countryside; maybe a flash of the fabled pampas. It was dark by the time we started moving.

We sat in the car and talked—noisy Americans. Joan changed the strings of her guitar, inserted some Kleenex at the high end of the neck and began to pick a little. She was dressed in knee-high brown boots and blue socks, blue denims with floral patterns sewn in circumference at the bottom of each leg, a white blouse, the blue suede vest of her blue suede pants suit, silver bracelet, silver ring, white on black against her dark brown skin. Effulgent.

She took off her boots and started singing; quietly, tentatively, gingerly placing her toe in the water, checking the temperature. Some paid no attention; others, both young and old, started to gather around our seats, at ease with the rhythmic sway of the choo-choo.

At first she acted as if this were all standard operating procedure; just noodling in her living room after another dinner at home. Then, voices began to speak. Haltingly, some in English. "I have all your records," said a young girl, shyly. "We saw you in Buenos Aires." "We will come to your concert tomorrow night in Rosario."

Joan smiled. The concert began. She sang "Gracias a la Vida," the title tune from her last A & M album and something of an anthem in this part of the world, a "Blowin' in the Wind," or "The Times They Are A'Changin'," or "Tenderly" or "Moonlight Serenade," but really none of these. The woman who wrote it—"Thanks to Life"—was Violeta Parra, a Chilean. She was, at 50, in love with a man of 30. She gave him every- thing, and he spurned her. She wrote her thanks to life, and killed herself.

"We are an emotional people," someone said.

Joan sang on as we lumbered through the darkness, an oil refinery fouling the air far longer than it took to pass. She sang "Guantanamera" and "The Night They Drove Old Dixie Down." Tired businessmen observed the scene with incomprehension. The silvery beauty of the voice was the only reality. But a baby toddled across the aisle, attired in a worn but spruce knitted baby suit, and Manny Greenhill took the child on his lap and Joan sang to the small person and that, at least, needed no introduction, no interpreter. And the train clattered on through the night.

HEROIC JOURNALIST BRAVES GUACAMOLE
August 15, 17 & 19, 1977

Now, finally, the truth can be told. When singer John Denver howls *"Faaaaan-tastic!"* and *"Faaaaaar-out!"* from the stage during his live appearances, he is not dutifully performing a programmed ritual to inflame his fans, he is being utterly, completely, indisputably himself.

"How does he know this?" you ask suspiciously, knowing full well that I have never even seen the Rocky Mountains, much less felt the sun on my shoulder.

I will tell you.

It was about 9:30 a.m. Friday, a time when decent folk are still asleep, and John (I call him John, even though at this point in the story, we had not yet been introduced) and I were bouncing along in a chartered bus on the concrete runways of Edwards Air Force Base in the Mojave Desert in company with his brother Danny, his father Henry John "Dutch" Deutschendorf Sr., several representatives of Harrah's Club, a spokesman or two from the National Aeronautics and Space Administration and my host, Mike Wash, a NASA engineer from Ames Research Center in Mountain View—now an enfeebled 37 but, in his youth, the man who trained all the Apollo astronauts in the lift-off and abort procedures for the moon flights.

We were there, deep in the burning, mysterious Southern California badlands, to witness the first free-flight test of the Space Shuttle Orbiter "Enterprise."

"But why was he there?" you ask suspiciously, knowing full well that, in the past at least, show biz has been my life.

Lissen, honey, show biz is everybody's life.

It had all started the day before.

"I tell you," I had told the Managing Editor on Thursday morning, "you gotta let me go. This is bigger than Led Zeppelin, bigger than

Gordon McRae—yes, bigger than Benji! Everyone will be there!"

He snorted, as Managing Editors are wont to do.

"C'mon," I cried, "tens of thousands of people are driving dozens of miles, risking sunburn and braving vicious rattlesnakes, prairie dogs and Senator Barry Goldwater to see this thing. And they don't even have BART down there!"

He lit up a contraband Cuban cigar, took several phone calls from people who demanded to know what had happened to Jack Rosenbaum's column, then turned back and regarded me with disguised contempt.

"How much'll it cost me?" he asked coldly, assuming the royal "Me," which is also expected of Managing Editors.

"Four ninety-five," I replied quickly, knowing what would be the next question. "Five bucks with tip."

He closed his eyes, leaned back and weighed the odds of me being run over by the space shuttle.

In desperation, I flipped my hole card. "Roy Rogers," I said evenly, betraying no emotion, "will be there...."

Without another word, he rose, beckoned me to follow him into the vault, reached into the extremely petty cash box and withdrew $5.10.

"But your highness," I mumbled, taken aback by the budget over-run, "why the extra dime?"

"Don't be such a cheapskate," he growled. "Headwaiters have to make a living, too."

At seven o'clock Thursday night, Mike Wash and I left the Sand Sailer motel in Lancaster for the nearby home of Colonel David R. Scott, moon astronaut (Apollo 15), now director of NASA's Dryden Flight Research Center at Edwards Air Force Base.

I was introduced to Colonel Scott. "Say, that's a mighty big bird you've got out there," I said with a casual wave toward the nearby desert (knowing that, in these parts, anything that flies, yet is not an insect, is called a "bird"). He nodded graciously, said he had to go check the atmosphere, and disappeared.

I looked around. It was a nice house with a large back lawn, a trampoline and a swimming pool shaped like a bottle of Tang. I moseyed over to the Mexican buffet dinner. The night air was warm, but gentle zephyrs, rustling through the turkey enchiladas, made it quite bearable.

I stood on the trampoline and unobtrusively surveyed the crowd. There was General Curtis LeMay, former head of the Strategic Air Command. Here was an assistant secretary of the Air Force, there was a gaggle of men who had trod on the moon. I spotted Dr. Carl Sagan, who graced last week's *Newsweek* cover. I spotted Jacques Cousteau, who was a member of Governor Jerry Brown's party. I spotted Governor Brown, who was a member of the Democratic party.

And—yes—Roy Rogers! I couldn't believe it. Roy Rogers. *Himself.* Surrounded by admirers. His hair looking not a day over 30. I craned my neck, peering around the encircling coterie. I craned and peered, peered and craned. But it was fruitless. *They* weren't there. No Dale, no Trigger.

Well, let's see, I thought to myself. One of them, I know, passed away recently and was stuffed. But which one? Trigger, probably. If it had been Dale, Roy could have carried her.

The Governor, a newly minted spacenik, was standing under the veranda. He is known for his piercing, granite-hard gaze. I engaged his attention by softly humming "Heart Like a Wheel." He whirled and focused his piercing, granite-hard gaze on me. I never wavered. He never wavered. I didn't blink. He didn't blink.

Then, abruptly, the Governor recoiled, as though struck in the face by a poltergeist blob of guacamole.

I smiled coolly and went about my business, still undefeated.

"Hey! What's that green gooey stuff on your fingers?" General LeMay cried as I wiped it off on his epaulets.

At 4:30 a.m., the wake-up call arrived. "Off we go, into the wild blue yonder..." warbled the motel telephone operator, Miss Spillet. I unsuccessfully tried to have the call traced. The last time I was up at 4:30 in the morning, I hadn't gone to bed. The first time, also. I put on my "Star Wars" Wookie mask so I wouldn't have to shave, gathered up my E-Z-Lurn Space Lingo handbook and hopped on a bus.

We arrived at the vast, desolate dry lake about 6:45 a.m. All the old gang from the party was there, plus Senator Goldwater, in a pink shirt, Michael McClure, who has just been appointed Poet Laureate for the Entire Universe, and John Denver, who had flown in that morning from Colorado—some say on his Lear jet; I say on a rainbow.

I spotted Dr. Sagan, the amiable exobiologist. "Hi," I said, "you live around here?"

Dr. Sagan and I discussed the pop music he has put on "Sounds of the Earth," a record he is sending out on the first Voyager spacecraft, which leaves Saturday for Jupiter, Saturn and, eventually, interstellar space. Among the tunes is "Johnny B. Goode."

"That's a happening tune, all right," I agreed. "How soon will it have a shot at becoming, literally, a universal hit?"

"Actually, not a long time by space standards," Dr. Sagan replied. "Maybe 40,000 years 'til it comes within 6,000,000,000,000 miles of another solar system."

"Jeez," I thought to myself, "and Chuck Berry's already 51...."

I was still glowing after having stumped the great Jacques Cousteau on a marine-life question *("In what habitat, sir, is one most likely to encounter the rare species troutus interruptus?")* when the mammoth Boeing 747 started moving on the Edwards Air Force Base runway, the space shuttle Enterprise perched on its back like a shark riding a whale.

The 747 taxied to, then fro. Suspense mounted as we peered through binoculars at the leviathan, perhaps a mile distant, or watched one of a dozen or so closed-circuit television screens while overhead speakers crackled with a last-minute conversation between the Enterprise and mission control at the Johnson Space Center in Houston.

"OK, Enterprise," came the voice from Houston, "this is Cap-Com and—"

"Whoa there, good buddy," broke in shuttle commander Fred Haise, "just take that pedal off the metal for a sec and tell me what's that there 'cap-com' handle you're tossin' into my convoy...?"

"Jesus, Fred, gimme a break," answered Houston, "how many times do I have to tell you—Cap-Com is short for 'capsule communicator.' I'm the communicator and you're the capsule, and you're not taking off till you get that straight...."

"Roger, Houston," said Haise. "I think I got it. Now what were you calling about? You couldn't have left it on my service?"

"Jesus, Fred," replied Houston, "this is no time for joking. We're just checking to make sure we copied the last computer read-out right. Now, that was a ham-on-rye, hold the mayo; a peanut butter-and-jelly; two chocolate shakes and a side of cow-pies...roger?"

"*Fries*, Houston," Haise snapped, "a side of fries...."

At 8:01 a.m. or thereabouts, the 747 started down the runway and, seemingly oblivious to its 250,000-pound passenger, soared into a blue sky peppered with deferential patches of stark white clouds and five sleek, tiny T-38 chase planes—goldfish to the shark on the whale. The Boeing climbed and circled for 45 minutes, then "pushed over" into a shallow dive, Houston calling out altitude and air speed as commander Haise and co-pilot Gordon Fullerton prepared for separation and the relatively tender one-G jolt that would accompany it.

Two minutes later, we turned from the television monitors to the sky as the shuttle came gliding silently across the desert, descending at the precipitous rate of 5,000 feet per minute, a speck evolving into a "DC-9 with no wings," as it has been described, heading directly for us, surrounded by the T-38 gnats nipping at its flanks.

Then, as Houston barked out the waning altitude in increments of 12 inches—"five feet from touchdown...four feet...three...two...one"— the Enterprise whooshed by within a hundred yards, its 200-mile-per-hour landing speed sending a hydroplane plume of sand and dirt showering in its wake.

Then it was over, and we left as we had come, each filled with new resolve.

Jacques Cousteau vowed to pursue *troutus interruptus* to the ends of the earth.

Carl Sagan determined to find out if Pacific Stereo would go for a 40,000-year warranty on parts and labor.

Governor Brown retired to practice his piercing, granite-hard gaze in anticipation of our next encounter.

Michael McClure was busily sketching out a new "gargoyle cartoon" about stuffing Roy Rogers.

And John Denver, his brother Dan and I boarded a bus for a sightseeing tour of Edwards and its awesome arsenal of fighting planes.

"Faaaaan-tastic," said John Denver with a big grin, shaking his head. *"Faaaaar-out."*

13

Wassy Goes 'Round the Bend

Great salty tears welled in my lovely wife Tacit's eyes as she
clutched the little nippers to her bosom.
"Doctor, doctor," she cried piteously. "Is there nothing that can
be done? No miracle drugs? Is there no way to save our Wassy?
Will he never type again?"
JLW

*How can you tell when someone you love is in danger, especially someone who
has always lived on the edge? Only by piecing things together now is it clear
to me that in 1978 John's life was spiraling out of control. On the surface,
things were going well. That year he received a big raise and the name of his
column "On the Town" was changed to JOHN L. WASSERMAN. People
at the* Chronicle *assumed that he was being groomed to take over Herb
Caen's column one day. John was a local celebrity, recognized on the street,*

approached in restaurants. Yet friends speak now of having sensed a deep sadness.

His hair was thinning and getting gray; he had lower back trouble and worried about emphysema. Despite many attempts to quit smoking, nothing had worked, not even hypnosis. Failed, too, was his resolve to write a book. There were an aborted biography of Joan Baez and other unrealized projects, including a proposed collection of his bad-movie reviews, a history of pop music (with stride piano player Mike Lipskin), and a biography of Bill Graham, which Simon and Schuster turned down because they didn't consider the rock producer a sufficiently prominent figure. Billy Abrahams, a literary editor, gave John encouragement and advice, as did novelist Herb Gold and Curt Gentry, whose book on the Manson murders, Helter Skelter, *was a runaway bestseller.*

It was Gold who suggested the Baez book as a natural for John, considering his interests and expertise and his friendship with the singer. After signing a book contract in 1973 with Atlantic Little, Brown, John traveled to South America with Joan and her entourage. But the project collapsed five months later, partly because he'd made little headway in the writing, partly because she was skittish about going public with aspects of her private life. Her manager insisted John sign a separate contract giving Joan the right of review. He felt hemmed in. "I want to write my own book," he wrote in a note to himself.

The fact is, he missed daily journalism—the first edition fresh off the press, the first appreciative response. When the book was scrapped, his strongest emotion was relief.

Throughout 1978 John continued doing the work of three, filling his days and nights as though afraid that if he stopped he would lose everything. Years of heavy drinking had taken a physical and emotional toll. As early as 1975 he had experienced alcoholic blackouts and paranoid delusions, but he'd always been able to bounce back. Now it was a lot harder. Yet his natural exuberance was so contagious, and the writing so good, that few people knew the extent of the problem. Occasionally, he tried to cut back on alcohol: writer Blake Green remembers a beach party in Marin County when John wasn't drinking. He sat miserably on the sand in his black clothes and left early.

Increasingly, there was a dark, even cynical edge to his humor.

A fast driver who considered yellow lights personal affronts and once set a world indoor speed record in the parking garage across from the

Chronicle *building (immortalized in one of Ron Fimrite's sports columns), John was a menace on the road. It wasn't just his drinking but his obsession with speed that caused most of his friends to refuse to drive with him. Just before his 40th birthday, he crashed his Datsun 280Z into a tree as he left a night club in northern Marin. He escaped with minor injuries, but the car was destroyed. Ashamed, he concealed the incident, then referred to it ironically in his birthday column.*

On January 31, 1979, his mentor and friend Kevin Wallace died suddenly of a heart attack. At the wake John told a Chronicle *colleague, "I don't think I'll outlive him by two weeks."*

BACK FROM VACATION

March 3 , 1975

Hi. My name is John Wasserman. I used to work here, back in the early '70s and the first two weeks of January.

Then I went on vacation. Or, so the paper claimed. Some thought otherwise. Rumors flew up and down Mission Street.

I was finished, they said...washed up. There was talk of demotion to the rank of critic. Some muttered darkly of a phallus coup in the sex-film department.

Nonsense. It was but a vacation. Vacations are important for balance. A time to sleep, a time to sew. To reflect, recharge the batteries and seek the elusive butterfly of perspective on one's life work and salary.

Who am I? What is the meaning of life? How does dust get on my phonograph when all the windows are closed?

Each year, I go on vacation and ponder these questions for five or 10 seconds. And turn once again for solace to Descartes: "Cogito, ergo sum."

"I think, therefore I can add."

I muse on the nature of my work. Truth. Integrity. Self-indulgence. Assessing the relative historical importance of Barbi Benton, the Rolling Stones, Little Jimmy Osmond and Werner Erhard.

Compared with that of Gerald Ford, Winston Churchill, Sonali

Das Gupta and the Reverend Ike.

A stand-off.

I think about significance. About profoundness. Meaningfulness. Art. I think a lot about Art. Ever since he split with Paul, you don't hear so much about him.

Music...what does it mean? I don't know. I only seek refuge in the words of Justice Potter Stewart as he wrestled with a definition of pornography for the United States Supreme Court: "I can't define it," he said, speaking for many of us, "but I know it when I hear it."

Yet there must be more than that. Music is all around us, in the trees and the elevators. It is the universal language if you don't count Esperanto. You can go up to someone in Bucharest, as I once did, and whistle "Lullabye of Birdland." And they will whistle back "George Shearing," quick as a wink. That is one of the reasons we have never gone to war with Rumania. They don't speak English.

And, for that matter, who can say, with absolute assurance, that the lyrics of Bob Dylan are of any less moment than the brassiere size of Adrienne Barbeau?

Much of this came home with searing impact as I re-read a letter I received from Mr. Joseph N. Boyce, the San Francisco Bureau Chief for *Time* magazine, in reply to a reference in this space some time ago to *Time* as "that august journal of irrelevance."

Mr. Boyce, stung by what he perceived as a ruthless and unwarranted attack, expressed both "irritation" and "amusement" at this humble pot calling the kettle of *Time* "irrelevant."

At any rate, regarding the matter of "irrelevance," Mr. Boyce concluded: "I hesitate (however), to take you to task on that—the assumption being that one as experienced as yourself in the day-to-day chronicling of the ambience of glitter rock, doll-decapitating transvestites and incompetent musicians is undoubtably an expert on the subject."

How true. Who, indeed, better qualified to judge irrelevancy after more than a decade of unrelenting exposure to every nitwit act in the Western Hemisphere?

But that eludes the point. Mr. Boyce assumed that a reference to *Time* as irrelevant would be intended archly and with disdain. Not at all. Irrelevance is among the highest planes to which we may aspire. Or, at least, it would appear so, for those we as a nation admire most have, almost without exception, attained that status.

Irrelevance is the very essence of being, you see.

Or, as Cyril Connolly said, regarding the writing of Ronald Firbank: "He recognized frivolity as the most insolent refinement of satire...."

I think I need a vacation.

UP THE BAYSHORE AT 30 M.P.H.

April 1, 1974

It was a dark and stormy Friday night as I trucked on down to the Circle Star in San Carlos to cast eyes on the Nicholas Brothers, Johnny Brown and Sammy Davis, Jr.

Opposite Levitz Furniture in South City, a strange thing happened. The front end of my auto commenced spewing steam at such a rate as to suggest a malfunction. I glanced at the temperature gauge. It was pegged on the right. Disaster. The radiator has blown up. I pulled over.

It is 8:12. There is no civilization within sight, including Levitz's. I begin chanting mantras to pass the time. At 8:27, a California Highway Patrol person pulls up behind me. I stiffen in terror. He probably won't even knock. I pop the rest of the salami sandwich in my mouth. No evidence, no case. Followed by a PepOmint Lifesaver. No breathalizer in the world can take that kind of pressure.

He gets out. My hands are on the steering wheel, in plain sight. He shines a flashlight in the car, revealing a Department of Motor Vehicles written test I had taken that very afternoon. One wrong. My license, expired since last August, has been renewed. Thank you, Vishnu.

"Stop trembling, you fool," he says. "What's the matter?" "Have you ever tried to eat a salami sandwich and a PepOmint Lifesaver at the same time?" I shoot back.

He calls Triple A for me. "I know nothing about the SLA," I continue. "My restaurant was called the Peking Duck."

Triple A arrives at 9:02. It is pouring rain. I've already missed the Nicholas Brothers. What, oh what to do? My head is swimming. So is the rest of my body, as I am underwater. The Triple A man attaches water-wings to my ears and tows me toward the closest gas station. "Say," I say, "could you possibly tow me to San Carlos?" He looks at his dog, a mammoth German shepherd. "Sic him, Klaus," he murmurs.

I take a cab to the airport and rent a car from Avis. It is now 9:30. I have missed Johnny Brown, as well. My car is a Dodge Dart, recommended by Joe Garagiola. I floor it. "The Circle Star," I snarl, "and don't spare the gas." There is a sign on the dashboard. "This Car Is Incapable Of Speeds Exceeding 30 Miles Per Hour." Terrific.

I rush into the theater and up to the box office. At least I'm in time to see Sammy. "One for me," I say casually, "and one for the Dart."

"You've been banned from the theater," the man says coldly. "Orders of Shirley Rhodes, Mr. Davis's aide. She says Mr. Davis is just as important as Tom Jones. Maybe more."

"And so's your grandmother," I retort with a withering glance as I break through the barrier of crippled children that has been erected in the lobby to keep me out.

The show begins. Sam is in fine fettle. He sings, he dances, he charms the capacity audience, he is gorgeous. An amazing man.

Back into the Dodge Dud and race for the city, for this is also the night that Sally Rand, the magnificent and ageless fan-dancer, is doing a benefit for one Katherine Marlow. Ms. Marlow is, according to my information, a former male person who is currently receiving sex-change assistance from the Stanford Medical Center. I whistle up the Bayshore at 29 miles per hour, passing an assortment of toads, turtles and small furry animals as if they were standing still, which, in most cases, they were.

I haven't seen Sal since about 1965 when she was a mere toddler of 62. The show, naturally, is over when I arrive, but the gala affair continues, enraptured in the throes of what "Peanuts" calls "touch-dancing." The John Cordoni band is playing "Charmaine."

Ah, nostalgia. Formals. Hair-dos. Wrist corsages. Sal is still there, dancing a rhumba. Her hair is blonde and all curls...Shirley Temple's fairy godmother. She is wearing a gold mini-dress which could be fairly described as a long tutu. Her legs are extraordinary. Mine should be as good when I'm 50.

Katherine, our host, is emceeing a dance contest. "OK, Rico," she calls gaily, no pun intended, "put your hand over the heads of the couples while they dance. The rest applaud your favorite." I choose the couple with the best looking heads and march briskly for the door.

Show business is my life.

WELCOME TO MY NIGHTMARE
December 19, 1975

"Come right in, doctor, don't be afraid. He can't hurt anybody now. We put him in a strait-jacket and glued his ankles together. But watch the teeth! He's already bitten through two tongue-depressors and maimed a Gray Lady."

"Thank you, nurse, I'm sure I'll be quite safe." The psychiatrist peered through thick spectacles at the sniveling wretch in front of him. The patient's eyes rolled back in his head, he was frothing at the mouth and tugged periodically at his bizarre clothing. He was wearing a suggestively low-cut flower-print prom dress and bunny rabbit ears. The doctor shook his head.

"An obvious case of the Blinder/Zeitlin syndrome," the doctor noted. "In God's name, what happened to him?"

The nurse nodded to a table the patient was nibbling on. On its surface was the police report:

"Officer Harms and Kinavey were cruising Nob Hill at approximately 12:07 a.m. Wednesday morning when they spotted the subject apparently attempting to immolate himself on a stolen baked Alaska in the middle of Mason Street, between California and Sacramento. When asked what he was doing by the arresting officers, subject replied that his name was Jane Friendly and he was Food Editor of *The San Francisco Chronicle*, a local newspaper. With that, subject assaulted Officer Harms with meringue, rendering him momentarily hors de combat, and asked Officer Kinavey to dance.

"He was subsequently subdued and booked at Central Station for assault with a deadly recipe, obstructing traffic, attempting suicide and dancing with a police officer.

"As nearly as we can recreate the events preceding the confrontation, through interviews with local chefs and the reading of a notepad subject was attempting to burn at the time of the arrest (he claimed to have spilled the brandy while in flight), subject's activities prior to 12:07 were as follows:

"He showed the first signs of cracking up while attending something called 'Get Down,' which is said to have opened at the Orpheum Theater earlier that evening. A souvenir program, found on subject's person, states that aforesaid show is 'A Rock Music Spectacular.' According to subject's own notes, there was a cast of seven musicians, six singers, 14 dancers and nine morons. While subject's notes become increasingly illegible during the 35 minutes he lasted, there seems to be some indication that 'Get Down' is a 'jive Las Vegas T & A spectacle,' to use subject's words, and that, while 'perfect' for the Sands or Sahara, was 'pathetic' in this context.

"Interviews with members of the Orpheum ushering staff indicate that, at approximately 9:20 p.m., subject ran screaming from the theater, attempting to throttle himself with a Flair felt-tip pen. Fortunately, no one was injured for the theater was nearly empty at the time.

"Subject apparently drove himself, or pushed his car—there were no witnesses—to the Fairmont Hotel for the opening of 'Barbi Benton.' Arresting officers have, so far, been unable to determine exactly what 'Barbi Benton' is.

"According to some eyewitness reports, 'Barbi Benton' is a great singer, an exhilarating conversationalist, a very lovely human being and the sexiest creature in show business. However, when we were finally able to locate a couple who had seen the show and were not employees of Hugh Hefner, the story was substantially different.

"Whatever the case, it seems that subject was not able to cope with 'Barbi Benton' on top of 'Get Down'—especially after, according to other reports, he had attended a 'press gala' in her suite following the show, and could not get an autograph.

"At that point, subject attempted to hurl himself into the bidet, was asked to leave, called room service and ordered a Hispano-Suiza, then shot into the kitchen, purloined the baked Alaska and fled toward Mason Street, tipping the doorman with a scoop of vanilla."

The psychiatrist looked up from the report and gazed sympathetically at the pathetic devil in front of him. For the first time, the patient spoke. "I did it, Doc," he said pitifully. "I'm guilty."

The doctor patted him on the head and knew he would never serve a day.

A classic case of justifiable pesticide.

THE BIG FOUR-OH

August 14, 1978

It is Sunday morning, Aug. 13, 1938. In faraway San Rafael, at little Cottage Hospital, a babe is born.

His parents beam down at the little nipper. "We will call him John," they say proudly, "in honor of the toilet."

And they wrapped him in old newspapers (swaddling clothes were already $11.98 a swaddle) and took him home to faraway Mill Valley, where they advertised him for sale in the *Mill Valley Record.* It was the Depression.

But no one would pay the tab, which was more than 40 dollars. So they reared the little shaver, and it was good.

Well, it was adequate.

And John, as he was known, grew straight and strong, and began tying up his little dolls with clothesline and flogging them with every ounce of strength in his little body.

And his parents saw this and said, "It is good. He should move to San Francisco."

So he packed up his roach-clips and petroleum jelly and moved across the Great Waters, to San Francisco. And he grew straighter and stronger, and began to smoke and drink to excess.

And his parents saw this, and said: "It is good. He should go to work for *The San Francisco Chronicle.*"

And he did, on July 1, 1963.

He started in the Drama Department, and was called Second Banana, and Flunky, and Leland the Benign, and unto him was given every stinko movie and stage production for hectares around. But diligent was he, and hard-working, and he learned his craft, which was mostly how to say "This movie sucks."

And his parents saw this, and said, "It is good. He should be a critic."

And the years flew by, and John, as he was now called, branched out to music, and clubs, and concerts, and porno musicals, and dog-and-pony shows. And many moons passed, and many suns, and many clouds, and many rains and many stars. And much water passed under the bridge, and there were many cold days in hell, and rocks were worn to pebbles and a whole new generation of morons came along.

And then it was Sunday, Aug. 13, 1978. And John sat at his loyal typewriter, Old Paint, and realized that he was 40 years old. And he said: "Hey, you're only as old as you feel."

And he felt 114.

And they felt good.

And then he looked back: on four decades of life, on 15 years with *The San Francisco Chronicle.* Back on nearly four thousand articles, and nearly two million words published. Camel feed to Herb Caen, of course, but several million more than, say, Herb Gold. And he thought of all the bad words he had written, not to mention the naughty ones, and knew that it was good.

He thought of his car, Old Paint, which had been mercilessly attacked and killed by a rogue tree near Nicasio, and of the other casualties: of the careers he'd ruined, in addition to his own, and of those he'd tried and failed. He thought of the gratuitous insults hurled, of payoffs received, of the friends he had made, and the enemas.

He reflected on the vagaries of life. How he'd grown tired of the few corrupting the many, of the moving pictures that pass for films, of the bellows in place of songs and the "artists" who aren't even craftsmen.

Much less craftspersons.

And he began to grow weary of his thinking, for he approached the end of the column, which would have been blank save for the big four-oh. He reached a last time for his favorite saying:

If you don't like it, get your own newspaper.

How simple those words, how nobly eloquent. Plato it was who said them first. Sure, it was different then, but that was because Plato didn't speak English:

If you don't like it, get your own chisel.

But the sediment lingers on. Fifteen years, 1.85 million words, give or take 85. And sew what? A new caftan?

Epilogue

On February 26, the day after John's death, the San Francisco Board of Supervisors adjourned their regular meeting, on a motion by Quentin Kopp, as a tribute to John. The next night a large crowd gathered at the Great American Music Hall, where the marquee read only JOHN L. WASSERMAN 1938-1979. David Allen arrived with Lily Tomlin on one arm and Robin Williams on the other. People hugged each other and wept. Some expressed anger at John for killing two others, himself and his talent. "Everyone is the product of heredity and environment, but we all are also responsible for our own actions," John had written in 1970. He would not have contradicted their anger.

There were no spoken eulogies, just music long into the night.

A wake the following Sunday at Zohn Artman's house brought John's worlds together: the *Chronicle,* the family, Mill Valley friends, including members of the Green-bellied Potfish Gang, lovers, comedians, musicians, actors, D.J.'s, producers, promoters, artists, writers. The place was filled with flowers, including some from Woody Allen, and you couldn't go five steps without bumping into a celebrity.

My younger brother Richey encountered Bill Graham, whom he hadn't seen since Richey was a roadie for Butterfield Blues Band and Seatrain. "John and I were more alike than anybody I knew," Graham said quietly. "That's why we fought so much."

Joan Baez invited the family upstairs to read the dedication to John of her new album, "Honest Lullabye." Later, other tributes would follow, including a dedication by Kenny Rankin of his album "After the Roses." The San Francisco Council on Entertainment created a John L. Wasserman Award for Lifetime Achievement, to be presented at the Cabaret Gold Awards, and William Hamilton, Curt Gentry and City Arts and Lectures head Sydney Goldstein started a memorial scholarship fund at the College of Marin, where John had studied and worked on the school paper. Arnold Schwarzenegger gave $500, and comedian Martin Mull, whose caustic humor John loved, staged a concert to benefit the fund. The awards are given every May.

John's personal collection of seven thousand record albums, many autographed and rare, were donated to the newly-organized Bay Area Music Archives, which, David Rubinson assured us, "is something John would have wanted." They were to become part of a Rock and Roll Museum that never materialized. Presently, their remains (the collection was vandalized in a previous site) are in boxes at Bill Graham Presents. The search continues for a home to fulfill the original intent of the gift.

At a private auction a few weeks after John's death, his friends bought mementos that included a complete set of Fillmore West posters, cases of vintage wines, black shirts and jackets, large floor pillows and original drawings by John's favorites—Charles Schulz, William Hamilton, Susan Hall, Gus Arriola, Dan O'Neill and Robert Bastian. Stephanie Salter, now a columnist for *The San Francisco Examiner,* purchased a framed photograph of the Richard M. Nixon family that John had hung above the toilet, and presented it to author Cyra McFadden, who displays it in a similar place of honor.

In 1980 Bethanie Kay Sample's mother filed a wrongful death suit against the Chronicle and John's estate, asking $1.5 million general damages and $2 million in punitive damages. The suit was settled out of court for a sum that remains undisclosed.

That July, bulldozers leveled 960 Bush Street—the site of the Boarding House and of John's last and best apartment—to make way for an upscale development of condominiums and shops.

"We shall not see his like again," Herb Caen said on the radio a week after John's death, but the truth is that we shall not see San Francisco as it was ever again.

Radio personality Dan Sorkin tells a story that preserves for me the freedom of the era and my brother's joyful spirit.

One beautiful afternoon in the late '60s, Dan, a glider pilot, took John sky-sailing over Fremont, east of San Francisco. Ascending, they caught a thermal and found themselves next to a red-tailed hawk who calmly accepted them as just another bird. Dan turned around in his seat to see John laughing out loud, eyes sparkling. They rode thermal to thermal for the rest of that glorious day, following the red-tailed hawk.

John's grave lies at the base of a small redwood grove in Fish Rock Cemetery, in the North Coast village of Anchor Bay. The gravestone is rough volcanic rock, and the bronze plaque reads simply, "John L. Wasserman, Journalist."

Inside This Hill

Michael McClure

*(A dream following John Wasserman's mortal accident—a remembrance
of the scene of the accident—and a return to the dream.)*

AND THERE WAS JOHN, TALL JOHN, WALKING, ACROSS
                                    THE GREENSWARD
of a campus—perhaps Kent State or Yale. He did not know
that he was dead, that he had died three weeks before
in a head-on car crash or that we
had seen the wreck on our way to view a film he
recommended in his column. We drove slowly
peering through the rain at the car overturned
in roadside blackness where it blazed orange-red
like a giant flaming match head.
Returning twenty minutes later from the sold-out
theater we saw the car again—John's car—beside the cinder
of the burned hulk. The front end had been pushed
concave and was in the front seat. I was stilled
by the thought of death there, and the quickness
of mortality—not knowing it was John. In the morning
Jane told me John had died on 280.

Now I have dreamed of John striding along a campus.

In the night, I ran after John shouting
but he did not hear. Then I remembered
the dead can return for a while to complete unfinished
business—but they do not know they are dead.
John was preoccupied—in his hand he held
a pad of paper—and he walked with mouth
half open, smiling to himself, looking young
and affable, and handsome in his gray hair
and black tee-shirt. I knew I must not tell John
that he was dead. He looked so abstracted, caught
in his business, and almost happy. I spoke
to him. I put my arm around his shoulder
but that embarrassed him. He pushed me away,
and walked on and I began to cry to see him dead.

It is March on Twin Peaks where I stop to write
this—there are new flowers—mauve mallow,
purple lupine, sorrel, buttercups, and golden
tracks of spring as if some joyous bear had walked here
with flowered feet and scattered prints
behind—and John is still here
in the generous beauty of his presence—but also
he is inside this hill where all spring flowers are black:
black mallow, black lupine, black sorrel,
black buttercups and black tracks of spring.

ACKNOWLEDGMENTS

Living with my brother's humor made this book a joy, as did meeting his friends. More than 100 talked with me about John, and I am deeply grateful to all of them, in particular Ward Dunham, Curt Gentry, Michael Kelly, Joel Pimsleur, Carole Vernier and Marian Zailian.

My son, Graham Rayman—researcher, confidant, voice of sanity—was essential to the project; my brother Richey, who knew John's world far better than I, added a perspective that balanced my own. Our mother was unfailingly encouraging. Every day I blessed my late father for so carefully preserving John's personal papers, articles, letters, tapes and memorabilia.

William Hamilton, Michael McClure, Grace Warnecke, Lani Mein, Peter Stein, Ted Betz, Fred Stimson, Sydney Goldstein and Joe Samberg generously offered photographs, illustrations, and, in Michael's case, a poem, for use in the book. Irvin Muchnick read an early draft and suggested a workable framework for the narrative sections.

Ideas, insights and material help came from Kevin Albert, Neva and Scott Beach, Gail Bernstein, Jeannie Bradshaw, Jon Carroll, Tom Clark, Charlotte Coe, Phelps Dewey, Mimi Fariña, Ron Fimrite, Bill German, Sigmund Gordon, Susan Hall, Dean Jennings, John Joss, Marc Libarle, Mary Lindheim, Mike McCone, Cyra McFadden, Frances Moffat, Phil Mumma, Kate Neri, Julia Poppy, Annie O'Toole, Alice K. Perry, Jo Rowlings, David Rubinson, Mary Miles Ryan, Joel Selvin, Charlene Spiller, John and Erica Stanley and Linnea Wicklund and most of all, Bernard and Dale Wasserman.

The library staff of *The San Francisco Chronicle,* especially Kathleen Rhodes, Sally Kibbee, Bob Britton and Richard Geiger, were stalwart and cheerful allies. Nion McEvoy and Charlotte Stone, my editors at Chronicle Books, worked with me in a spirit of collaboration and celebration.

Potter Wickware gave me two things I couldn't live without: loving friendship and unsentimental editing.

ABOUT THE AUTHORS

John L. Wasserman wrote on entertainment for *The San Francisco Chronicle* from 1963 until his death in 1979 at age 40. His column "On the Town" and reviews were famous for their brilliance, acerbic humor, iconoclasm and, often, pure joy. John Wasserman believed that San Francisco was the most beautiful and culturally alive city in the world.

Abby Wasserman, John's younger sister, left California in 1963 as a Peace Corps volunteer and returned home to stay 20 years later. Notable among her interim resting places were Colombia, Turkey, Honduras, Nigeria, Connecticut and Washington, D.C., where she wrote freelance art and dance criticism and researched Tom Wicker's book, *One of Us: Richard M. Nixon and the American Dream.* She is the author of *Portfolio* (1986), a catalog of 11 Native American artists, and is currently the editor of the quarterly magazine of the Oakland Museum.

Michael McClure is a prolific poet, essayist and playwright. His books of verse include *Jaguar Skies, September Blackberries* and *Fragments of Perseus,* from which the poem "Inside This Hill" about his friend John Wasserman's death is taken. He has been working in recent years with the keyboardist of The Doors, Ray Manzarek, doing performances of poetry and music. His latest book is *Rebel Lions.*

INDEX

A

Abrahams, Billy, *198*
Adler, Kurt Herbert, *184*
Albright, Lola, *14*
Albright, Thomas, *6*
Allen, David, *163-4, 172, 175, 207*
Allen, Woody, *7, 97, 98-9, 105,*
163, 174, 207
Amaya, Carmen, *126*
Ananda, Leah, *155*
Andre the Giant, *36-7*
Andress, Ursula, *80-1*
Ann-Margret, *79, 93, 97*
Anspacher, Carolyn, *6*
Arriola, Gus, *208*
Artman, Zohn, *123, 207*
Asher, Don, *6*
Astaire, Fred, *85, 158*
Avengers, The, *146-7*

B

Baez, Joan, *3, 7, 39, 165, 189-91,*
198, 208, (photo spread p. *xv*)
Balin, Marty, *121, 124, 134*
Balsam, Martin, *91*
Bandersnatch, Joaquin, *9, 60*
Banducci, Enrico, *163, 183*
Barca, Capt. Charles, *124*
Barkan, Todd, *159*
Barrow, Cliff, *39*
Barry, Bob, *166*
Barry, Dave, *35*
Barton, Noelle, *128*
Bastian, Robert, *208*
Bay Area Jazz Foundation, The, *7,*
177-8
Beach, Scott, *111*
Beatles, The, *38, 49, 90-1*
Beckton, Clarence, *161*
Bell, Richard, *126*
Bennett, Tony, *178*
Benson, Irving, *46*
Benton, Barbi, *199, 204*
Bierce, Ambrose, *3-4*

Big Al (Al Falgiano), *44*
Big Brother and the Holding
Company, *124-6*
Bisset, Jacqueline, *92*
Blackman, Gary, *124*
Bladen, Barbara, *97*
Bleiweiss, Nancy, *118-19*
Bleiweiss, Roberta, *119*
Blinder, Martin, *56, 203*
Blossoms, The, *27*
Boarding House, The, *164-5, 172,*
175, 208
Bo Donaldson and the Heywoods, *23*
Borreta, Voss, *44*
Bowie, David, *139*
Boyce, Joseph N., *200*
Boyle, Peter, *103*
Bradshaw, Jeanne, *57*
Bradshaw, Tom, *57*
Brand, Stewart, *124*
Brechin, Jeanne, *125*
Brecht, Bertolt, *133*
Breinig, Peter, *152*
Brooks, Christopher, *113*
Brown, Buster, *158*
Brown, Jerry, *193, 195*
Brown, Willie, *57, 63, 66*
Bruce, Lenny, *167-8, 169*
Buckner, Milt, *158*
Buffett, Jimmy, *165*
Bull, Sandy, *125*
Burns, Marilyn, *76-7*
Bush, George, *42*

C

Caen, Herb, *6, 67, 122, 178, 197,*
206, 209
Camp, Joe, *89*
Campbell, Brad, *126*
Caron, Leslie, *85*
Carson, Johnny, *118, 164, 165*
Casady, Jack, *134-5*
Cash, Johnny, *139*
Chambers, Marilyn, *56-7, 65, 66-7*
Channing, Carol, *118*
Chayevsky, Paddy, *101-2*

Clapton, Eric, *137*
Cohen, Bob, *124*
Colombu, Franco, *52-3*
Coltrane, Alice, *155*
Committee, The, *110-11*
Condor, The, *41-4*
Conner, Bruce, *111-12*
Connolly, Cyril, *201*
Cook, Paul, *148*
Cooper, Alice, *139*
Cooper, Gary, *97*
Cooper, Ray, *143*
Coppola, Francis Ford, *95*
Cordoni, John, *202*
Corey, Professor Irwin, *112,*
163, 167
Corney, Ed, *49, 52*
Cosby, Bill, *163, 168, 173-4*
Country Joe and the Fish, *121, 132*
Cousteau, Jacques, *193, 194, 195*
Creach, Papa John, *134-5*
Crist, Judith, *16, 18-19*
Crosby, Norm, *27, 112*
Crystal, Billy, *91, 164, 165*
Cushing, Peter, *105*

D

Daltry, Roger, *126*
Damiano, Gerald, *68*
Danniebelles, The, *39*
Davis, Clive, *140*
Davis, Miles, *152*
Davis, R.G. (Ronny), *122*
Davis Jr., Sammy, *50, 57, 66-7,*
201, 202
Deason, Paul, *76*
Dee Dee, *44*
Dee, Kiki, *142*
Delaplane, Stanton, *6*
DeNiro, Robert, *14, 103*
Denver, John, *140, 191, 193, 195*
Deodato, Eumir, *32*
deRenzy, Alex, *55, 64*
Digard, Uschi, *76*
Dill, Frank, *22*
Divine, *106-7*

214